Eventually David would learn the truth

She had to accept that point. She could easily imagine him stopping by a gallery and asking the proprietor to locate a Jenny Marshall painting. The proprietor would check his list and inform David that no such artist existed.

That scenario was painful.

But at least she wouldn't be there to watch him put together the pieces and finally grasp her deception. She wouldn't have to witness the collapse of his trust. Or the hurt and betrayal she knew he'd feel.

She stared blankly ahead and concluded she had no choice. Her only course was to continue the deceit. She'd take the enchanted days remaining to her and hope the memories would be enough to balance the lonely nights waiting for her at home. And she prayed that one day she could forgive herself for throwing away her second chance at happiness.

ABOUT THE AUTHOR

Early in life, Margaret St. George set two goals:
to publish a book and to be ravished by Burt
Reynolds. Obviously she has achieved her first
goal; she has not given up on the second. This is
Margaret's eighth novel, most of which have
been historical romances. She lives with her
husband and family in Colorado.

Books by Margaret St. George

Castles and Fairy Tales
MARGARET ST. GEORGE

Harlequin Books

TORONTO • NEW YORK • LONDON
AMSTERDAM • PARIS • SYDNEY • HAMBURG
STOCKHOLM • ATHENS • TOKYO • MILAN

Published July 1986

First printing May 1986

ISBN 0-373-16159-X

Printed in Canada

Chapter One

Oh, no. Jenny Marshall peered over the top of her sunglasses toward the man emerging from the ocean. He shaded his eyes and looked toward the line of cabanas and beach loungers where Jenny was sitting.

It couldn't be him, Jenny thought. God wouldn't do this to her. She blinked at the towel shrouding her sunburned legs, at the oversize shirt protecting her sunburned arms and shoulders, touched the dead-white zinc oxide smeared across her nose and murmured a quick prayer. "Please, God, let that man be anyone on earth except David Foster. Let it be anyone else and I will never again cheat on a diet or mail a letter with postage due. The minute I get back to Denver I'll clean the oven, Lord. Cross my heart and hope to die."

After taking another look at the man on the beach she concluded that God was not in a bargaining mood. The man on the beach looked exactly as Jenny had always imagined David Foster would look after fifteen years, even more handsome than when she'd known him in college. It had to be him. He had David Foster's dark, curly hair, David Foster's lean, muscled body, David Foster's confident, lopsided smile.

And he was walking up the beach toward her. Clearly, God was not going to send an earthquake to rescue Jenny Marshall from a ghastly embarrassment. No fairy godmother was going to whisk away the zinc oxide, her head scarf and the faded old shirt. Nor would Fate divert David Foster. The long-ago object of her sorority daydreams focused on the two empty loungers beside Jenny and, followed by a young beauty in a very brief bikini, moved toward her.

This wasn't how it was supposed to happen.

In her fantasies, Jenny ran into David Foster when she was wearing something chic and slinky, casually draped by a million-dollar mink coat and shimmering with diamonds and drenched in a perfume that drove men to their knees. How she had acquired these items the fantasy didn't explain, but she had them and she wore them with panache. In the fantasy, she glanced out the window of a chauffeur-driven Mercedes and smiled pityingly at David in his battered VW, exchanged a few gracious pleasantries with him, then drove away. She left him devastated, ready to kill himself that he hadn't begged her to marry him when he'd had the chance.

Not once had zinc oxide and a sunburn figured in her fantasy. Jenny studied the smile of the man approaching her and doubted that suicide was uppermost in his thoughts.

But it was right up there in hers. If he recognized her, Jenny swore she would nod pleasantly, then walk into the ocean and keep going until she drowned or reached Europe.

"Jenny? What's the matter?" Pam Alder pushed up in her lounger. "You look funny."

Didn't she know it. "Shh. Don't say a word." There wasn't time to run. Jenny pushed her sunglasses back on her nose and hastily tucked stray wisps of hair under her scarf. "If you say my name, Pam, I'll never speak to you again."

"What?"

"Later," Jenny whispered, lifting her book as David Foster stopped beside her.

"Excuse me. Are these lounge chairs taken?"

"Mmm." Staring at her book, Jenny shrugged and waved toward the loungers. It was him. She would have recognized his voice anywhere—deep, easy, a voice to send shivers down female spines. She turned a page of her book, watching from the corner of her eye as David Foster spread a towel over the nearest lounger and his companion pulled the second one out from under the protective shade of the cabana and into the Mexican sun.

The girl was stunning, Jenny admitted, one of the two million Gorgeous Young Things populating the beaches and the hotel and making Jenny feel ancient, overweight and flat-chested by comparison. Fortunately, she had a theory about GYTs to make herself feel a tiny bit better.

God had created GYTs to keep ordinary women from getting too vain and arrogant. God didn't want to do it, but He had to. Otherwise, unemployment would have run rampant. Without GYTs making ordinary women wild with envy, there would have been no exercise salons, no jogging suits, no diet books and consequently fewer women's magazines, no diet pills, no cosmetic surgery, no false eyelashes or padded bras. A lot of people would have been out of work.

So God had to create Gorgeous Young Things; anyone could see that. He gave them flawless beauty, curvaceous bodies, perfect teeth and hair. Then, because God wanted to be fair about this, He balanced things out by giving them the intellect of a small appliance.

Jenny took comfort from this thought as she watched David's GYT lean forward to examine her toes, thereby exposing a canyon-deep cleavage above a red bikini the girl had probably packed in a thimble. A Mexican waiter serving iced beer to the hotel guests stopped dead in his tracks, and his eyes bulged.

Jenny sighed and wished she, too, had a gorgeous tan instead of being beet-red beneath the towel spread over her legs. She wished she'd worn makeup to the beach and that the zinc oxide painted over her nose would vanish. She wished the hair hidden beneath her scarf was curled and fluffy. She wondered if there was any truth to the evil rumors about cellulite and wished she had the courage to examine the backs of her thighs.

Most of all, she wished Pam Alder, her neighbor and best friend, had not convinced her to come to Cancún. At least not this week. This week the Palenque Hotel was sponsoring a singles' week. The entire hotel had been taken over by singles, most of whom were between the ages of seventeen and nineteen, or so it seemed to Jenny. She was sure she had bras older than most of the people on the beach. She peeked at David spreading sun lotion on the GYT and felt as old as the Mayan pyramid she planned to tour tomorrow.

Could the girl be David's daughter? she wondered hopefully. The GYT wiggled voluptuously as David rubbed lotion across her shoulders. "Oooh, that feels so gooood." The voice dripped Southern honey. Nope, not his daughter. And it certainly wasn't Marilyn Cody, the girl David had left Jenny to marry.

Pam poked Jenny's arm and Jenny bit back a yelp of pain. "Sorry, I forgot about your burn," Pam said. "What's going on?"

Jenny glared over the top of her sunglasses and waved Pam to silence. But Pam wasn't the type to remain silent long. What she needed was a good escape before David recognized her. Jenny didn't think recognition was likely, considering her scarf, sunglasses, zinc oxide, oversize shirt and towel-covered legs. Plus, she was fifteen years older and five pounds heavier than when she'd been in college. Okay, maybe ten pounds heavier. A woman's weight was between herself and God, and was not the pressing problem of the moment. If Pam didn't say her name and if Jenny didn't speak, it was possible she could escape. She would rather have crawled over glowing lava than have David Foster see her as she looked this minute.

The problem was how to escape when her legs had turned to Jell-O. Being this close to David Foster seemed to have paralyzed her. She cast him a sidelong look and suddenly felt twenty again and shaky inside.

The GYT fluffed damp hair that was drying in—wouldn't you know it?—beautifully natural curls. "I just love Cancún. How far above sea level are we here?" she asked.

David stared at her. "About three feet."

The girl blinked at the ocean, then fluttered scarlet fingertips and pulled her lip between her teeth. "Sure. Silly ol' me."

Jenny grinned. The girl was a toaster. A two-slot toaster, not even a four-slotter. *Thank you, God.* David Foster stared at the girl for a long moment, then he released an audible sigh and turned toward Jenny.

He smiled at her. And when David Foster smiled, the sun burst from behind the clouds, birds sang and movie music swelled out of nowhere. Jenny caught a breath and wished the sand would swallow her.

"Is this yours?"

"Mmm?" She was strangling, she knew it.

"This book."

Jenny stared at the book, *Single Parenting*, as if she'd never seen it before. To the other side of her, she could sense Pam's interest.

"No hablo inglés, señor," she muttered, pulling out one of the two Spanish phrases she knew and pitching her voice an octave higher. Pam's eyebrows shot toward her hairline as David answered in Spanish. Fate was being nasty today; who would have guessed he spoke Spanish? Jenny shrugged and spread her hands. *"No hablo español, señor."* So, if she didn't speak English and didn't speak Spanish, what language did she speak that he didn't?

Jumping to her feet, Jenny rapidly gathered her belongings into her beach bag, ignoring the book, which was in English and thus couldn't be hers. Pam was watching her with openmouthed astonishment, and David Foster had tilted a curious eyebrow.

Jenny struck a worldly pose and smiled at them both, then shrugged and said every German word she could think of. *"Fräulein Munich Wiener Schnitzel."* She gestured toward the water rolling up the beach. *"Achtung nein Lederhosen, ja?"* She laughed gaily in her phony high-pitched voice as if she'd made a stunning bon mot, then gave what she hoped was a Germanlike wave. *"Adiós."*

Adiós? Never mind. Ducking her head, she fled across the beach, paused to wash the sand from her feet, then hurried through the hotel lobby and into the elevator that would whisk her to the safety of the room she shared with Pam.

Inside, she stood still a moment, enjoying the flow of cooled air over her flushed face. David Foster, here in Cancún. How often had she thought of him during the past fifteen years?

"About a million times," she said aloud, seating herself before the mirror. One didn't forget one's first love. It was like being vaccinated; the scar was there for the rest of your life.

Slowly she pulled the scarf from her head and shook out her hair. David had loved her hair. He'd said it reminded him of wheat-colored silk. At the time Jenny had thought it was the most romantic comment she'd ever heard. Had it really been fifteen years ago?

She stared into the mirror, hating the zinc oxide on her nose. Yes, it had been fifteen years. And looking at herself in the mirror and thinking about all the GYTs strolling about the hotel, she felt every one of those years.

"Are you crazy?" Pam said, shutting the door behind her. "A great-looking guy sits down beside you, one who isn't a teenybopper, I might add, and you act like the sun fried your brains." She sat on the edge of the bed and brushed sand from her feet. "And what on earth was that *Wiener Schnitzel* business?"

"You know what I like best about you, Pam?"

"What?"

"I like it that you're my age and flat-chested."

"Well, thanks a lot."

"Tell me the truth—all things considered, how do I look for a person my age?"

"At the moment you look like hell."

"I knew it."

"Usually, you're gorgeous." Pam rummaged in her beach bag for a cigarette, lit it and squinted through the smoke. "Mind telling me what this is all about?"

"Did I ever tell you about David Foster?"

"Only a hundred times."

Jenny drew a breath. "Well, that was him."

"Who was him?"

"The man sitting next to me."

Pam sat up straighter. "The bronzed-god type with the graying temples?" Jenny nodded. "The gorgeous hunk with hair on his chest and the teenager on his arm?"

"The very one."

"Well, well." Pam looked suitably awestruck. "Now I understand the *Wiener Schnitzel*."

"What could I do? I didn't want him to see me like this."

Jenny stared into the mirror, seeing flaws where none existed. All her insecurities surged to the surface. She wasn't a modern-day princess who owned a chauffeur-driven Mercedes. She didn't own a mink coat or any diamonds. She was a divorced mother of two with more bills than income. In the great rat race of life, the rats were several lengths ahead. Jenny supposed that anyone who had known her in college—like David Foster—would say she hadn't lived up to her early potential. Somehow the potential had gotten lost along the way.

There just hadn't been enough time. Everything else came first. She'd told herself she would develop her painting after Walter's business got off the ground. But before that happened, Deuce had arrived and then Rhonda. The years had passed in a blur of diapers, preschools, PTA meetings, then Scouts and baseball and soccer and parties for Walter's business associates. Finally, Jenny had blinked and looked around and Walter was gone, the kids were teenagers, and she'd achieved none of her dreams. All she had was enough potential to earn a living painting greeting-card covers. Which was nothing like real painting.

"Pam, what am I going to do?"

"Are you kidding? Fix yourself up and go find David Foster."

"It isn't that simple." Nothing ever was. "When David and I were dating, he thought I was...special. At least that's what he said."

"You are special."

"No, I'm not. I'm a thirty-seven-year-old divorced housewife."

"An artist."

"A dauber. It's not the same thing. But David... David is very successful." She'd kept up with him through the alumni newsletter. "Have you heard of Foster/Beta computers?"

Pam rolled her eyes. "Anyone living in the twentieth century has heard of Foster/Beta computers. It's the success story of the decade. Two guys working in their garage come up with a state-of-the-art computer and make millions."

"Right. David Foster is the Foster in Foster/Beta."

Pam stared. "You mean a guy who looks like that is rich, too?" She fell backward on the bed and looked at the ceiling. "If you don't take him, I will."

Jenny laughed. "You're married. Remember old what's-his-name, your husband?"

"Tom is in Denver, baby-sitting. I could get a quickie Mexican divorce; he'd never know."

"Any man who will baby-sit while you fly off to Cancún for a week is worth keeping," Jenny said, smiling. Pam was a travel agent and part of her job was to inspect sites for the agency. Three times a year she flew off to exotic locations, all expenses paid. This time, because Jenny's kids were visiting their dad, Pam had convinced Jenny to come along.

So far the trip hadn't been an unqualified success. They had arrived yesterday morning to discover it was singles' week at the hotel; Jenny had crisped herself on the beach the first afternoon; she was still worried about charging the trip on her VISA card, and now David Foster had appeared.

"Maybe he's leaving tonight," she said hopefully.

"Nope. I heard Miss Boobs-of-the-World ask how long he's staying. He arrived this morning and he's staying ten days."

"Oh." Jenny pushed a finger against the top of her thigh and watched her pink skin flare white, then redden again. "You know," she said thoughtfully, "it's really dangerous for me to leave the room. I could get sun fever or something. I probably should stay right here for the rest of the week."

Pam bent to the small refrigerator and opened two Cokes, giving one to Jenny. "Is this guy that important?" she asked shrewdly.

"He was once."

"What happened?"

Jenny rolled the icy bottle across her forehead. "I had a chance to study in Rome. For a year." She shrugged. "I thought David would be there when I returned. I even asked Marilyn to keep an eye on him for me."

"A really stupid idea."

"Right. My trusty sorority sister married him."

Pam looked at her watch. "There's a get-acquainted cocktail party and buffet on the terrace in an hour and a half. We have ninety minutes to get gorgeous."

"Maybe I'll order something from room service."

"Come on, is this the same Jenny Marshall I know? The same Jenny Marshall who faced down a librarian with a book three months overdue? The same Jenny Marshall who roller-skated to the PTA bake sale when the car broke down? The fearless Jenny Marshall who coaches girls' interscholastic soccer and deals with enraged soccer parents once a week?"

"Don't remind me. This is a vacation, remember?" Jenny grinned; then the smile faded. "I don't know, Pam. David has been so successful and I—" she bit her lip "—I saw his picture in *Time* magazine, for heaven's sake. Receiving some kind of award." Her hands lifted and fell. "I'm not in that league."

"We're not talking about marriage here, Jen. We're talking about an hour. You say: 'Long time no see.' He says: 'How are you?' You say: 'Fine. How are you?' And that's it. He collects ole Marilyn or Miss Boobs-of-the-World and drifts away, and you and I look around and see if we can find you a man over twenty."

"Will you stop matchmaking? I'm fine."

"Walter's been gone for two years. Are you still carrying a torch for him?"

"For Walter?" Jenny laughed. "Walter's a nice man and he gave me the two greatest kids in the world. But Walter's a flake, Pam. He always was a flake. A nice flake, granted, but not the kind of man to build a life around. No, I'm not carrying any torch. We shouldn't have gotten married in the first place. We're better friends since the divorce than we ever were when we were married."

"Well. We now have seventy-four minutes to get gorgeous. Do you want the shower first?"

WHEN JENNY FINISHED showering she wiped steam from the mirror and stared into it. Where were the fairy godmothers when you really needed them?

First, she had to do something with her hair. Second, she needed to do something with her face. And third, she needed to lose five pounds in the next thirty minutes. Fourth, she needed to wear her new black confidence-building ultrasexy underwear to compensate for the five pounds she wasn't going to lose in the next thirty minutes.

Jenny sighed. She had a theory about weight loss. Matter could not be destroyed, right? Einstein had said so, and who was she to refute Einstein? So. If matter couldn't be destroyed and weight was matter, then, when someone dieted away ten pounds, exactly where did the lost fat go?

She knew where. The fat floated around in the air just waiting for some poor soul like Jenny Marshall to step out onto the back porch. And then—*wham!* The ten pounds zoomed down and clamped onto Jenny's thighs. Or onto any other part of her unfortunate enough to be exposed on the porch when ten pounds were looking for a home. The answer was physics; her theory was irrefutable. Dieting was therefore hopeless. A person had to go out onto the porch sometimes. And that's what did you in.

So much for losing five or ten pounds. She wound her hair around hot curlers and studied her face, trying to see it as David Foster would. Actually, the sunburn made her look healthy and glowing. Radiant, maybe. Next to her flushed skin, her eyes were a startling cornflower blue. Eye shadow? No, if destiny had wanted her to have green eyelids, she would have been born with gills. But definitely mascara, lots of mascara. And a lush, moist lipstick. Hot pink to match...match what?

"Pam! What am I going to wear?" She stared into the closet in dismay. Tomorrow she might get into the new clothes she'd charged, but her burn was still too raw to manage even tiny sleeves tonight.

"Try my black silk camisole. It'll be great with your cream-colored skirt."

Jenny dropped it over her head, luxuriating in the feel of silk next to her bare skin. But—did mothers of teenagers go out without bras? She asked Pam.

"What century are you living in?" Pam said, leaning toward the mirror to apply lipstick. "Nobody wears a bra anymore. Besides, you have a terrific figure."

"This feels positively indecent." Jenny examined herself from the side and from the front. "I love it." She smiled. "Marilyn Cody, eat your heart out." If she remembered right, Marilyn Cody had been notably flat-chested, the type who looked marvelously elegant in high-fashion clothing and lousy in a swimsuit.

It gave Jenny a moment's wicked pleasure to remember that David and Marilyn lived in California, where people spent half their lives in swimsuits.

"Ready?" Pam asked, giving her springy red hair a final pat.

"Ready." And eager. Pam was right, Jenny thought. This wasn't a life-or-death matter. It was an opportunity to satisfy her curiosity about David Foster. They'd chat for a while, exchange a few "remember whens," then Jenny would drift away. David would gaze after her with bittersweet longing, knowing his life would have been fuller and richer if he'd married Jenny when he had the opportunity.

Fat chance. She thought of his photo in *Time*, thought of the celebrities he probably knew, the parties he and Marilyn probably gave. And her shoulders slumped for a moment. He would speak of being on the board of directors of Foster/Beta, and Jenny would brightly offer having served as president of the PTA for three terms. He would mention leading a giant corporation to greatness; she would mention coaching her girls' soccer team to a winning season. He would ooze financial security; she would think of the bills stuffed in her desk drawer. He would toss off a reference to an intimate party at the White House; she would remember the last party she had attended—a slumber party thrown by her twelve-year-old daughter.

She gave Pam a glum look while they waited for the elevator.

"Cinderella was one lucky girl, do you know that?" she said. "One tap of a wand and all the drudgery vanished. Princess for a night."

Too bad it couldn't happen to Jenny Marshall.

Chapter Two

David Foster stood near the stone wall separating the terrace from the beach, cradling a Scotch-and-water in one hand. He glanced over the noisy crowd, absently avoiding Mary Sue or Mary Ellen or whatever Miss Bikini's name had been. When he saw her, he moved nearer the steps leading to the lobby, placing a palm tree in her line of vision. The girl was lovely, but talking to her was like attempting to communicate with a creature from Planet X. She wanted to be a hairdresser someday and she read palms. She knew the names of all the current rock groups.

He tasted his Scotch and idly wondered if he had ever been as young as the people around him. Or as old. Today's college kids wore the faces of youth masked with a canny wisdom he didn't remember having fifteen years ago. There had been an innocence then, an idealism he found lacking in today's students. Yesterday's youth had seemed to focus on the outer world; today, their phrase was "What's in it for me?"

"Hi. I'm Laurie and I'm a Scorpio. Who are you?"

"I'm David and I remember when people had last names instead of astrological signs." He smiled at the girl standing before him and decided she couldn't be more than six or seven years older than his daughter. "How old are you? Eighteen? Nineteen?"

"Old enough," she said with a wink. Wide green eyes dipped to his Rolex watch, paused a moment at the ruby in his tiepin. "I like it that you wore a tie and jacket." She dismissed the crowded terrace with a sweeping wave and gave him a nod of infinite wisdom. "I like mature men who know how to dress. The kids of today are so gross about clothes. You know?"

A hint of a smile wavered about his mouth as he swept a glance over her designer jeans and the T-shirt with All Yours spelled across the front in sequins. He had no idea what to say to her.

She ran a coy finger down the length of his tie and looked at him from beneath a sweep of dark lashes. "I just love older men. They're so... well, so..."

"Much older?" he supplied, smiling.

"Yeah. Mature men know how to take care of a woman, you know?"

He knew. Mature men had things like bank accounts and American Express cards, Rolex watches and ruby tiepins.

"Are you getting hungry? How about you and me...?"

He couldn't even imagine it. Hastily he removed her fingers from his tie. "You go on ahead. I need to speak to the manager." Earlier he'd spotted Hernan Mortiz standing near the steam tables. After giving Laurie the Scorpio a gentle push toward a muscled football type, David made his escape across the terrace.

It would be flattering to think Mary Sue and now Laurie the Scorpio were devastated by his looks and charm. But he doubted it. A wry smile brushed his lips as he stepped between two good-looking kids who looked as if they had spent their entire lives on surfboards or as quarterbacks for their home teams. These were the two young men that Mary Sue and Laurie should have been making up to rather than David Foster, thirty-eight-year-old conservative with graying hair and wrinkles around the eyes. But David Foster had the bank account and the American Express card. And everyone was in a hurry. Why wait for the good life? Why not find a man who already had it?

David frowned, realizing he had arrived back at square one: *Is it me or my money she likes?* The eternal suspicion of the man with the bank account. Or two or three.

He shook hands with Hernan Mortiz, the Palenque's manager. "Am I imagining it, Hernan, or are there a hundred females for every man?"

Hernan Mortiz laughed. "Actually we have about sixty more males than females this time."

"How many total?"

"Hard to say. We have two hundred and thirty rooms, with a capacity for, say, four hundred. But during singles' week it gets crazy. They sneak in friends we don't know about, pack four and five to a room." He shrugged broadly.

David knew the Palenque had two hundred and thirty-four rooms, with a capacity for four hundred and twenty-eight—four hundred and forty-two, if the roll-away beds were all used. He knew exactly what the Palenque had grossed last year and how much was net. If pressed, David could have given an accurate estimate of how many employees were on the Palenque payroll and how many piña coladas were sold each day from the thatched poolside bar. The exact break-downs were in his briefcase in his room.

"And, of course, we have a few married couples," Hernan was saying. "And a couple of travel agents and a Méxicana flight crew."

"But mostly college students?"

"Probably. We set singles' week to coincide with spring break."

David nodded. It was a good business move. Cancún was a new city, just beginning to be known as a vacation spot. Fifteen years ago, there had been nothing here but rocks and jungle. As little as five or six years ago, the new residents were killing rattlesnakes and bushmasters on the city streets. Now luxury hotels lined the strip, some backing the lagoon, some offering the soft beaches of the Caribbean. The city was as modern as any in Mexico. All that was needed were tourists to rave about the climate and the limestone beaches, about the reefs for diving and snorkeling, the clear sailing waters and the glittering discos. The college kids would go home and tell everyone they knew about Cancún. And they would come back, along with parents and friends.

His instinct had been right. Now was the time to invest in Cancún, before it became as famous as he sensed it would be in the not-so-distant future.

"When does Spenser arrive?" Rob Spenser was the lawyer putting together the syndication of the Palenque. "Friday?" When Hernan confirmed it, David nodded. That gave him three days to explore on his own before receiving an official tour.

After finishing his Scotch, he watched the people going through the buffet·line and noticed that most had aligned into couples. And why not? A full orange moon hung above the ocean waves, and the night air was warm and fragrant. A mariachi band swung into a Mexican love song. For a moment he missed having someone of his own. It wouldn't have been difficult to arrange a companion for dinner and maybe something more, he'd seen that. But he wasn't the type for one-night stands. Wrong generation, he supposed. So he'd dine alone, as he usually did. Worse things could happen.

Then he saw the statuesque blonde descending the lobby stairs. She was a stunning woman. Moreover, there was something familiar about her. David studied her a moment before experiencing a shock of recognition.

Jenny. It was Jenny Tucker. His chest tightened as it hadn't done in years at the sight of a woman. But Jenny had always had that effect. God, he'd been crazy about her. Emotional enough that he'd never been able to forget her completely. His first instinct was to rush across the terrace and sweep her into an embrace and babble something incoherent about coincidence and finding her again. Thankfully, he restrained himself. Good sense dictated that he wait at least until he discovered if she was with someone, a husband for example. Impatient, he leaned against the palm tree and watched her descend the stairs, her fingers trailing the banister, and he remembered the first time he'd seen her. How long ago? Too long, much too long.

He'd been at the Denver Art Museum, waiting for someone whose name he had now forgotten, peering up the staircase between glances at his watch. Then Jenny had appeared. Her face had been flushed with cold, making her eyes as bright as blue stars. She wore a red coat and a red tam pulled to one side of her wheat-colored hair, and she was laughing. He had stared at her and thought her the most vividly alive person he'd ever seen. Most of the girls he'd known then had dulled themselves to suit their idea of sophistication. They didn't clatter down the stairs or dash from painting to painting clapping with enthusiasm.

He laughed softly at the memory, his smile widening as he watched Jenny bend to examine a small statue almost hidden in greenery. She was still doing it, seeing things other people missed, viewing the world through her own unique perspective.

Lord, he'd missed her. He hadn't known how much until this moment, but he'd missed having Jenny Tucker in his life. He'd missed her simplicity, the way she had of reducing complications to basics. He'd missed the clear, open honesty of her smile, and her light humor and genuine warmth.

He started toward her, then paused.

Would Jenny want to see him again? They hadn't discussed it during the time they'd been seeing each other, but there had been an unspoken understanding that someday—when he was on his feet financially and Jenny had established herself as an artist—someday they would marry. Then she'd been offered the chance to study in Rome, and pride had stopped him from asking her not to go. And later, without quite realizing how it had happened, he'd found himself pinned to Marilyn Cody. And the letters from Rome had stopped.

Lord, that was fifteen years ago. Was he so conceited as to think she'd been hurt enough to carry a grudge for fifteen years? She probably hadn't thought of him once since she stepped off the plane in Rome.

He watched her a moment, enjoying the vivacity in her expression, drawn to her maturity. Next to Jenny, the college girls reminded him of blank pages. Life hadn't yet stamped a readable impression. But there was character in Jenny's face. A crinkling about the eyes that told of frequent laughter; a slight tug at the corner of her lips that suggested she'd had her share of disappointments. But it was her eyes that captivated him. If the poets were right, and eyes were the windows to the soul, then Jenny had a lovely soul. Her eyes were curious and alert, eager for life's next moment.

There was no hint of the boredom he'd been accustomed to in Marilyn's expression. No secrecy.

He looked behind her to see if she was followed by a husband and was surprised at the intensity of his relief when no man moved forward.

The least he could do was say hello.

"THERE HE IS!" Jenny saw him standing near the buffet line looking more handsome than any man had a right to be. Dark trousers, light-colored jacket, pink shirt and maroon tie. "Act natural."

Pam rolled her eyes. "I can't stand this. Why didn't I bring Tom instead of you?"

"You felt sorry for me, because the kids were with Walter and I was starting to clean house."

"When you clean house, I know you're going bananas. You needed a real vacation."

Jenny took a plate and stepped into the buffet line. "He's coming this way. Do I look all right?"

"I should look so good."

"Jenny? Jenny Tucker?"

"David Foster! What a surprise." She smiled into his dark eyes and her heart lurched into overdrive. The years fell away and she felt like a giddy college girl again. "What are you doing here?" Why did people always ask that sort of stupid thing? Why didn't they just come out and say: "Kiss me, you fool; I'm yours."

"You look wonderful, Ms Tucker."

"It's Marshall now. Jenny Marshall." Was that disappointment in his eyes? Should she tell him immediately that she was divorced? Or would that be too obvious? And where was good ol' Marilyn Cody and/or Miss Boobs-of-the-World?

David smiled at Pam. "I'm David Foster. Jenny and I went to school together."

"Really? I'm Pam Alder, Jenny's neighbor."

"I'm sorry, I should have introduced you." One look into those velvety dark eyes and her mind had turned to mush. Jenny spooned a mound of something onto her plate and tried to sound as if encountering her first true love was an ordinary occurrence, no big deal. "So. How are you?"

How banal could one get? Dull, she sounded dull. But what did one say after fifteen years?

His shoulder brushed hers as he extended his plate for pink slices of roast beef. "Fine. And you?"

"Sunburned." As if he couldn't see that. She'd been more interesting when she was muttering about *Wiener Schnitzel* and *Achtung*. "I don't know what caused it." Oh, God, she was sounding as idiotic as the GYT on the beach.

"Probably that big hot thing up in the sky," Pam murmured. Jenny jabbed her elbow in Pam's ribs.

"Are you putting anything on it?"

"Solarcaine. I always travel with Solarcaine. Just in case." When all else failed, Jenny had a tried-and-true conversational plan—babble. She was good at babbling.

"Would you ladies mind if I joined you?"

Mind? Would she mind? Did paint come in tubes? Wasn't she practically panting? "We'd be delighted."

She managed to reach the table without spilling her plate down her skirt. A major accomplishment, as her hands were shaking. Who would have imagined David Foster would still have this effect on her?

After smoothing her napkin across her lap, Jenny listened with enjoyment to the self-confidence in his baritone voice as David ordered wine. Walter had never been able to order wine. After a few years of mangling French labels, he'd finally given up and simply requested the house wine. In contrast, David studied the wine list, then ordered something French and elegant-sounding. It underscored the difference in his life and Jenny's. He knew about wine, whereas she was convinced every bottle contained the same vintage simply labeled and priced differently. It was the theory of creative labeling for people with indiscriminate taste buds.

"Is it suitable?" David asked when the wine had been poured.

Jenny had no idea. Actually, she would have enjoyed cherry Kool-Aid just as much. The thought depressed her. She needed to get out more. "Very nice, don't you think so, Pam?"

"Well, I'll be darned," Pam said. She peered across the tables and candlelight. "I believe that's . . . yes, it is. Well, if this isn't old home week. Do you see that couple seated by the mariachi band? That's my cousin Sam and his wife. From Des Moines.'' Smiling, and speaking in a voice as phony as plastic, Pam pushed from the table and gathered up her plate, purse and silverware. ''If you two don't mind, I'll just go say hello to Fred...''

''Sam,'' Jenny corrected.

''...and see how things are doing in Des Moines.''

When Pam had disappeared in the direction of the band, Jenny and David smiled at each other. ''I like your friend,'' David said.

''She doesn't have a cousin in Des Moines.''

''I didn't think so.''

Now what? Jenny looked across the terrace. ''I didn't know it was singles' week when Pam convinced me to come here. They all look so...''

''Young.''

''I know. I'm feeling ancient by comparison. I keep thinking I'm smelling clouds of acne medicine.''

David laughed. ''I can't tell you how nice it is to talk to someone who remembers Janis Joplin and a time when Simon and Garfunkel were partners.''

They smiled at each other, and Jenny couldn't have swallowed a bite if her life had depended upon it. A million questions hovered on her tongue, but for once in her life, she managed not to blurt them out.

It occurred to her that, for the moment, she and Cinderella shared a lot in common, after all. An airborne coach had whisked her away from a life that right now seemed humdrum, and had deposited her in a setting as foreign to Jenny as the palace must have been to Cinderella. Like Cinderella, she had new clothes, courtesy of VISA rather than a fairy godmother, and she was sitting across a candlelit table from a handsome prince. She inhaled the coconut fragrance of suntan lotion and the tang of salt and sea and soft breezes. Palm trees rustled overhead. She felt enchanted.

"You haven't changed at all," David observed softly. "You're as beautiful as you were fifteen years ago."

Jenny blushed with pleasure. Seeing the admiration in his dark eyes, she felt beautiful. Usually she felt like a mother. With Rhonda and Deuce she felt useful, exasperated, loving, guilty, affectionate, and all those other emotions that one experienced in parenthood. She seldom had time to think about her appearance. Besides, it required a man's gaze to make a woman feel beautiful. And tonight, right now, she blossomed beneath the interested approval in David's eyes.

"Tell me about yourself," she said, sipping the wine without tasting it. "After graduation you married, uh…" Jenny snapped her fingers and screwed her face into a frown of concentration, pretending she didn't have Marilyn Cody's name burned into her brain.

Actually, Jenny remembered Marilyn as vividly as if she'd seen her yesterday. Marilyn was one of those perfect people who made everyone else look bad by comparison. Organized, efficient, cool under fire, Marilyn had managed the sorority as deliberately and as smoothly as she managed her life. Nothing was left to chance; everything was calculated and calibrated well in advance.

Marilyn had never had a hair out of place, knew every detail of etiquette, always sported a golden tan, could organize absolutely anything and, even in college, had subscribed to *Vogue* and *House Beautiful*.

Her bones were tidily arranged on an elegant frame that would never know the tortures of dieting.

Had Jenny been running the world, perfect people like Marilyn Cody would have been drowned at birth.

David supplied the name. "Marilyn. Marilyn Cody." He looked into his wine, then drained the glass. "We're divorced."

"Oh. That's a shame," Jenny commented cheerfully. There was justice after all. "I've kept track of you somewhat, through the alumni newsletter. I know you and Marilyn moved to California, where you and a friend developed Foster/Beta Computer Systems."

"A lucky accident, actually."

"You're being too modest. That isn't what the newsmagazines said. I remember words like 'brilliant,' 'genius' and so on."

"Exaggerations." He grinned. "Do I look like a genius to you?"

He looked like heaven to her. Like a dream come true. "As I remember it, you were no slouch in the intellect department." When he shrugged, she added, "I read something recently that said Foster/Beta had been sold to IBM. For a fabulous sum. That's wonderful, David. You've been as successful as everyone who knew you guessed you would be."

He looked uncomfortable. "We sold to IBM, that's true. As to the price...you know how the media exaggerate."

The media were a mystery to Jenny, but she was flattered that he seemed to think she would know how it operated. On the other hand, his expression and gestures made light of his accomplishments, indicating he wasn't the fabulous success she'd believed him to be. Still, David Foster was probably richer than anyone she knew. But, clearly, he didn't want to discuss Foster/Beta.

"So. What are you doing now?" she asked.

"Now?" He gestured to the waiter for more wine. "I guess you could say I'm an investment broker."

"Oh." Obviously the media and the alumni newspaper had indeed exaggerated. Millionaires didn't go to work like ordinary people, at least she didn't think so. It was curious. Since reading the article in *Time*, Jenny had assumed David had netted enough from the sale of Foster/Beta to free him from ever having to work again. Apparently the article had inflated the company's sale price. Or maybe Foster/Beta had been heavily in debt at the time of the sale. Or maybe a million wasn't what it used to be. "Do you like being an investment broker?"

"It's time-consuming, but..." He gazed at her across the candles. "Enough about me. Tell me everything about Jenny Marshall. Where is Mr. Marshall?"

"Walter and I are divorced."

His eyes met hers and she saw the tawny glow of warm candlelight deep within. "I'd like to say I'm sorry, but that would be a lie. I'm glad there's no Mr. Marshall."

Jenny's heart thundered against her ribs before she placed her feet firmly on the tile beneath her sandals. *Whoa, girl,* she told herself. *Just because we're both divorced doesn't mean anything. Think this through.*

After this week, David would fly back to California and she would fly home to Colorado. This was a case of ships passing in the night, nothing more. Besides, people changed in fifteen years. Even if David wasn't the gazillionaire she had supposed, that didn't change the fact that his life had been and still was very different from hers. She glanced at the flash of gold on his wrist and doubted he had a stack of unpaid bills in his desk drawer as she did. And he had been photographed for *Time* magazine. He'd taken an idea and built it into a national company important enough to catch the interest of IBM. David had a solid base of accomplishment behind him; he'd lived up to his potential and was worthy of admiration. While she . . .

"Any children?"

"Two." Jenny's face lit up as it always did at the mention of her children. "Deuce is thirteen and Rhonda is twelve going on thirty."

"I understand. I have a twelve-year-old daughter, too. Also going on thirty." He smiled. "Deuce is an unusual name."

"It stands for Walter Marshall the second." Jenny smiled softly, suddenly missing her children. "They're in California right now, visiting Walter during spring break."

"Walter lives in California, then."

Jenny nodded and smiled. "Walter went berserk when he turned forty, two years ago. He decided he had to find himself. Apparently he wasn't in Denver, so he bought a motorcycle and went to California to see if he was out there." She looked at her hands. "Apparently he was."

David reached across the table and lightly covered her hand. "That was the reason for the divorce?"

"Yes and no." Jenny sighed. "Actually, Walter and I probably should never have married. We just drifted into it. By the time we realized we had little in common, Deuce was toddling around the house and Rhonda was on the way."

David studied her. "Odd. Usually when divorced people speak of ex-spouses, there's bitterness in their voices. But I don't hear any in yours."

Jenny's eyebrows lifted. "Why should I be bitter? Walter and I are both nice people. He tried and I tried; we just couldn't make it work."

"No hurt feelings?"

"Yes, there are hurts," Jenny said after some hesitation. "To be fair, though, I suspect I gave as good as I got. No one emerges from a divorce unscathed." Curiosity flickered in her eyes. "Is there a lot of bitterness between you and Marilyn?"

"I'm afraid so." For a moment he stared at a point in space. Then the lines between his brows smoothed and he smiled. "Now, tell me about your art. Are you famous? What happened to you after Rome?"

There it was, the question she had dreaded.

How had Cinderella handled this? At some point the handsome prince must have insisted they sit out a dance. And they would have talked. The handsome prince would have gazed into Cinderella's eyes as David was gazing into hers, and he would have said something like: *"Well, m'dear, what do you do when you aren't attending fabulous balls? Do you have a career or anything? What is your life like?"*

Would Cinderella have explained that she was the family cleaning lady? That she spent her time cooking and sweeping up the castle? Would she have admitted that balls and palaces and splendid new gowns weren't her usual bill of fare? Or would she have decided to prolong the magic of the evening by not shattering the prince's illusion?

This was what it came down to: Would Cinderella have lied through her teeth, like any sensible girl, to remain admirable in the prince's eyes? Would she have taken steps to preserve her one perfect evening?

Of course she would have.

Jenny thought of her unpaid bills, her cluttered house. She thought of the weighty responsibilities of being a single parent. A parade of PTA meetings and soccer games marched through her mind. Laundry on Monday, cleaning on Friday, roast beef on Sunday. Dull stuff, though it didn't seem so when she was living it. But details, nonetheless, that weren't likely to interest a handsome prince.

As for her art—she didn't regard the greeting-card covers she painted as art, or even as very interesting. They provided her with bread-and-butter money, allowed her to keep the wolf from the door, but that was about it. The cover boards she mailed to New York paid the bills without satisfying the soul. It wasn't real art. The covers she painted for New Image Greeting Cards didn't approach the masterpieces she had dreamed of painting when she first met David.

"Jenny?"

"I'm sorry, I was daydreaming for a moment. I was remembering the day I first met you. At an art museum. I told you then that, someday, one of my paintings would hang in a museum."

He pressed her hand. "I remember. Let me guess— one of your paintings is now hanging in the Denver Art Museum."

Okay, Cinderella. Here we go. Jenny drew a long breath and listened to herself with something akin to amazement. "Not one—but two." She couldn't believe she was doing this.

"Two? Congratulations, Jenny. I always knew you'd be a success!" His smile warmed with genuine pleasure. He was happy for her.

His smile convinced Jenny that she and Cinderella had made the right decision. After all, what harm could it do? After this week she and David would fly back to their separate lives and that would be the end of that. But her pride would be intact and she'd have had the fun of living out a long-standing fantasy of what might have been.

"Start at the beginning. How did you get from being a student in Rome to having your work hung in the Denver Art Museum? And in others as well, I imagine."

She nodded and hoped the odd expression in her eyes could be mistaken for modesty. Then she told him about studying in Rome, most of it the truth, but omitting her loneliness and how much she had missed him.

"Maestro Frascotti used to lean over my shoulder and breathe garlic on my cheek," she said, smiling at the memory. Within a week her palette and paints had reeked of it. Even now she couldn't smell garlic without remembering Frascotti and Rome. That garlic-saturated studio had been washed in light that seemed golden with promise.

Then, one day, six months after she'd begun her studies with Frascotti, an envelope had arrived, and the simple cream-colored invitation inside had changed her life. *Mr. and Mrs. Archibald Cody request the honor of your presence at the marriage of their daughter, Marilyn Elizabeth Cody, to David Westridge Foster.*

"Under Frascotti's tutelage, my work improved and matured."

Frascotti had praised her to the skies. Until the wedding invitation arrived. Knowing she had lost David undercut her confidence. She'd wandered Rome's narrow lanes wondering what was wrong with her that David had left her for someone else. She'd compared herself to Marilyn Cody and found herself wanting. In those dark moments, she had decided Marilyn was prettier, smarter, better than Jenny Tucker in every way.

"The year ended with an exhibition. And Frascotti featured my work."

That's how it might have been, should have been. But it hadn't worked out that way. Her confidence in herself had eroded until she no longer believed she had talent. Instead of seeing what was right with her canvases, she stared at them in silent agony and saw nothing but the flaws. Frascotti, not a patient man, had shouted at her, had tried to goad her into working. Her selective mind had heard the criticism, not the praise.

"I won a prize at the exhibition, and that launched my career."

This was a lie, granted, but based on a grain of truth. When it became evident that Jenny was too frozen to paint, Frascotti had been forced to dismiss her; too many students were waiting and praying for her slot in Maestro Frascotti's small, select group.

Frascotti had summoned her into his tiny, cramped office and had stared at her from beneath heavy dark brows that reminded Jenny of two fuzzy caterpillars. He told her how disappointed he was. He told her he'd expected to feature her work in the exhibition, and that he'd expected her to take the top prize. He castigated her for letting love—he spit the word—ruin her talent: "Love is supposed to inspire, not expunge."

But Jenny had been twenty-one. And she had believed her heart was broken forever. She had never suffered emotional pain before and had no experience to tell her she would recover. At loose ends, her confidence at its lowest ebb, she had silently packed her supplies and flown home to Denver. Defeated.

"Go on," David said, bringing her back to the present.

Firmly, Jenny put the past's reality aside and spun a tale of the future she had dreamed of. It seemed very real while she was telling it; she could almost believe it had happened that way. She spoke of beginning by selling a few paintings here and there, and then of her first showing in a minor gallery.

"It must have been exciting."

"It was," she agreed, beginning to enjoy herself. These were dreams of bygone days, no less powerful for not having been dusted off and examined in years. It was fun remembering her hopes and plans, and fun hearing them spoken about aloud. If only her life had actually unfolded that way.

Warming to the story of her imagined success, she spoke modestly of building a growing reputation. She spoke of private showings and public triumphs. She hinted at champagne receptions and media acclaim. She placed herself firmly in David's world, a world of glittering parties, celebrities and financial success. And it was intoxicating. Marvelous fun to give rein to her imagination and romp through the world of might-have-been.

"Jenny." David took both her hands and gazed into her eyes. "I'm so proud of you. You achieved everything you set out to win. That says a lot about you. No, don't be modest. It can't have been easy doing everything you did—while raising children and coping with all that goes along with being a parent."

The approval she'd wanted so badly to see in his eyes was there. For a moment their eyes held, and Jenny felt she was drowning in warm chocolate. When she finally made herself look away from him, she discovered they were the only guests remaining on the terrace.

"Good heavens. What time is it?"

A line of waiters stood by the emptied buffet, yawning and quietly talking. The tables had been stripped and reset for breakfast.

"It's after midnight."

Jenny groaned. "And I have to be up at seven o'clock to catch the tour to Chichén Itzá."

He held her chair, his hands brushing electricity across her shoulders. "Do you have time for a nightcap?"

"Just one." She didn't want this magical evening to end.

David tucked her hand through his arm and they entered the lobby. He lifted an eyebrow and smiled down at her. "The disco or the bar?"

The distant thump of disco music emanated from a door surrounded by flashing neon. But Jenny looked toward the deep chairs of the piano bar. "I'm sorry, but strobe lights give me a headache. Would you think me terribly old-fashioned if I admitted I'm no disco duck?"

There were three things she didn't understand about the world at large and didn't want to. Machinery, bank statements and disco music. Some evil genius had designed all three to confound people and wreck their lives. Jenny was convinced more people had jumped off a bridge because their lawn mower had turned on them than had ever leaped for love. As for bank statements, those hair-tearing items had been handed down from the days of the Inquisition; Jenny was sure of it. No sane person had invented bank statements. And no sane person could twist into the demented postures required by disco, or emerge with eardrums intact.

David grinned. "Thank God. For an awful moment there, I had visions of you dragging me onto a dance floor."

Jenny's eyes twinkled as she laughed up at him. "I seem to remember you and I won a dance contest way back when. Or was that a different David Foster?"

"Lord, I'd forgotten. The Saint Patrick's Day dance, wasn't it? In the gymnasium. You wore a green dress and I borrowed a green jackct from someone."

"Jerry Kelly."

"We danced rings around the competition." He ordered drinks and gave her a mock frown. "What happened to our prize? Did you keep it? I sense an injustice here."

Laughing, Jenny admitted she still had their trophy, although she hadn't seen it in a decade and couldn't remember where it was. Probably somewhere amidst the chaos in her basement. But only a masochist would venture into her basement. Someday she was going to restore it to order.

"Jerry Kelly. I haven't thought of him in years. What happened to him?"

"The last I heard, he was..."

IT WAS PAST TWO when the elevator stopped at Jenny's floor. The time had sped past in a blink.

"David, thank you. This was a wonderful evening." The most wonderful she could remember. "It was so nice seeing you again." He was standing against the elevator doors to keep them from closing, prolonging the moment.

"You say that as if we won't be seeing each other again." His smile seemed to light the corridor. "Didn't you mention you were touring Chichén Itzá tomorrow? Today, that is?"

"Yes."

"So am I—if you'll tell me where to sign up." When she'd told him, her own smile wide with pleasure, David placed his hand on her cheek. "Good night, Jenny." His thumb lightly traced the curve of her lips. "I'm very glad to have found you again."

She watched the elevator doors close, continuing to feel the imprint of his warmth on her cheek and lips. Then she floated—there was no other word for it—to her room.

Pam's sleepy voice muttered from the darkness. "Jenny? Is that you?"

"No, it's Cinderella."

"How are you feeling?"

"Like springtime. Like a twenty-year-old."

"No, dummy. I meant your sunburn. *Achtung, Wiener Schnitzel* and Jenny Marshall cooked to medium rare. That sunburn."

"Fine. I feel fine." She'd forgotten all about it. Stepping out onto the balcony, she turned a radiant smile to the moonlight ribboned across the ocean waves. This was the first real vacation she'd had in years. And it promised to be all she had hoped and more. Palm trees, tropical flowers, white beaches and sparkling water.

And David Foster.

Clearly, the age of miracles had not passed.

Chapter Three

"Pam, are you sure you won't join us for the Chichén Itzá tour?" Jenny called from the shower.

Stifling a yawn, Jenny closed her eyes and let the water flow over her head, hoping it would wake her. There were night people and morning people; she was a night person.

Unfortunately, there seemed to be more morning people than night people, and they had structured the world to suit themselves. The morning types had decided school must start at an hour when mothers and children should still be in bed. They were directly responsible for morning rush hour. Morning people took great glee in making night people feel guilty for still being in their bathrobes when the morning people started phoning around to discuss items they'd learned about on *Good Morning America*. Obviously, morning people had also decided what time bus tours would depart. It was criminal, Jenny concluded. Someone should organize the night people and demand fair treatment.

"I've been to Chichén Itzá. Besides, I'm working, remember? I'm supposed to check out some of the other hotels and restaurants."

"Was that room service at the door?"

"Coffee and orange juice await."

"Thank heavens." Wrapping her hair in a towel, Jenny tied her robe and poured two cups of coffee, taking one to the desk Pam was using. "Too bad you can't inject the stuff." She tasted her coffee and sighed with the pleasure of a true addict. "I'm sorry I woke you last night."

"I take it the reunion was a success?"

"It was wonderful. Thanks, by the way, for finding your cousin."

They smiled at each other, pleased by the perks of a long friendship.

"Now, don't you feel silly about worrying whether or not David Foster would like you after all these years? You sell yourself short, Jenny."

"Well..." Sooner or later, she would have to tell Pam how she'd elevated herself to an artist of national repute. But not now. "I've got twenty minutes to pull myself together and get down to the lobby!" She gulped her coffee and poured another, and carried it to the double vanity. "Where's the blow dryer? How could I have lost my mascara already? What am I going to wear?"

Laughing, Pam shook her head. "I swear, you're the most disorganized person I know."

"Somehow it always works out."

"I know. I'm continually amazed."

JENNY WASN'T SURE David would be waiting in the lobby until she saw him. Last night had been so perfect she could easily have convinced herself that she had imagined the whole thing.

He stood when she emerged from the elevator and gave a long, low whistle. "You look beautiful."

"I look half awake." But seeing the approval in his stare, she was glad she'd chosen her blue slacks and blue-and-lemon top. And, for once, her hair had behaved, falling in soft waves to her shoulders.

"You should always wear that shade of blue. It matches your eyes."

"Flatterer. You look pretty good yourself for a man who's had only a few hours' sleep." Today he was wearing khaki jeans and a navy pullover. And when he smiled, Jenny was certain angels peeped over the rim of heaven and swooned.

"Don't remind me," he groaned. "Some crazy woman kept me up half the night, plying me with drinks and stories about people she knew in college."

Jenny grinned. "I don't remember you complaining."

"I'm not, I'm not. I enjoyed every minute. It's just that they start these damned tours so early."

"You're a night person!" The joy of discovery lifted her voice.

"You, too? We suffer the slings and arrows of a world addicted to dawn." He rolled his eyes and looked mournful as Jenny laughed.

"Chichén Itzá. All those on the tour to Chichén Itzá over here, please." A man whose cheerful smile identified him as a morning person waved them forward and pointed toward a waiting bus.

Jenny smiled. Watching David Foster board a bus was a little like watching Prince Charles open his own car door. Despite her long-held fantasy of driving her imaginary Mercedes past David, who was behind the wheel of a battered VW, she never really pictured him that way. She envisioned him as the type for chauffeur-driven limos. The type who strolled into a restaurant and immediately the staff snapped to, saluted and bowed low.

"What's funny?" David asked when they were settled on the bus beside a large tinted window.

"I don't know. Somehow I just never imagined a genius like you—someone who could bring IBM to its knees—would take a bus tour. I always supposed you VIPs toured in limos."

"What about you? Don't world-famous artists rate a limo?"

Lord, she'd forgotten. Luckily, she was spared a reply, because the guide chose that moment to begin an introductory speech as the bus pulled from the hotel grounds.

"We have a small group today," the guide began. He introduced himself as Carlos, mentioned that there was Coca-Cola and beer for sale at the front of the bus, and explained it would take two hours and twenty minutes to reach Chichén Itzá. "We'll make a rest stop in about an hour and forty-five minutes. You can refresh yourself and buy souvenirs. In the meantime, relax and enjoy the scenery, and please ask me anything if you have questions."

"An hour and forty-five minutes until we can have a cup of coffee?" David placed a hand on his heart and pretended to collapse.

"Ah." Jenny smiled. "One of us anticipated such a catastrophe and came prepared." She reached in her travel bag and pushed aside her camera and wallet and produced two paper cups with steam escaping from the lids. "Voilà. Room service provided the coffee,

Pam produced the cups and I had the good sense to fill and pack them.''

"You are a rare treasure, Jenny, love.'' He sipped the coffee with a deep sigh of pleasure. "I do appreciate a woman who thinks ahead.''

"Thank you. I admit I'm not usually this organized. But when it comes to coffee..."

It was so easy to talk to him; he was so unlike the few men she'd dated since the divorce. Jenny had begun to despair that whatever conversational skills she'd possessed had turned rusty from disuse. Her dates had been punctuated by pauses and silences, by conversational dead ends followed by a rush of words to fill the spaces. The get-acquainted process had seemed awkward and uncomfortable. She suspected she didn't handle it well. It always surprised her when she was invited out a second and third time.

The guide, Carlos, was moving through the bus, pausing here and there to answer questions. He stopped beside them and smiled. "And you are Mr. and Mrs....?''

Jenny and David looked at each other and laughed. "Jenny Marshall and David Foster,'' David said.

Carlos glanced through his registration tickets and grinned apologetically. "Any questions?''

"Are the tours usually this light?'' David had counted about fourteen people on a bus that would easily hold forty.

"There are many students in Cancún this week, *señor*. Most would rather snorkel, sail and play on the beaches than ride a bus.'' A crisp white jacket rose around his shoulders as he shrugged. "It is the older group that is interested in the ruins. Next week, *señor*, this bus will be filled.''

"Thank you." What Carlos had said indicated that Cancún appealed to all age groups. There was something to interest everyone. David nodded thoughtfully.

Jenny looked at the dense jungle growth crowding the road. "Are there snakes out there?" she asked.

"Oh, yes, *señorita*. But we won't see any today."

"Are you sure? Isn't Chichén Itzá in the jungle?"

"Yes, but the grounds are cleared and there are tobacco plants on the perimeters."

"Tobacco plants?"

"Snakes don't like tobacco." Carlos knelt in the aisle and pointed out the window. "Do you see that small village? I grew up in such a village. And each night my father placed a line of tobacco in front of the door. You will see a tobacco plant near each hut."

"Pam is going to love this," Jenny said when Carlos had moved on. "Finally, a good reason to smoke. It keeps the snakes away. Although I'm not sure I believe that." She peered from the window at huts constructed of poles and thatch. "But there does seem to be a tobacco plant near each house."

The bus passed through a succession of villages and they examined each with interest. Carlos had explained that under Mexican law the villagers could earn the deed to as much land as they could clear, fence and maintain. Plot after fenced plot passed by the bus windows. Jenny and David saw women washing clothes in front of the pole huts, men clearing jungle growth with machetes, children feeding chickens and pigs.

"It looks like a hard life," Jenny commented.

"I suppose. But there's something appealing about the simplicity."

"Are you serious?"

David finished his coffee. "Life today has become increasingly complicated, don't you agree? And our values have suffered. It isn't enough to have a house anymore; we have to have a showplace. We don't have jobs; we have careers. People aren't measured by their integrity and strength of character, but by the fatness of their bank accounts. Money is the yardstick of success in our society. And I'm not convinced that's such a good thing. A man may be a bastard in every sense of the word, but if he has enough money, he's accepted—and even admired."

"Are you suggesting successful people lose their values?"

"Some do." He'd seen it happen again and again. Even in his own marriage.

As Foster/Beta began to earn unimaginable sums a few years back, Marilyn had changed. Or maybe she hadn't, maybe he'd just begun to notice. At any rate, labels assumed an importance they hadn't held in the early days of their marriage. If a dress or a chair or a set of dinnerware didn't carry the "right" label, it was considered worthless. And people whose possessions didn't have the "right" labels were no longer "our kind." Eventually, David noticed he and Marilyn no longer saw friends he'd had for years, friends whose incomes had not kept pace with his. He found himself living in a house more pretentious than comfortable, and Marilyn was waging a battle to have it featured in *House Beautiful*, and doing so with all the intensity of a general going to war.

But the event that had opened his eyes to what was happening involved Marilyn only indirectly. His daughter had set aside a Christmas gift from her

Grandmother Foster because it didn't have the "right" label. And he had seen the flare of approval in Marilyn's eyes.

"That's one of the many things I like about you," he said, taking Jenny's hand. "You're successful, but it hasn't changed you. You aren't wearing a shirt with some designer's name on the sleeve. You're still open and honest." The expression on her face made him laugh. "That was a compliment, you're supposed to smile."

"Well, I'll admit I've never wanted to be a sandwich board for a designer. Let them do their own advertising." Of course, she couldn't afford to put her principles to the test by buying designer clothing. The conversation had taken an uncomfortable turn and she bounced it back to him. "Has success changed you?"

"I hope not!"

"Well, your theory seems to postulate that wealth corrupts values." Theories always interested her.

David shifted on the seat. "You're assuming I'm wealthy." The reply seemed to require further comment. "IBM bought a lot of companies the same year they bought ours. We were simply one of many. As I said, the media exaggerated the buy-out."

His response was instinctive, a reaction he'd developed over the years. He tended to minimize his financial success as a protective device. Although, he admitted ruefully, the ploy wasn't always effective. Somehow the deal makers always sniffed out people with money, as did friends and relatives. The problem was with their motives. David would have liked to believe he was sought for his business acumen, but he suspected his bank balance was the primary draw. Unfortunately, wealth made its owner a desirable target. And everyone had something to sell, be it an investment or friendship or whatever. The only way, in his view, that he could lead something approximating a normal life, was to downplay the extent of his wealth.

Additionally, he'd discovered that being single at this stage of his life was much different than the last time. Then it hadn't been necessary to ask himself if the lady on his arm was interested in him or in his money, or if she would have been there if he were still a computer engineer earning a weekly paycheck.

Jenny turned on the seat to face him. "David, are you doubting your success? Forgive me, but that's nonsense. Foster/Beta products are known for being state-of-the-art. And you helped develop them. That's success, and an impressive accomplishment that you can be proud of!"

"Ah, Jenny." He rolled his head across the back of the seat and looked into her blue eyes, warming to the sincerity he read there. He squeezed her hand. "I can't tell you how glad I am to have found you again."

They looked at each other for a moment that seemed to stretch toward eternity. "How long have you been single?" Jenny asked, to take her thoughts off his mouth and dark eyes. There were still blanks about his life to fill in.

"Nearly a year. How about you?"

"It's been two years since Walter burned his neckties, bought two pounds of gold chains and roared off to California."

"I'm starting to get a very strange picture of Walter," David laughed.

Jenny grinned. "Walter is stuck in the sixties. He wants to be a hippie, a flower child." She tilted her head. "Actually, I suppose Walter is searching for what you mentioned earlier—simplicity. I don't know. I think he simply tired of juggling mortgage payments and dentist bills and all the other responsibilities."

He looked at her in surprise. "I wouldn't think you'd have any financial problems. You mentioned that Walter's law practice was successful, and didn't you say you have regular showings at Melton's Gallery? If I remember correctly, paintings from Melton's generally cost four or five thousand dollars each."

"Oh. Well, yes. But Walter refused to use any of my money. Pride, I guess." In truth, Walter would have jumped at any extra money. Jenny almost laughed. She would have jumped at it, too. She still would.

"Do you like being single, Jenny?"

"Lord, no. I liked everything about being married except Walter." Did that sound too suggestive? "Being single has its good points, of course," she amended hastily. She just couldn't think of any at the moment.

"Like loneliness and silence?"

"You, too?" she asked softly, thinking he had the darkest, gentlest eyes she'd ever seen.

"Me, too."

His gaze steadied on her mouth, and Jenny felt a tingle of response shoot up her spine. He still had that lopsided smile that had sent her heart into double time years ago. New lines cut across his brow, but they added character and interest. Suddenly she wondered what it would be like if he kissed her. The thought raised a smile to her lips. She sounded like Rhonda and her girlfriends, giggling behind their hands at the love scenes on TV.

But she remembered. One night in particular rose in her memory. She and David had studied together, and had then walked back to Jenny's sorority house from the library, swinging hands and hurrying to meet her curfew. Snow swirled out of the night sky, blurring the outlines of the University of Colorado's sandstone buildings. It had been so cold Jenny's teeth chattered. Then, on the porch of her sorority house, David had taken her into his arms and his warm lips had melted the snow and the cold night.

Why this particular memory surfaced, Jenny didn't really know; there had been many such nights together, many kisses. Perhaps it was because that night was the night she first recognized how much she wanted him and sensed they would eventually go to bed together. She had looked at the snow on his lashes, at the desire in his dark eyes, and what she saw had both exhilarated and frightened her.

"A penny for your thoughts, Ms Marshall."

"I was remembering the library and the hours we spent there," Jenny hedged. "If it hadn't been for you, I'd have flunked all my math classes."

"Remember your theory? Math professors hate blue-eyed blondes."

"I'm still convinced of it." Jenny laughed.

At the rest stop they bought ice-cream cones for themselves and souvenirs for the kids. After much vacillation, Jenny chose an onyx chess set for Deuce and a shell necklace for Rhonda. David paused before a display of gold earrings, then ended by choosing a shell necklace for his daughter similar to the one Jenny had selected for Rhonda. She watched him curiously.

Had he decided against the gold earrings because he couldn't afford them? That didn't seem likely. On the other hand, Jenny admitted to a growing confusion. She was picking up mixed signals. The expensive watch and all she'd previously known suggested David enjoyed a very comfortable standard of living. But, he'd also made it clear he didn't have the wealth she'd guessed, and that he was working as an investment broker, which had surprised her. She didn't care if he was as rich as Howard Hughes or if he had a drawer full of unpaid bills, as she did. He was still David.

"Look what I bought for me," she said when they were again ensconced on the bus. Carefully she eased open a small painted box and showed him the collection of tiny figures inside. "Mayan worry people," she explained. "You put them under your pillow and they absorb all your worries while you sleep."

"They're better than sleeping pills." He examined one of the tiny painted figures. "But what would a famous artist have to worry about?"

Jenny wasn't at all sure she was good at this. She kept forgetting her Cinderella tale. "Well, for starters, an artist worries if the painting is really any good. And will it sell? That kind of thing."

"With your track record, I doubt you'll have much need for worry people."

She wished it were so. All of it. She wished she had the time and the confidence to return to her real art, wished she could afford to have the house painted and the screen door fixed. She wished she didn't feel so guilty spending money on a vacation, money that was needed in a hundred other ways. Wished she knew for certain if New Image Greeting Cards was going to like the Thanksgiving series she'd already begun. Although it was April, New Image operated on a six-month lead time, and she'd need to have her Thanksgiving designs in the mail by May first. Oh, yes. She had plenty to worry about.

When the bus finally reached Chichén Itzá, Jenny was awestruck. "For the first time since I set foot on the Yucatán peninsula I feel positively young, like an infant," she said, staring at the massive stone ruins.

David laughed. "Good. Then you won't mind climbing to the top of Kukulcán's temple."

"You're kidding." Shading her eyes, Jenny studied the pyramid that dominated the central clearing where they were standing with Carlos and his group. The pyramid overwhelmed her by its size and by the fact of its existence. A broad staircase soared up four sides to a temple at a squared top. She groaned. "Carlos says there are ninety-one steps—straight up. We're talking steep here, David, my friend. Steep."

"Don't tell me you'd come this far and then not climb it? Are you a woman or a wimp?"

"Is that a challenge?"

"I believe it is."

She waved a hand airily. "A mere piffle for a woman who can arrange coffee at the crack of eight." They smiled at each other. "Let's go."

The climb was easier described than done. Jenny was panting when she reached the top, and muttering darkly about losing an extra five pounds if it killed her. But the view was spectacular. Oceans of green jungle surrounded the clearing, and here and there the tops of ruins protruded above the dense foliage. "Breathtaking," she pronounced.

"I agree," David said, looking down at her.

"I meant the view."

Their eyes met and held, and suddenly Jenny felt as she had on that snowy night long ago. Tension drew her stomach tight, and an electric heat seemed to draw her toward him. Her gaze dropped to his wide, warm mouth, and she caught her breath as butterflies fluttered inside her stomach. Jenny leaned against the stone wall of the temple and looked up at him, helpless, in a tide of emotion as primitive as the structure she leaned against.

"Jenny..." David began.

A man wearing a T-shirt that read Remember the Alamo touched Jenny's arm. "Would you mind taking a picture of me and the missus?" He pushed a camera into her hands.

Jenny laughed, the tension relaxing from her body. "Not at all. I'd be glad to." But her hands were trembling enough that she suspected she'd clipped the heads off the smiling couple.

They inspected the famous Mayan ball court, the sacrificial well and the Temple of the Warriors. Within the Temple of the Warriors was a stone statue of a reclining *chacmool* who held a bowl in his lap, which, Carlos explained, was to receive the hearts of sacrificial victims.

Jenny's eyes rounded. "There's a restaurant in Cancún called the Chacmool! Ugh!"

David laughed and snapped a photo of Jenny sitting in the *chacmool*'s lap.

By the time they returned, hand in hand, to the bus, Jenny was exhausted. It seemed the most natural thing in the world to rest her head on David's shoulder as the bus eased from the lot and began the long journey back to Cancún.

David put his arm around her and drew her closer. "Where do you suppose the Mayans went when they disappeared?"

"I have a theory about that," Jenny murmured drowsily.

"As I remember it, you have a theory about everything." David's low chuckle sounded near her ear. "Want to tell me the Jenny Marshall theory to explain the disappearance of the Mayans? Why did they abandon an absolutely awesome city?"

"It's elementary, my dear Foster. It has to do with early women's liberation."

Jenny smiled when he groaned.

"Someone had to clean those pyramids, and guess who that was? Right. Women." She tilted her head to look up at him. "One day a group of women were hauling their vacuum cleaners up the side of Kukulcán's temple and one of them said: 'Girls, this thing has four sides, with ninety-one steps to each side, for a total of three hundred and sixty-four steps we have to sweep.' And another one said: 'Nuts to this; let's go on strike.' So they did. When the place got knee-deep in sacrificial leftovers, the men gave up and moved everyone to a new city only one-story high. I predict that someday archaeologists will find a thriving civilization living in this jungle, in nice easy-to-clean one-story houses."

"Vacuum cleaners?" David smiled.

"Do you have any idea how hard it is to clean dirt and snakes off stone steps?" His shoulder felt just right under her cheek, and she could smell the faint essence of an expensive after-shave. "And what did the ladies get for their trouble? The chance to be sacrificed."

"Not the most inspirational motivation, I'll admit."

"I rest my case." Before she snuggled deeper into his shoulder and dozed, Jenny thought his lips brushed her hair, but she wasn't sure. The next thing she heard was Carlos's voice crackling over the loudspeaker.

"Siesta's over, my friends. Here's the hotel."

Jenny sat up and stretched, then smiled sheepishly at David. "I fell asleep. Sorry."

"So did I. It was nice sleeping with you."

She returned his smile and felt a blush beneath her sunburn. Some things she hadn't managed to outgrow.

In the lobby, David glanced at his watch. "It's six o'clock now; suppose I meet you and Pam at eight o'clock for dinner. There's a restaurant in town called La Habichuela that has lobster in three sizes: normal, jumbo and colossal."

"Colossal? I can't wait." She touched his cheek lightly. "See you at eight o'clock."

"I CAN'T BELIEVE IT," Pam said when she'd heard Jenny's story about becoming nationally famous. "Jenny Marshall, you just aren't the type to lie."

"It isn't really a lie," Jenny said, feeling uncomfortable. She glanced at Pam in the mirror, then bent forward to apply her lipstick.

"What do you call it, then?"

"Airplane truth."

Pam rolled her eyes. "And what is that?"

"You travel more than I do, so you should know. It's when you pour out the intimate details of your life to an absolute stranger."

After buttoning her silk blouse and zipping her skirt, Pam nodded. "Okay, I know what you mean. But there's a flaw here, Jen. There isn't a grain of truth to the details you're pouring out."

"But it's the same thing. The person next to you on the plane doesn't really care what you're saying. In an hour or so you'll go your separate ways. You can tell him anything, actually, and there's no harm done."

Pam looked at her. "Are you sure you and David are going separate ways?"

"He lives in California; I live in Denver. He has his life; I have mine." Jenny sighed. "We're ships passing in the night."

"Sometimes ships collide."

How she wished these two would, but it didn't seem likely. Jenny would have her Cinderella week with the handsome prince, then she would return to suburban obscurity. There were no fairy godmothers in real life. Worse luck.

"You won't give me away, will you?" Turning from the mirror, she looked at Pam anxiously.

"Of course not. But ol' Aunt Pam thinks you should 'fess up. And the sooner the better."

"Thanks for the advice, Aunt Pam, but I'm having too much fun dreaming out loud." Jenny held her hairbrush like a microphone and solemnly intoned, "Ladies and gentlemen, we're fortunate to have with us today that internationally known artist Jenny Marshall. Mrs. Marshall, tell us how it feels to grace the cover of *Time* magazine."

Pam smiled and pushed at her springy red hair. "Okay, madam artist. But, remember what the poet said? 'Oh, what a tangled web we weave, when first we practice to deceive!'"

"Tell it to Cinderella."

"Come along, Cindy. Prince Foster is waiting for us."

THE MARGARITAS at La Habichuela were icy and just tart enough, the colossal lobsters were everything David had promised.

"I didn't know such huge lobsters existed." Pam sighed.

"Or that I could actually eat that much," Jenny agreed.

Pleased, David ordered flan for dessert. He lit Pam's cigarette and they sipped brandy while waiting for the flan.

Their table was in a tropical garden, lit by subtly concealed colored lights. Giant flowers dropped from the tree limbs overhead, ferns and banana plants intertwined the lush foliage marking the garden's perimeter. Jenny decided paradise must look like this.

"Have you attended Jenny's showings?" David asked Pam.

"I can honestly say I haven't missed any showing Jenny has had," Pam replied after a tiny hesitation.

"Even the international showings?" David pressed Jenny's hand. "Now, that's a friend."

"Well, I am a travel agent," Pam explained, with a quick, narrowed glance at Jenny's innocent smile. "I can usually travel free."

"Tell me about your paintings, Jenny, love. Is there a recurrent theme? Or are they all different?"

How easily he'd slipped into his pet name for her. And how nice and comfortable it sounded. "Portraits mostly. As I wanted to do in college." She didn't look at Pam. "Faces interest me. Particularly the faces of the West—Indians, the old cowboys."

"I still have the painting you gave me before you left for Rome, did I tell you that?"

"The old man standing beside the horse?"

David smiled. "It's probably worth a fortune today. An early Jenny Marshall."

If one considered six dollars and fifty-three cents—the cost of the paint and canvas—a fortune. Considering the price of hamburger, Jenny decided it was.

"What's the worst part about being famous?"

Pam smiled sweetly. "Yes, Jenny, I'd like to know, too. What do you hate most about being internationally acclaimed?"

Jenny was enjoying herself too much to pay any attention to Pam. "Autographs, I think," she said grandly. "It's very strange having people ask for my autograph."

"I'll bet," Pam commented dryly.

"I'd think it would be flattering," David said, pride glowing in his dark eyes.

"Well, I leave my autograph for the milkman every Monday and he's notably unimpressed." She was pleased to see that Pam joined David's laughter.

The evening passed in a dream, in a blur of enchantment. Jenny was surprised and slightly ashamed of how easily the details of her invented life rolled off her tongue. Under David's interested questioning she spoke of glittering receptions, exhaustive media interviews, a life that was glamorous and exciting. She sounded like a woman who wouldn't recognize a can of furniture polish if one dropped into her lap, like a woman who was confident and sure of her place in the world. She sparkled with happiness.

Outside the door to their room, Pam fitted her key into the lock. "Thanks for including me, David." She looked at them a moment, then stepped inside and closed the door behind her.

Heart thumping against her ribs, Jenny raised her eyes. "It was a wonderful day." Usually she thrust out her hand, pumped her date's hand in a cheerful handshake and closed the door in his face. But this was David. And she wanted him to kiss her. All day a tension had been building between them, an intimacy of brushed shoulders, hands that clasped naturally, her head against the warmth of his shoulder. She looked into his steady gaze and knew she hadn't felt like this in years.

"Jenny. My beautiful Jenny."

Gently his hands framed her face and tilted her mouth upward. His lips brushed hers lightly in a kiss as tantalizing as a promise. Then he kissed her eyelids as he drew her into his arms and pressed her against the long, hard length of his body.

Jenny's heart accelerated and her knees turned to water. His mouth covered hers in a kiss that deepened with an urgency that snatched her breath away. Her arms circled his neck, and she felt her breasts crushing against his chest as she buried her fingers in his thick dark hair.

A wild pulse thundered in her ears and heat swirled through her body. When his lips released hers, she pulled slightly away and stared at him with wide eyes. Being struck by a lightning bolt would feel like this.

"Wow," he said in a hoarse voice.

She managed a wobbly smile. "I feel like a teenager—necking in a hallway."

Warm fingers brushed a strand of honey-colored hair from her cheek. "I've missed you, Jenny, love. I let you get away once. I'm not going to be that big a fool again."

Jenny examined the in ensity in his eyes and her heart soared. How often had she imagined David Foster saying those words? Only about a million times. Who said dreams didn't come true? "I've thought about you so often," she said. The understatement of the century. "Wondered what your life was like, where you were, if you were happy."

"I am now. Happier than I've been in a very long time."

Radiance glowed in her eyes and she felt more alive than she could ever remember being. "Me, too."

"I warn you, I'm going to monopolize your vacation."

The heat of his strong thighs pressed to hers seemed to melt through her light silk dress. Before he kissed her again, she murmured in a throaty voice, "I hope you do."

"I'll see you at breakfast," he said, fitting Jenny's key into the door. "About nine o'clock?"

"A most sensible hour."

Inside the room, Jenny leaned against the door, wishing she had packed her paints. Instead of feeling sleepy, she tingled with creative urgency. Right now she wanted to paint something dreamy and softly romantic. Lovers perhaps, reuniting after years of separation.

Pam's voice interrupted her thoughts. "I don't know about this, Jen. That guy is crazy about you. What's he going to think when he learns you've been pulling the wool over his eyes?"

"Don't be a wet blanket, Pam. I've fantasized a week like this for years. Nothing is going to spoil it."

"Well—I hope you know what you're doing."

"I'm taking one day at a time and enjoying every fabulous minute! We famous artists do that, you know."

There was nothing that could diminish the natural high raised by David's kiss. There was no obstacle Jenny couldn't conquer, no pyramid she couldn't climb. She flung out her arms and spun in a circle of sheer happiness.

If life got any better than this, she couldn't imagine it.

Chapter Four

They had breakfast on the hotel terrace. Sunlight sparkled off the Caribbean and spun Jenny's hair to gold. In David's eyes she didn't seem a day older than she had in college. It looked as though her sunburn would fade to a smooth, golden tan; a light sprinkling of freckles dusted her nose. Today she wore pink shorts and a halter top that drew his eyes. She was relaxed, confident and beautiful.

Thinking of the girl he'd known in college, he was glad for her, pleased by the changes time had worked. She had always been flip and a little brash, quick with an amusing comeback. It wasn't until he'd known her better that he'd grasped her vulnerability and understood she wasn't as confident as she appeared.

Now, with the passage of years, it seemed Jenny had come into her own. She'd blossomed with her success. Maturity had given her an unforgettable face and a better figure than he remembered. There were still traces of vulnerability, a sudden expression, or a look in her eyes, but he hoped it was a quality she'd never lose. And she still concocted those crazy theories, he thought with a smile. But she also had the self-possession of a woman who knew she could cope with life's obstacles. It didn't sound as though there were many problems in her life, but he imagined she met those that came along with humor and assurance.

And her painting made her financially secure. Jenny Marshall clearly was not looking for a man to take care of her. For all the talk about women wanting careers, it had been David's experience that most women were still looking for a husband to ride in on his white charger and ensconce them in a mansion on the hill. He was fair enough to admit that not all women fitted this description. But those from his circle of friends seemed to. If the women had careers, their careers were more in line with hobbies, something to occupy them while their husbands did battle downtown and brought home the spoils to assure that life in *House Beautiful* continued at a suitably lavish level.

It was a relief to find a woman who was genuinely committed to an important career, successful at it, yet who had remained warm and definitely feminine. A woman financially independent, but able to admit honestly that she preferred marriage to being single. Jenny would love a man for what he was, not for what he could give her. But David had always known that.

"Is there anyone important in your life right now?" he asked. "A man?"

"I date occasionally, but...no, there's no one special."

"Good. I'm glad to hear it." He wanted to make love to her. Right here, right now.

"David, if you don't stop looking at me like that, we're going to be arrested." Jenny wet her lips and felt her heart flip over in her breast. She could sense the heat of his legs inches from hers under the table. And she was experiencing physical urges she'd supposed she had under control. Wrong.

"There's no place else I'd rather be, Jenny, love, than here with you."

She looked into his dark eyes and thought of melting chocolate chips. "Me, too," she whispered. His hand covered hers and she felt the warm strength of his touch flash up her arm like electricity.

"What would you like to do today?"

"I don't think it's legal," she said.

Laughing, he squeezed her fingers. "Why not? We're unattached adults, aren't we?"

Jenny had a theory about that. No one was truly unattached. Invisible threads tied people to children, parents, friends, ex-spouses, houses, possessions and creditors. Sometimes the threads were loose; sometimes they exerted a stranglehold. At the moment her threads were comfortably loose. She nodded, looking at his mouth.

"Then—how would you like to take the ferry to Isla Mujeres? I understand there's a wonderful French restaurant there. We can snorkel, tour the island...and catch the morning ferry back to Cancún."

"The morning ferry?"

"I've been told there's a charming inn above the French restaurant."

She met his eyes and what she saw in his steady gaze made her catch a quick breath and hold it. The sky seemed to spin above her, and she felt breathless. And she wanted to say yes. She hadn't said yes to any man since the divorce.

"David . . ."

"If I'm rushing things, just say so. I'll understand."

"You're rushing things." But the days were flying past and she wouldn't have this chance again. Though Jenny was the last person to indulge in a quick fling, she also knew this week was a block of time outside reality. She was a new person, not bound by the rules and regulations of everyday life. The new glamorous persona she had created for herself would not have turned prudish and rigid. Besides, she had set aside this one week to revel in fantasy. "And, yes," she added softly, "I'd love to go to Isla Mujeres with you."

His face lit up. "Are you sure, Jenny, love?"

"Very sure." Gazing into his eyes, feeling the sudden tension in the pit of her stomach, the tremble on her lips, she'd never been more sure of anything. Finally she looked away and pushed herself from the table. "I'll pack a bag."

"I'll arrange for the ferry and meet you in the lobby in, say, an hour and a half?"

"Perfect."

He tilted her face up to his and dropped a kiss on her nose. Then he drew his finger lightly over her chin and down the curve of her throat. "Until then."

Conscious of David watching, Jenny crossed the terrace and mounted the steps to the lobby certain that her feet didn't touch the ground. She'd been wrong. Life could get better, it could be a waking dream. Smiling, she decided she was living out a glorious illusion, without a problem in the world.

Wrong. She stopped in her tracks and stared at nothing. She had a problem all right—a big one. A problem she hadn't thought of in two years. Sex. More accurately, birth control.

Striding forward, she flew into the lobby and looked about frantically for Pam. When she saw Pam head to head with the Palenque's manager, Jenny dashed over and interrupted the conversation.

"Excuse me." Speaking from the corner of her mouth, she whispered to Pam. "Big trouble. I need to talk to you."

Pam smiled at Hernan Mortiz, then drew Jenny aside. "Jenny! This is a business meeting."

"I'm talking an emergency, Pamela. A big-time emergency. Meet me in the room in five minutes." Turning, she grabbed Hernan Mortiz's hand and gave it a firm shake. "Lovely hotel, lovely." Distracted, she shot a pleading gaze at Pam. "Nice ocean. Great sun. Keep up the good work."

When Pam arrived in the room, Jenny was pacing and coughing through the smoke of one of Pam's cigarettes. "This had better be good, Jen," Pam said, flinging herself in one of the chairs.

"How do you ask a man if he's had a vasectomy?"

Pam's mouth dropped then clamped in a line. "You called me out of a business meeting for *that*?"

"How would you like to be an unwed mother at age thirty-seven? If this isn't an emergency, I don't know what is."

"All right. You've got a point." After lighting a cigarette, Pam squinted up at Jenny. "Would I be correct to assume I'll have the room to myself tonight?"

"If I can work this out." Jenny drew on the cigarette, choked and exhaled. "I haven't thought about this in years. What am I going to do?"

"Aren't you taking the pill?"

"Why should I pay for pills when there's no need? I haven't met a man I wanted to... never mind. The fact is, I'd like to spend the night with David, but I don't want to end up pregnant at my age. It's too late to gulp down a pill, and I ain't got rhythm, so what's left?"

"Well, I hate to be indelicate, but..."

"If you're about to suggest one of those little flat packages some men carry around in their wallets, forget it. Rhonda is living proof there's a flaw in that system."

Pam looked interested. "Really? How come you never told me that before?"

"This subject never came up before. Speaking of which, what do I say? Something like: 'I had the dog spayed recently, David, old friend. That reminds me—how about yourself, have you been spayed by any chance?'"

"Real subtle," Pam laughed. "Tact is not your long suit, my dear. I don't suppose you're willing to make this relationship platonic?"

"Pam, all I have is a few days. Then it's over. Plus—I know this sounds stupid, but I haven't felt this starry-eyed since... well, since college."

"Don't I recall someone named Walter? About two kids ago?"

"It wasn't like this with Walter." Jenny stubbed out the cigarette and spread her hands. "Walter was just—there. But it wasn't a grand passion."

"Oh, boy. Here it comes. Romeo and Juliet. Héloïse and Abélard. David and Jenny."

Jenny smiled. "That's it. So how do I find out if he's had a vasectomy?"

"I haven't the vaguest idea."

"Maybe I should just ask him outright. What do you think?"

"The honest approach? What a charming idea."

Jenny made a face and paced toward the balcony. "You know—have you ever thought about vasectomies? Really thought about them?"

"Not in living memory."

"I mean, as I understand the procedure, the man keeps manufacturing sperm. So where does it go?"

"God, Jenny. How do you think of these things?"

"It goes into the bloodstream, that must be it. Do you realize what this means?"

"You probably have a theory, right?"

"It means that after a few years, the bloodstream must be lousy with sperm." A new thought occurred to her. "Pam, don't ever help an old guy who's bleeding. You'll get pregnant just like that." She snapped her fingers.

Grinning, Pam shook her head. "As it appears you've been the victim of poor planning, you seem to have two choices."

"Which are?"

"Keep this relationship platonic or take your chances. You'll look great in maternity clothes."

Jenny groaned. "I look like a pear in maternity clothes. A giant pear." She stared at the ceiling. "I am too old to be an unwed mother."

"Hey, it's the fashion nowadays. Half of Hollywood is turning up forty and pregnant."

"Pam, be sensible. Most of those Hollywood types are having first babies; they don't already have two teenagers—well, one and twelve-thirteenths teenagers. What they have is money for nannies, nurses and such. I don't. What I have is a long memory. I remember night feedings and diapers and overall sticky." She stared hard at Pam. "Tell me the truth. Would you like to be pregnant now, at our age?"

Pam considered. "After two seconds of brief but intense thought, I can truthfully say I'd rather run naked through the stadium during the halftime period of a nationally televised Bronco game, thereby exposing these thighs to worldwide ridicule, than be pregnant again just when I've reached the point where I can finally go to the bathroom without having a child watching me."

"There you are. I couldn't have said it better myself." Jenny waved a hand. "I can't do this, can I? I can't run off to Isla Mujeres and have a mad fantasy fling."

"Well," Pam said, standing and looking at her watch. "As it seems we've exhausted all options but a vasectomy, I'd say you have to think of a way to ask the gentleman. Then make your decision."

Jenny tried to think of something while she packed her overnight bag. Nothing came to mind. To ask seemed tacky beyond words. How did single people handle this?

In her case, the problem hadn't arisen before. Until David, she hadn't met anyone she cared enough about to let things go that far. When she'd noticed that certain gleam in her dates' eyes, she'd refused further dates. Avoidance: it was still the best form of birth control.

"UH, DO WE HAVE TIME for a quick cup of coffee?" she asked when she met David in the lobby. Nervously, she gripped the handle of her overnight bag. She'd thought she could handle her disappointment if things didn't work out as she'd hoped. But a warm shiver of anticipation heated her body when David smiled at her.

"Having second thoughts?"

"Oh, no, no," Jenny lied. "Just a sudden craving for caffeine."

They ordered coffee from the poolside cabana and found seats where they could watch the waves rolling up the beach. Jenny drew a long breath and gazed into her coffee cup. "Do you remember Bill Hanson and Marian Anderson? They got married right after graduation."

"I don't think so. The names don't sound familiar."

Jenny would have been amazed if they had, as she had only now made them up. "Poor Marian is pregnant." She shook her head pityingly. "She's the same age as I am, thirty-seven. And pregnant."

"Hmm."

"I'd sure hate to be starting over again, just when I've reached an age when I can go out without hunting up a baby-sitter. Wouldn't you?"

"Frankly, babies terrify me." He passed her the cream and sugar. "Did you bring snorkeling gear?"

"No."

"We'll rent some. The manager tells me the best snorkeling in the world is off the reef near Isla Mujeres."

Jenny tried again. "Yes, the last time I talked to Marian, she was distraught, poor thing."

"Who?"

"Marian Anderson. Our pregnant classmate."

"Oh, yes."

Jenny stirred her coffee. "Just imagine. Pablum and Pampers again. At my age."

David nodded companionably. "I've heard it can be dangerous to be pregnant at that age."

Jenny emphatically agreed. "Oh, it is! The wife of Walter's partner got pregnant when she was forty." Jenny shuddered. "She almost died." What she had nearly died of was shock at being pregnant, but Jenny didn't think it necessary to explain this. This wasn't going well; maybe she would have to ask him outright.

"Did you bring your swimsuit?"

"Yes."

"I can't wait to see you in it," he said, his gaze slipping briefly to her halter top.

She decided to give it one more try. "I was talking to Marian Anderson about swimming the other day..."

"The woman who's pregnant?"

"At my age. And..."

Comprehension dawned in David's dark eyes. He burst into laughter. "Jenny, are we talking about birth control?"

Thank God. "Well, now that you bring it up..." Heat flooded her cheeks. This was worse than her Great Sex Talk with Deuce and Rhonda. Cheeks flaming, she made herself look at him. "I haven't taken the pill in two years and..."

"And you'd like me to take care of things?"

"Ah, the thought has crossed my mind." Constantly. Every few seconds.

"I had a vasectomy years ago," he said gently. Clasping her hand, he pressed it with understanding.

"And, before you tell me about another friend who is dying of some dread social disease . . ."

Her blush deepened to scarlet. There was a whole lot about being single in today's world that she didn't know. In fact, the first time she'd heard about herpes, she'd thought the conversation referred to a minor deity from Greek mythology until Pam told her how dumb she was.

"I'm being silly, aren't I?"

"Not at all. You're being careful and that's smart." Smiling, he looked at his watch, then stroked her cheek. "Now can we go? Or is there anything else you'd like to know?"

"One more thing—where have you been all my life?"

He laughed, then his eyes sobered. "Waiting for you, Jenny, love." His eyes swept her face, making love to her. "Waiting for you."

THEY TOOK THE FERRY from Puerto Juárez to Isla Mujeres and passed the five-mile trip listening to the guide speak of a history rich with conquistadores, pirates and hidden treasure.

The town, a sleepy fishing village, was located on the northern tip of the island. Wide sidewalks framed narrow streets; lively music drifted from the town square. Scarlet bougainvillea climbed the balconies of the small inn facing the square.

Jenny gazed about the lobby as David led her inside. A polished floor gleamed in the sunlight falling from tall windows, lush greenery contrasted with light-colored furnishings, the tantalizing scent of French sauces wafted through the dining room doors.

As David approached the registration desk, Jenny bit her lip and pretended great interest in the painting hung near the door. This was the moment that separated the sophisticates from the provincials. And she was undeniably provincial. Disgustingly old-fashioned. When it came to checking into a hotel, the GYTs had it all over her. Any GYT worth her salt would have waltzed up to the desk with David and been as natural as vanilla pudding. She would not have skulked around the door, hiding behind a potted palm as Jenny was doing.

When it seemed enough time had passed to register the entire Yucatán peninsula, Jenny peered through the leaves of the palm and discovered the desk clerk watching her with a curious expression. She was positive the desk clerk bore a certain family resemblance to her Uncle Larry, her mother's brother. Had Uncle Larry ever mentioned a trip to Mexico—or any engaging *señoritas*? Feeling slightly panicked, Jenny let the palm leaves snap together as she imagined the desk clerk dropping a note to her mother: "Dear Aunt Mary, I thought you should know that your daughter checked into our hotel today with a man who was not Walter, and I noticed she was wearing no wedding ring...."

"I am not cut out for this," Jenny muttered. "I am hopelessly square."

She prided herself on keeping track of what was happening in the world. On occasion she even adopted a worldly air. In fact, she heartily approved of the new relaxed atmosphere that allowed men and women to test their relationship before making long-term commitments. Had she done so with Walter they would never have made the mistake of getting married. The new system was excellent, beneficial for all. A good thing. Sensible.

But not for her. With a sigh Jenny admitted she belonged to the generation who made commitments first and then jumped into the sack. Dumb, but what was a person to do? She'd never checked into a hotel with a man in her entire life except with Walter, and he didn't count because they'd been married. Even then she had felt guilty.

It had to do with her mother theory. A woman could be eighty-years-old, but her mother was still there, frowning over her shoulder and whispering such guilt-inducing items as: "Be sure your underwear is respectable—you could be in an accident"; or "A tidy home is a happy home"; or "Nice girls don't go to hotels with strange men."

But David isn't a stranger, Jenny thought. She'd met his family, albeit long ago; she'd shared his dreams and innermost thoughts. She knew David Foster. Knew his kindness and generosity, knew his strength and integrity. Slowly, she began to relax.

"The bellboy will put our bags in the room," David said, smiling when she jumped at the sound of his voice. "You might want to get your swimsuit first."

Relaxed? She was kidding herself. All she had to do was glance at his mouth or feel the warmth of his hand against her back and her nerves leaped to the surface of her skin. "I have it right here," she said, patting the side of her beach bag.

He cupped her shoulders with his palms and smiled gently into her wide eyes. "Jenny, the desk clerk doesn't know who we are and couldn't care less."

"Was I that transparent?" Crestfallen, she bit her lip.

"Not at all," he teased her. "I imagine he's used to ladies hiding in the ferns." His thumbs brushed across her bare shoulders as his expression sobered. "I'm glad you aren't accustomed to checking into hotels, Jenny, love. I like that about you."

For a moment she waged an inner battle. It seemed to Jenny that her new famous and worldly self would not quake at registering into a hotel. She considered remaining in character and trying to brazen it out by denying she'd been hiding. But a value system founded in bedrock won out. She doubted she could have been convincing anyway.

"I'm hopelessly old-fashioned," she admitted, a trace of annoyance in her voice.

"I know. And I couldn't be happier."

They held hands in the taxi taking them to the southern tip of the island and El Garrafon beach. David smiled, thinking how comfortable and how right it felt to have Jenny's shoulder against his. He looked at their interlaced fingers and wondered how he had let her slip out of his life. Why hadn't he gone to Rome with her? Why hadn't he waited until she returned?

Pride maybe. A youthful pride that had demanded unreasonable proof of love. He'd been young and green and had believed she wouldn't go if she really loved him. Instead of encouraging her and being proud that Frascotti had accepted her, he'd been wounded that she needed something in her life besides him.

Thank God he'd grown up. And thank God Jenny had had the sense not to give up Rome and the opportunity to study with Frascotti. In his youth and ignorance he might have cost her the chance for self-fulfillment and independence.

"Have I told you how much I admire you?" he asked.

"Whatever for?"

"For having the courage to follow your dream. For not letting circumstances or people stand in your way. For not giving up." Tipping her face up to his, he brushed a light kiss across her lips. She had the softest mouth. "And for not letting success change the wonderful person you are."

"I don't think I deserve all that."

Two dots of color flamed in her cheeks, and he laughed at her modesty, liking her for it, wanting to kiss her again. But if he'd learned anything over the years, he'd learned that anticipation lay at the center of romance. Neither of them were kids anymore; they could wait and enjoy the slow building of tension and need. They no longer required the instant gratification of youth. There were pleasures in delay he hadn't suspected when he was in college.

"Well, what do you think of Isla Mujeres?"

Jenny glanced out the window. "Beautiful. Less commercial than Cancún."

David nodded agreement. The surf was stronger here, the beaches unspoiled. A wild tangle of growth encroached upon the twisting road. "I'm afraid it will be twenty years or more before Isla Mujeres is ready for development."

"Spoken like a true businessman."

"That's why I'm here, to look over the area for possible investment."

"For one of your clients?"

He hesitated, then said yes. In truth, he had only one client: himself. Managing his investments had become a full-time job. There were stocks and bonds, treasury notes, oil debentures, real estate holdings and several small companies. He didn't mistrust Jenny's motives, and he would have cleared up any confusion she had regarding his financial position, but he could think of no way to do so without appearing pretentious or as if he were boasting. "I'm meeting Rob Spenser tomorrow afternoon. He's the attorney who's putting together an investment package for the Palenque."

"Looks like a good investment to me."

"Would you be interested in part of the syndication?" Jenny stared at him a moment, an odd smile on her lips. Possibly she was offended that he hadn't mentioned this before. After apologizing, he explained the deal, ending with, "You can invest as little as a hundred thousand, or as much as half a million. The return percentages will be figured when the syndication is complete."

"Thank you for thinking of me, David. But, actually, my money is tied up right now." She made an airy wave, and for some reason David suddenly imagined her draped in mink and diamonds instead of wearing shorts and a halter top. He smiled at the illusion. "Otherwise," she continued, "I might have been very interested."

The moment was thrilling for Jenny. She'd never imagined that anyone would mention Jenny Marshall and a hundred thousand dollars in the same breath. What a strange and marvelous week this was turning out to be. And what a large world there was beyond her doorstep. It was a glorious thing to be part of that larger world, even for a short while.

Smiling at nothing, she laughed aloud. When David smiled and raised an eyebrow, she pressed his hand. "It's nothing. I'm just happy."

And her happiness continued to grow. They inspected the red-and-white lighthouse above El Garrafon beach, then walked hand in hand along the sand, laughing when the surf bubbled up around their knees. After renting snorkeling gear, they paddled about the reef, pointing out to each other thousands of brilliantly colored fish. Jenny gloried in the darting flashes of color, wishing she could capture such brilliance on canvas.

Later, David stretched out in the sun and Jenny reclined a few feet away beneath the protective thatching of the beach cabana.

For a long moment, they faced each other, looking deeply into each other's eyes. Then David said softly, "Do you think I could persuade you to put some lotion on my back?"

Jenny knelt in the sand beside him and poured coconut oil over his shoulders. She drew a breath, then smoothed the oil over David's back. His skin was firm and warm from the sun. She could feel muscle and sinew beneath her fingertips. A soft breeze played through her hair; someone nearby was strumming a guitar accompanied by the whisper of the surf rolling up the sand.

A tightness drew across her stomach. A flush appeared in her cheeks.

"Now you," David said. His voice had dropped to a lower register. And when he looked at her, Jenny saw an intensity in his eyes that made her feel light-headed.

"Yes," she whispered, sliding her beach cover off her shoulders.

"You are so lovely."

She held her breath as the oil touched her. And then his hands. His fingers stroked the oil over her skin as gently as a caress. She felt each touch as a tiny explosion of heat; each sliding stroke brought her nerve endings singing upward. The languid warmth of the oil and the sensual touch of his hands made her feel . . . liquid inside, and yet restlessly tense, as if her body had stirred into a yearning entity with a life of its own.

When he gently turned her to face him, his hands on her arms, Jenny lifted her fingertips to his shoulders and touched the cords of muscle beneath the warm oil. For an instant, it seemed that her awareness centered in her fingers. Heat, muscle, bone. And when his hands framed her shoulders, she tingled, fully alive and vibrant.

"Jenny . . ."

She stared at him helplessly, caught in an emotional whirlpool. The beach, the sky, the rest of the world vanished. There was only David. Dark eyes staring intently into hers; his mouth—his firm, eager mouth—moving toward hers.

When he kissed her, Jenny melted into his arms. She clung to him and surrendered completely to the force of his lips, to the urgency of his seeking tongue. Time ceased to exist, and she was aware only of his warm skin against her own, of the sweetness of his mouth, of the waves of urgency rocketing through her body. When he released her, she was shaken to her toes.

David stared into her eyes for a long moment; then he stood up and extended his hand to her. Wordlessly they gathered their belongings, then they burst into simultaneous laughter and ran hand in hand toward the taxi that would take them back to the hotel.

Chapter Five

Their room was charming. Brightly upholstered chairs carved from Mexican hardwood furnished the sitting room, along with small tables draped by handmade lace. Hand-crafted throw rugs were scattered across a cool tile floor. Good lithographs adorned the walls, and the balcony faced a breathtaking view of the ocean. There were fresh flowers on the tables and a well-stocked bar in the corner.

Best of all, Jenny realized, there were no ghosts here. Marilyn Cody had not decided the color scheme; Walter Marshall had not dropped his shirt over that chair. The rooms and the memories to be made here belonged exclusively to her and David, shared with no one.

"Would you like a glass of wine? I saw a split of Chablis in the fridge."

"Sounds wonderful," Jenny said.

Once, they would have fallen on each other the minute the door closed behind them. Now, by tacit agreement, they prolonged the moment, letting their anticipation build. There were advantages to maturity, Jenny decided with a smile.

She kicked off her sandals and walked toward the balcony, enjoying the sensation of cool tiles against her warm feet. Leaning against the wrought-iron railing, she viewed the scenery with a painter's eye.

Never had colors seemed so vivid. The sea undulated in tones of bright greenish-blue tipped with snowy foam. A cobalt sky stretched overhead. The beach was dazzling white, and the bougainvillea blossoms nodding between the balcony's rails were brilliant sparks of pink and scarlet. The palm trees reminded her of lush green feather dusters sweeping the sky. This, then, was heaven's palette.

"Jenny?"

Her fingers brushed David's as she took the wine he offered, and the brief contact was like a heated force flying from her fingertips through her body. She looked up at him—acutely aware of his strong, tanned face, the flash of white teeth as he smiled—alive to the controlled heat in his gaze. Hereafter, Jenny would think of passion in tones of bronze, white and tawny-brown as warm and deep as David's eyes.

He leaned beside her, their shoulders touching as they toasted the spectacular view. Open to sensation, Jenny inhaled the voluptuous scent of the coconut lotion oiling their bodies and knew it would forever remind her of Mexican sunsets and soft ocean breezes. And David Foster.

Time spiraled backward and she remembered the first time they had made love, more than fifteen years ago. She'd been frightened and eager, curious and reluctant—and so innocent of the ways of men and women.

She cast a sidelong glance at David's profile and recalled that their first encounter hadn't been an immediate success. Both had been painfully self-conscious. Jenny remembered the evening as a parade of anxieties. Would David's roommate return at an embarrassing moment? Would she have a red mark around her waist from the band of her ski pants? Would it hurt? Would he be disappointed in her? Or she in him? What would they say to each other afterward?

As if reading her mind, David looked at her, his lopsided smile bathed in sunset tones of orange and gold. "Remember the first time?" he asked softly.

"Yes." Jenny smiled into her wineglass. "It was awful, wasn't it?"

"All I could think about was how beautiful you were. I was half crazy worrying that the experience would end too quickly and that I wouldn't make your first time a happy one." Lightly he touched her cheek. "I remember concentrating on math that night. Because if I thought about you, I knew I couldn't prolong the moment for you."

"And I kept thinking about my knees. I didn't know what to do with them. I could have sworn I had fourteen knees that night, and all of them were in the way." They smiled at each other.

"It was snowing. Remember?"

"I remember." She closed her eyes, feeling the heat radiating from his body to hers. Remembering his hands on her naked skin. Her knees—all fourteen of them—suddenly felt as if they had turned to straw.

David's fingertip traced her jawline from temple to chin. His thumb brushed the curve of her lips, feeling the tremble there. "Beautiful Jenny."

Looking down into her eyes, he removed Jenny's wineglass from her nerveless fingers, then gently cupped her face between his hands. He tilted her head upward and kissed her with slow deliberation, exploring the contours of her mouth with a delicious lack of haste.

Jenny's arms rose to circle his neck and, as he guided her toward him, she fitted herself against the curves and angles of his body, blending into him. She felt his rising passion as his arms tightened around her, and she trembled lightly at the answering tension drawing her stomach. Her lips parted beneath his, and she knew she was slipping away on a tide of desire both emotional and physical. When his mouth released hers, she stared into his eyes, shaken.

Bending, he lifted her into his arms as effortlessly as if she weighed no more than the flowers filling their bedroom. The fragrance surrounded her as he carried her inside and gently laid her on the bed. A nervous flutter began in the pit of Jenny's stomach and spread upward and down. A rush of heat warmed her skin as she watched him remove his shirt, revealing a thatch of dark hair across the muscles tightening his chest.

Fingers trembling, Jenny unfastened the clasp of her halter top, her large, blue eyes not leaving his intent gaze. Almost shyly she opened the halter to reveal a soft swell of creamy flesh beneath the glow that was slowly fading to a golden tan.

A low sound broke from David's throat. Stepping to the bed, he gathered her into his arms. The explosion of warmth against her breasts sent a ripple down Jenny's spine. She pressed her face into the warm crease at his neck and touched the hair on his chest with wonder, remembering the texture of his skin, the hard length of his body pressed against hers.

His lips whispered across her hair, her forehead and then her eyelids. The heels of his hands felt like flames against the sides of her breasts. With a soft moan, Jenny lifted her mouth and returned his kiss with a mounting desire that swept all thought from her mind. Their tongues met and teased, as he stretched out beside her, her body adjusted to the hollows and curves of his as if it were only yesterday they had held each other.

Reaching behind her, David unzipped her shorts and guided them over her hips. "Lovely," he whispered when she lay naked before his gaze. "So lovely."

"Oh, David." She looked at him, loving the lean, strong grace of his body, his firm mouth, the smooth touch of his oiled skin. Shivers of anticipation flowed over her and she knew it had not been yesterday they had held each other and loved—it had been a lifetime ago. Eons ago.

She pressed her forehead against his shoulder and held him so fiercely she could feel the steady pulse of his heartbeat. "Hold me, David. Hold me and tell me this is real."

His gentle hands stroked the ridge along her spine, softly touched the curve of her buttocks. Warm, wine-scented breath stirred the tendrils of hair brushing her ear. "This is real, Jenny, love."

His words reassured her, and Jenny moaned softly as her head fell backward against the pillow and her body arched toward the strength and warmth of his.

Slowly, deliberately, not rushing, although Jenny felt his need hard and demanding against her thigh, David kissed her throat, whispered against the pulse thudding at the base of her neck. Her fingers twined in his dark hair, guiding him to her breasts. And then his tongue circled and teased until her nipples rose like hard little buttons to meet his attention.

A slide of heat followed his hand along the curve of her waist and over her hips. She gasped with pleasure as his fingers trailed along the inside of her thighs—approaching, then withdrawing in tantalizing suggestion. Jenny's stomach wound into coils of urgency, her nerves felt raw and exposed. Heated breath rushed past her parted lips as his mouth brushed kisses across her stomach and kindled wild, dark fires.

She whispered his name without realizing she did so. Her eyes closed, and her fingers shook lightly on his shoulders.

Then his lips were where his teasing fingers had been, climbing the tender swell of her thighs. And her breath burned in her throat, and her body trembled on the edge of something warm and moist and explosive.

When his tongue found her center, Jenny cried out with exquisite pleasure. Her head pushed against the pillow as she lifted to him, and each breath seared her lungs. Her body flamed into life.

Expertly, skillfully, David stroked, coaxed, until Jenny felt a gasp building in her throat, until tension quivered on her skin like a live thing, and she felt she could not bear another second of such sweet torment without exploding, without melting.

Reaching blindly, frantically, she pulled him up to her and saw in his eyes, in the velvet rigidity of his body, that he was as urgently ready as she. His kiss was no longer gentle but hard and satisfying and bruising in his need, a need that matched her own.

Twining her long legs around his body, Jenny guided him into her, releasing a quick breath as he filled the emptiness she'd been unaware of until now.

She breathed the intoxicating scent of wine and flowers and coconut oil. And she opened to David as totally as never before, giving herself completely.

They sensed each other's rhythms and paced themselves to give, as well as to receive, the greatest pleasure. Deep kisses accelerated the pace, soft fluttering caresses slowed it. Jenny brushed damp hair from David's forehead and smiled into his eyes.

Then, as if her smile had been a signal they had both awaited, their bodies meshed in a final urgent blending that soared and rocketed toward an explosive, shattering union. Jenny's body arched to meet his, and she clung to his damp skin as if she were drowning. His shoulders contracted under her fingertips and his head dropped to her throat.

They held each other, neither wanting the magic to end, waiting until their breathing had quieted. Then David lifted his head and smiled into Jenny's softly shining eyes. "Happy?"

"I've never been happier," Jenny whispered truthfully. "Unless—were you by any chance thinking about math?" A teasing sparkle danced in her eyes.

"Not a chance," he said, grinning. "Believe me, math was the furthest thing from my mind."

They smiled, facing across the pillows, legs intertwined, hands clasped.

"Is there a Jenny Marshall theory regarding sex?"

"There is. I'm in favor of it."

"I suspected as much." David dropped a kiss on her left breast, then leaned on an elbow to smile down at her. "And?"

"My theory postulates sex is only good if the two people involved care about each other," Jenny said slowly.

"Agreed."

"Otherwise, the whole thing borders on the ridiculous. If people could watch themselves making love, they would collapse in hysterical laughter. David, this isn't funny." But she smiled at his loud guffaw. "It's a good thing God arranged body parts so no one can clearly see what's going on. This foresight has preserved the human race from extinction. If our eyes were on stems, we'd be goners."

David kissed her soundly. "Jenny, love, I adore you. And maybe I should thank you for not laughing a few minutes ago."

She looked up at him with love in her eyes and said softly, "Believe me, I wasn't laughing."

"Are you hungry?"

"I'm famished." Savory smells drifted through the open windows from the kitchen below. The throaty voice of Edith Piaf singing a French love song could be heard on a scratchy recording being played somewhere nearby. Jenny kissed David lightly. "Thank you, David, for making this the most memorable vacation in my life."

"I should thank you—for turning a routine business trip into something magic. And for turning up in my life again." His hands circled her waist and he held her against him. "Maybe you'll understand this, Jenny; I hope so. For the last year I've drifted emotionally. Until you walked down the lobby steps, I'd begun to wonder if love and romance were anything more than a temporary illusion. I'd begun to doubt the existence of women like you."

"Like me?"

"Honest, open, warm. Generous of spirit. I was losing sight of the fact that there are women who can be trusted. Women who can meet a man on equal grounds; who aren't—I don't know—looking for something beyond a compatible relationship based on mutual honesty and trust. Does any of this make sense?''

"Perfect sense. Divorce is shattering."

"You know, don't you, that I'm not talking about losing Marilyn. By the time Marilyn left, all I felt was relief. For me, the damage of divorce was that it shook my basic values. It seemed as if I'd lost everything I'd once prized. Can you understand that?''

"I think divorce rattles the basic values of everyone who undergoes it, David,'' Jenny answered gently.

When she emerged from the shower, she returned to the same topic. "When Walter decided to become a hippie or a flower child, or whatever they call them now, there was a period of time when I envied him. I wished I, too, could walk away from responsibility. Just close the door and never look back.'' She toweled her hair. "For a while everything was mixed up in my mind.'' After shaking out her hair, she shrugged. "Finally I realized I like my life as it is. Responsibilities included. I don't want to be a hippie.'' She grinned at him. "I'm hippy enough."

"Perfect, if you ask me,'' David called from the shower.

THE DINING ROOM was a small slice of France transported to Mexico. Candles inside wax-dripped bottles sat in the middle of checkered tablecloths. Framed pictures of Paris scenes covered the stucco walls. A waiter with Gallic features wore an apron that ended below his knees.

"This menu rivals the one at Maxim's," David marveled. "Don't you think so?"

A famous artist would be expected to have visited Paris, center of the art world, so Jenny pretended she had. "Absolutely. It's amazing." After studying the menu she threw up her hands. "I can't decide, everything looks wonderful." The menu was in French and she couldn't read French. She could spot the snails and onion soup, but that was about it. And she hated snails. The idea of eating something that people stepped on was revolting. "You order for me."

"All right."

He ordered the snails and onion soup and tender medallions of veal covered with a sauce that Jenny equated with paradise. But eating the snails, which she struggled through, was like consuming garlic-drenched erasers.

When they'd ordered from the pastry cart, and had been served coffee with thick cream, Jenny looked at him across the candlelit table.

"David, when you said you'd lost everything you valued, did that include Marilyn?"

He stared at her. "Good Lord, no." After pressing her hand, he stirred his coffee. "Marilyn and I never had a terrific marriage. I think we stayed together during the early years because neither of us knew what to expect; we didn't know a terrific marriage was possible. I think we believed everyone had what we did."

He had come to believe that people's lives ran in cycles. When the college cycle ended, the marriage cycle began, running concurrently with the career cycle. He hadn't questioned this setup at the time. In his mind it had been time to marry, time to begin the serious business of life. If his marriage wasn't all he had hoped for, still, being married identified him as a solid citizen, a man of responsibility. With that area of his life taken care of, he could devote his energies to his career. But his marriage hadn't been satisfying.

"I know what you mean." Jenny sighed. "At that age it's easy to convince yourself that the two of you have everything in common. I like pizza; you like pizza—let's get married." She returned David's smile. "The important things aren't taken under consideration. People don't discuss money and in-laws and how to discipline children and . . . all the other things that will make such a difference."

"Value systems and friends." He nodded. "You think you know someone, then discover you don't know your partner at all."

Jenny ducked her head and bit her lip, then looked at him again. She drew a small breath. "Is that what happened with you and Marilyn?"

"That and other things." It wasn't simple to dissect a marriage. "I don't know, Jenny. People change. Or maybe they don't. Maybe if I hadn't been in such a hurry to get on with my life, I'd have seen the things in Marilyn that were such a problem later. Maybe we'd each have found someone better suited."

"You don't have to talk about this, David." Oddly, there was no satisfaction in learning that Marilyn had possessed feet of clay and might not have been the perfect person Jenny had always imagined her to be.

David's eyes met hers and his thumb stroked her palm. "Jenny, for most of my life I've had a feeling that I was waiting for something, an elusive feeling that something was just around the corner. I didn't know what that something was until I saw you walking down the lobby steps. I've been waiting for *you*, Jenny."

Unable to speak, Jenny just looked at him, loving the candlelight in his eyes, the silver threads flowing back from his temples. In her secret heart, she had dreamed of David Foster saying such words. It was an exquisitely perfect moment. One that she, too, had awaited.

"And I have a feeling that maybe it's that way for you." When Jenny nodded, his eyes darkened. "This could become very serious very fast, Jenny, love."

"I know," she whispered. It already had. And she didn't know if that was good or bad. Her enchanted week was leading her down a path she hadn't anticipated. Already she understood that saying goodbye to him would be wrenchingly painful.

"So I want you to know what happened between Marilyn and me."

"That isn't necessary, David." Jenny voiced the polite words, but in truth she was overcome with curiosity. She was the type who doggedly finished every book she picked up. No matter how disappointing or dull the story might be, she wanted to know how it ended.

"I don't want any secrets or gray areas between us," David said, He gazed into his wineglass, gathering his thoughts, and so missed the shadow that crossed Jenny's face. "Marilyn was—is—perfect," he finally began, "in so many, many ways."

Jenny released a sigh. Imperfect women didn't really want to hear about perfect women. On the other hand, the news came as no surprise. She'd always known Marilyn Cody was perfect. The entire sorority had held her up as a role model. Marilyn was the person everyone else wanted to be like. She was the girl who could wear a linen suit all day long without having it wrinkle. She made straight A's and made it look effortless. She never came in late, never incurred the housemother's disapproval. When in doubt, all the sorority sisters had looked to Marilyn Cody and followed her lead. She was the last word in proper behavior.

David pushed a hand through his hair and looked at Jenny. "Do you know how difficult it is to live with a perfect person?"

Jenny's eyebrows arched. Such a thought had never occurred to her.

"At first I felt lucky to have a perfect wife. Marilyn never complained when I worked late, and I worked late hours more often than not during the first years of our marriage. There was always a gourmet dinner waiting in the oven, no matter what time I got home. Never a word of complaint. Our home ran smoothly and efficiently whether I was there or not.

"But after a while, I began to feel guilty. As nutty as this sounds, I wanted her to complain. I began to wish—I don't know—that the plumbing would burst or something, and Marilyn wouldn't be able to handle the situation. That she'd call and rage at me to fix it. I began to wish she weren't so understanding about the long hours and the low paycheck."

"Her perfection made you feel somehow inadequate?" Jenny asked softly, remembering how Marilyn had made her feel.

"I suppose so," David admitted. "What I didn't understand was that Marilyn had inadequacies, too. They just didn't show on the surface. It wasn't until Foster/Beta got off the ground that her imperfections began to emerge." He looked out the window. "To be fair, maybe what I think of as Marilyn's flaws wouldn't be flaws to someone else. But they were to me."

"Such as?"

"Money did something to Marilyn. It opened new vistas, and did so almost overnight. Suddenly we were able to afford things we couldn't have had before. Instead of shopping at Penney's, Marilyn shopped in designer boutiques. Before I knew what had happened, we were living in a walled mansion with a dozen servants and two gardeners. We no longer had a few friends over for a backyard barbecue; we hosted lavish dinner parties. And the people sitting at our table were people who regularly appeared in the society columns." He lifted troubled eyes to Jenny. "It became important to be seen with the right people, to wear the right clothes, to eat at the right restaurants."

"I suppose having lots of money would naturally change your life-style," Jenny said, groping for words.

She tried to imagine her own response if she were suddenly wealthy. First, she'd buy every container of lemon ice cream in the state, eat it herself, then go to a fat farm for a month. She'd pay all her bills, fix the damned screen door, paint the house and...then what? She didn't need or want designer gowns to paint in; she had no idea who made up Denver's society list, and as for servants—long ago she had convinced herself that dust had nutritional value, and having a bit of dust around the house was a healthy thing. She could no more imagine herself ordering a servant to polish the silver than she could imagine owning silver.

She would, of course, buy a fur coat if she suddenly had a gazillion dollars. Even if it hung in her closet forever after. Jenny had a theory about fur. The way men and women responded to fur was genetically ingrained. Evidence to support this theory showed up in the cradle. You saw it the moment you gave your child a teddy bear. Little boys stared at the teddy bear and dreamed of hunting it. Little girls clutched the teddy bear and dreamed of skinning and wearing it. In a perfect world, all women would be issued a fur coat and a crystal decanter of Chanel No 5 when they reached the age of twenty. They could then sally forth with their deepest longings satisfied.

"It wasn't just our life-style that changed; our values changed also. Unless people were somebody, they were nobody."

"Social climbing?"

David nodded. "We judged things by different criteria. We didn't buy things because we needed them, we bought for show. Because a mansion is more impressive than a tract home. Because an antique is more valuable than something purchased off a showroom floor. We didn't buy a Rolls because it ran better, but because it looked better parked in a mansion's garage."

"A Rolls? You used to want a Porsche when you were in college." Jenny tilted her head. "You keep saying 'we,' David. But this doesn't sound like you."

"In the beginning I think it was me, although I'm not proud to admit it. I guess I wanted the world to know I'd become a success. So I didn't fight too hard at the trappings of success."

"But?"

"But after a time, I realized that the people we saw looked at me the same way I looked at them—as dollar signs. As contacts." He grinned suddenly. "You know, there wasn't a single comfortable chair in that whole damned house? Not one chair where a person could sit at ease and watch TV. Anyway, it didn't take long to understand that none of the people attending our parties cared about either of us, not really. There wasn't a soul among them I considered a friend. They were living, breathing business opportunities, that's all. Not one among them I'd want to phone in a personal crisis."

"And that's what led to your divorce?"

"Partly. I didn't want Sara growing up in an unreal world where men and women didn't get their hands dirty. Where values were all screwed up."

"Sara?"

"My daughter. She was starting to judge people by their addresses instead of by who they were inside. She was beginning to think everyone commanded a platoon of servants—or should. That's when I realized how shallow our lives had become. And the arguments started."

"I'm sorry, David."

"To be honest, I think eventually Marilyn and I might have found a middle ground we both could have lived with—less pretentious house, public school for Sara, fewer servants and more privacy. We might have stumbled on for years, thinking this or that might make it better." He ran a hand through his hair. "But that wasn't possible. Because inside, Marilyn was the one thing I cannot abide and cannot forgive. And I couldn't live with it."

"What is that?" Jenny asked. A sudden sense of foreboding swept over her, causing the back of her neck to prickle.

"Marilyn was a liar."

The joy went out of the evening and Jenny's heart hit her toes.

Chapter Six

Sleep was impossible. Without making a sound, Jenny carefully eased from the protective curve of David's arms and slipped out of bed. Moving quietly, she put on her robe, then crossed the room and stepped onto the balcony, inhaling the soft, fragrant scent of night-blooming flowers.

A pale moon hung suspended above the ocean waves, dipping toward a lemony arch that fanned across the eastern sky signaling the onset of dawn. Jenny had passed the better part of the night tossing and turning and staring sleeplessly at the ceiling fan's lazy revolutions.

Marilyn Cody hadn't been perfect after all; she had been a liar. And Marilyn's lies had torn David's marriage apart. What had he said? "Lying is the one thing I can't forgive. Lying is the refuge of cowards."

Didn't Jenny know it! She bit her lip and dropped her head, and thought about everything David had said.

He had gone on to explain Marilyn's deceptions, how she had begun by misstating the price of small items, had progressed to misrepresenting anything that didn't enhance her image of herself and her position in the world. She had invented a background for herself and for David more befitting their new social status than the truth. Eventually, David had discovered that Marilyn's lies had kept old friends from intruding on their new life; lies had kept him from seeking them out. Anything that threatened Marilyn's perception of herself as perfect was covered by a lie. Once he accepted the unthinkable, that his wife was a liar, he understood that lies had permeated their relationship from the beginning. He'd turned a blind eye because he hadn't wanted to believe it.

David had said more, much more, Jenny remembered. He'd talked about Marilyn's refusal to seek professional help, about the affair she had drifted into and the resultant painful deceptions. He'd told Jenny about moving out of the mansion and the lengthy custody battle for Sara. He'd spoken of starting over, of returning to basics, of getting reacquainted with himself and with Sara, of slowing the pace of his life and his business obligations.

Jenny listened with a frozen expression, frowning with sympathy when sympathy was required, smiling at his anecdotes regarding the move across country with a teenaged girl. Her responses were wooden and automatic and she comprehended only half of what he said.

Because her thoughts were centered on those damning words: "Marilyn was a liar" and "the one thing I cannot forgive."

While David had talked about buying a house in a normal middle-American suburb and enrolling his daughter in public school, Jenny had been thinking about her Cinderella tales.

Her lies.

David's baritone faded into the background as she remembered her own voice stating that Jenny Marshall paintings hung in the Denver Art Museum. An inner whisper reminded her that she'd told David about showings and subsequent sales at the Melton Gallery, about interviews and awards, receptions in her honor and high acclaim. She had blanked out large chunks of David's history since the divorce, not listening, lost in her own horrifying realization of what she'd done.

She hadn't heard everything David said but she had heard her own deceptions loud and clear, presenting dreams as reality, what might have been as truth.

"Damn," she whispered now, pulling her lower lip between her teeth. By playing Cinderella, she'd plunked herself squarely in the middle of a mess. By stepping out of character for one fleeting interval, she'd made herself into someone David Foster would despise.

A liar. She had no doubt that was how David would see it. There was no excuse she could offer that would be acceptable. He'd heard all the excuses and explanations a hundred times before. The instant he learned that Jenny had lied, the magic between them would vanish like steam from a boiling pot.

There could be no shared future.

Jenny hadn't planned on sharing David's future when she first saw him striding up the beach toward her. Nor had she consciously considered such a possibility when he joined her for dinner that night. What had she said? Ships passing in the night. A brief encounter, nothing more.

But somewhere, somehow, that had changed. Emotions she hadn't experienced in years had flamed to life. Although she hadn't allowed herself to examine where her emotions might be leading, she understood their intensity. In her heart, and in David's eyes, she had comprehended, as Pam had predicted, that their ships had collided. Meeting David again wasn't intended to be a brief encounter. Fate had given them a second chance. And Jenny had ruined it.

"Damn," she said again, softly pounding her fist against the balcony railing. "Damn, damn, damn!"

Why hadn't she just been herself? Why hadn't she simply shrugged and admitted things hadn't worked out as she'd once hoped? There was no disgrace in painting greeting-card covers. In fact, most of the time she was proud to be earning a living with her painting.

Okay, it wasn't real art. The Melton Gallery wasn't interested in showing greeting-card covers. But it *was* art. She'd kept her hand in. And someday, when the kids were raised and she didn't need a regular income, she fully intended to paint a masterpiece. It was there, in the back of her mind, waiting only for time and confidence. When the moment came, she knew what she would paint, and how she would approach the canvas and the colors that would spread across her palette. Who could say? Maybe she really did have a masterpiece in her, one that could hang in the Denver Art Museum, or one that the Melton Gallery would beg to show. It was possible. All things were possible.

That thought brought her back to David. Was it possible to get out of this mess and salvage their relationship? How could she make him understand that, even though she had lied about so many things, she wasn't really a liar?

"This is the point where the fairy godmother steps in and rescues the day," she muttered under her breath. The lemony sky was deepening to blue, the colors a blend of pink and gold and turquoise. Jenny closed her eyes and released a long, hopeless sigh.

She didn't need a fairy godmother to tell her this wasn't going to work. No matter how she glossed it over, the fact remained. She had lied. And her lies had all been so unnecessary.

Now she could see that David would have understood if she'd admitted she hadn't achieved the potential she had aspired to so long ago. It wouldn't have mattered to him that she had lived a less than exciting life. Or that she was far from financially secure, that she had a desk drawer full of bills.

She hesitated on this last point. There had been hints that David was sensitive to people's underlying motives. If he'd known how she hovered over the mailbox, waiting for the checks from New York, would he have questioned her interest in him?

This thought raised another. Exactly what was the status of David's finances? When he was telling her about Marilyn and his life in California, she'd had the definite impression of great wealth. And yet, when she'd said, "I can't imagine money like you're talking about," a curtain had dropped over his eyes and he'd shrugged, saying, "It sounds better than it is."

At some point, trying to understand, Jenny had asked, "Were you hurt financially by the divorce?" She was looking for an explanation for the difference between then and now. He had nodded bitterly, indicating the divorce had resulted in a financial beating.

Not that it mattered, but her conception of his financial status was murky at best. Sometimes it sounded as if he were another Fort Knox; other times it sounded as if he needed to count every dime he spent.

Certainly, he was a bit odd on the subject. When he'd noticed her glancing at his Rolex, he'd covered the face of the watch with his hand and had murmured, "It was a gift from my daughter." As if he felt he needed to apologize for wearing something expensive. "Marilyn bought it for Sara to give me on Father's Day a few years ago."

Jenny gave herself a shake. She was straying from the problem that had nothing to do with David and everything to do with her. When David learned the truth, would he forgive her?

Not a chance, she thought helplessly. In his eyes she would look the same as Marilyn. He would see a liar.

So. Where did that leave her?

Pain darkened the color of her eyes to navy. Although she knew she should immediately confess what she'd done, she couldn't. Not now. The thought of watching David's expression change from loving to contemptuous shot an arrow through her heart. She couldn't do it. No way.

The only acceptable option was to continue the deception through to the end. She would maintain the charade until it was time to say goodbye. Then she would return to Denver, and David would fly off to California and that would be the end of a perfect vacation.

She covered her eyes, hating herself. She sounded like Marilyn. Protect the situation, keep it perfect. Don't expose yourself to the imperfect truth. God, is that what had started all this?

Jenny gripped the balcony railing and stared at the ocean. Eventually David would learn the truth. She had to accept that point. She could easily imagine him stopping by a gallery and asking the proprietor to locate a Jenny Marshall painting. The proprietor would check his lists and inform David that no such artist existed. The image hurt.

But at least she wouldn't be there to watch him put together the pieces and finally grasp her deception. She wouldn't have to witness the collapse of his trust. Or the hurt and betrayal she knew he'd feel.

She stared hard at nothing and concluded she had no choice. Her only course was to continue the deceit while trying to hide her anguish. She'd take the enchanted days remaining to her, and hope the memories she made would be enough to balance the lonely nights waiting for her at home. And she prayed that one day she could forgive herself for throwing away her second chance at happiness.

Tears swam in her eyes before she dashed them away with the back of her hand. "Oh, David," she whispered. "I'm sorry. I'm so sorry."

She waited until the sun had edged above the horizon; then she tiptoed into the bedroom and slid into bed. "David?" she said softly. "David, are you awake?"

He opened one eye. "Mmmm."

Jenny kissed his tousled hair, feeling her heart swell. "Make love to me, David. I need you so much right now."

Both eyes blinked open, and he smiled at her. "I thought you weren't a morning person."

"I'm not," she said, sliding into his arms, "but this morning is special."

"I think," he said, looking into her eyes, "that every morning with you is special."

Slowly his hands moved over her body, quickening her pulse and turning her breath to ragged gasps. Instinctively, he sensed her urgency and deep need and didn't tease her. Instead, he came to her immediately, filling her with a bittersweet joy. Jenny clung to him, trying to imprint the texture of his skin upon her memory, etching the sound of his murmur inside her ear, wanting desperately to make the moment last.

When coffee had been ordered from room service, David smoothed Jenny's damp hair back over her temples and guided her into the curve of his arm. He kissed the top of her head and placed his lips near her ear.

"I love you, Jenny."

She was glad he couldn't see the pain drawing her mouth. A small kernel of despair exploded near her heart and swept through her body. "Oh, David," she whispered. "Don't say that."

He didn't respond for a moment, but she sensed his puzzled expression. There had been a hint of expectation in his voice when he said he loved her, a hope that she would say she loved him, too. But she couldn't say it, even though she knew it was true. If she admitted her feelings, the next step would inevitably be to discuss their future together. And liars had no future with David.

Gently, he turned her in his arms until she faced him. "I know this may seem fast, Jenny, but it really isn't. We aren't strangers. I know you and I love you. I've loved you most of my life."

"David . . ."

"And I think you love me, too."

Jenny reached a trembling hand to her lips. "I... I don't know. There are things I haven't told you. You don't know me as well as you think."

He laughed and kissed her nose. "I know everything that's important." His eyes sobered as he examined her expression. "I don't want to rush you, Jenny, love. I don't want to push you into saying something you don't mean and aren't ready for."

"Thank you. I..."

"But I am ready. And I am sure. I love you." His thumb caressed her lips. "And neither of us is going away this time. This time we're going to give ourselves a chance."

Jenny bit her lip and looked at him. "David, some things just aren't meant to be." The words stuck to the roof of her mouth. A sense of unreality overwhelmed her. David was saying words she'd longed to hear. He was offering a dream come true. And, heaven help her, she was rejecting him. It was a crazy Alice-in-Wonderland world.

"I admire your caution," he said, swinging from the bed in response to room service's knock at their door. He belted a blue terry robe, a cheerful smile on his face. "But I warn you, I know what I want and I won't give up. Everywhere you go, Jenny Marshall, I'll be right behind you, pleading my case. The shadow behind you is going to be me. There's nothing you can say or do that will change my mind. I love you. And I think you love me."

"Nothing?"

"Nothing," he said firmly.

But of course that wasn't true. Nor was it true that David would be pursuing her. Even if Jenny hadn't messed things up, theirs would have been a long-distance romance. Not an insurmountable obstacle, but not the romantic togetherness he spoke of, either. For the first time since she'd gazed into his warm chocolate eyes, the thought of the distance separating them provided relief instead of misery.

But the misery was there, too. In spades.

SOMETHING HAD CHANGED, David could almost pinpoint the moment when the radiance had faded from Jenny's expression and a look of deep sadness had entered her eyes. It had happened while he was telling her about Marilyn and the divorce and the fight to gain custody of Sara.

What had he said to upset her? Had she and Marilyn been better friends than he'd suspected? Had he placed Jenny in a position where her loyalty to an old friend warred with learning unpleasant facts about that friend?

Frowning, he swung his golf club and watched the ball zing down the fairway. He had tried to be fair. He hadn't soft-pedaled his own role in the breakup of his marriage. He'd told Jenny how he'd worked too many nights, how he hadn't spent enough time with his family. He'd admitted a lack of understanding for Marilyn's problems. He'd even admitted his own anguish at the thought that perhaps he had pushed Marilyn into lying. Maybe she had believed lying was the best way to avoid arousing his anger; maybe she had believed they couldn't communicate unless she smoothed the way with lies. He didn't think these excuses were true, but maybe they were.

He'd worried these questions for months after the divorce without reaching a satisfactory answer. In the end he'd decided the reasons for Marilyn's deceptions weren't as important as the fact that he couldn't live with them.

But how had that sounded to Jenny? He watched her walking down the fairway beside him, a distracted look on her face. Had he seemed unfair? Rigid? Unforgiving?

Maybe he was. But he'd reached a point where nothing in his marriage was acceptable. He couldn't bear what was happening to his daughter, couldn't pretend he didn't know Marilyn was having an affair, couldn't swallow one more lie. His reservoir of forgiveness had run dry.

"Nice shot," Jenny said.

"Thanks."

She looked as relieved as he that this was the last hole. Puzzled, David watched her walk toward the women's lockers to change for the ferry back to Cancún. Finding her again was the best thing that had happened to him in the past few years. And he'd been so certain she felt the same way. They had fit together as naturally as two pieces of a jigsaw puzzle. He'd known it that first night on the terrace. It was as if the intervening years had dropped away and they were twenty again, in love, and filled with a thousand ideas and opinions they wanted to share with each other.

Now, after a night he knew he would never forget, strained silences opened between them and he didn't know why. Was he pushing Jenny into something she didn't want? Was that it? Was it possible he'd misinterpreted her glances and soft touches? Maybe she didn't feel what he did. The thought tightened his stomach and raised a frown on his brow.

It was impossible to talk above the thumping of the ferry's cranky engine and the sound of spray hissing up from the bow. But when they'd returned to the Palenque, David touched Jenny's elbow and looked down into her face. "How does a piña colada sound?"

"Actually, I thought I'd take a short nap. I didn't sleep well last night."

"Jenny, what's wrong?"

"Wrong?" She smiled brightly. "Nothing's wrong. I had a wonderful time on Isla Mujeres. Thank you."

"Please, Jenny. Tell me anything, but don't lie to me; I can't stand lying, even about small things. Something's wrong. I can feel it."

Misery etched her expression and she edged toward the elevator. Frustration tightened David's shoulders, and he wished to God she'd tell him what was troubling her. Something obviously was.

"I'm just tired. That's all."

"Well, then, enjoy your nap and I'll see you for dinner. Okay?" Maybe he was imagining shadows where there were none. That's what he wanted to think.

"Mr. Foster? You have a call from the States." A white-coated hotel clerk extended a message slip.

"Thank you." He watched Jenny until the elevator doors closed, not understanding the struggle in her eyes. She looked vulnerable and unhappy, and it mystified him.

Still thinking about her, he returned to his room and dialed the number on the message slip.

"David?" Rob Spenser's cheerful voice boomed through the wires. "What do you think of Cancún?"

"I think it's lucky." David smiled. Rob Spenser was a good friend as well as his attorney. "So, where are you? I expected to have dinner with you tonight to talk about syndicating the Palenque."

"I missed my plane. Got tied up in a new corporate war; big case coming in. How about lunch tomorrow?"

"Why do I sense I'm not going to like this?"

Rob laughed. "Because I want you to come here."

"San Diego?"

"Nothing to it. Or did you fly commercial?"

"Commercial."

"I might have guessed. Well, call your pilot and tell him to fly down there and pick you up. He'll have you here by noon and back in Cancún for dinner."

David hesitated. He didn't want to miss a minute with Jenny. "All right," he said after a moment. "I'll be bringing a guest."

"Oh, ho!" Rob crowed. David could feel Rob's grin at the far end of the line. "Cancún *has* been lucky for you."

"Believe it, friend. You'll understand when you see her."

"All I've got to say is: It's about time."

JENNY'S MOUTH DROPPED. "We're going to San Diego? For lunch?"

"That isn't the worst of it," David said, laughing at her expression. "The plane leaves at eight in the morning."

She groaned. But she was also impressed. Books and movies were full of this sort of jet-set thing, but Jenny had never imagined herself jetting off to another country for lunch.

For the first time since they'd entered the hotel's dining room, she laughed. "You live in a strange magic world, David."

He covered her hand and smiled into her eyes. "You have a wonderful laugh, did you know that? I'm glad you're feeling better. Want to tell me what was bothering you?"

Jenny bit her lip and dropped her eyes before arranging a bright smile on her lips. "It wasn't important. What's important is the time with you." She knew she was giving him conflicting signals, but she couldn't help it. What on earth had ol' Cinderella done when the prince assumed tomorrow? Had she discovered, as Jenny was discovering, that a person could be simultaneously happy and miserable?

David waved aside the waiter offering after-dinner drinks and looked into Jenny's eyes. "Being an artist, Jenny, love, I wonder if you'd like to inspect the etchings in my room."

Forcibly, Jenny pushed away all depressing thoughts. She rolled her eyes, then smiled. "Mr. Foster, I would be delighted to see your etchings."

Later, when dawn tinted the sky and David kissed her glowing face in front of her door, Jenny laughed softly and leaned her forehead against his shoulder. "We forgot to look at your etchings."

Smiling, he tilted her mouth up to his and kissed her. "We'll try again tomorrow night."

THOUGH SHE TRIED TO PRETEND she was a famous artist, jaded and sophisticated enough not to shout, "Wow," Jenny's eyes widened when she stepped aboard the private plane. She'd never seen such luxury outside a movie theater. Instead of seats, the interior was furnished with deep, velvet-upholstered wing chairs. The rose-colored carpet was three inches thick, and tiers of crystal decanters twinkled from an elaborate private bar. Two smartly clad flight attendants fussed over eggs Benedict, which would be served on gold-edged china.

"Imagine how many hot dogs you could buy for what this cost," Jenny blurted, saying the first thing that came into her head.

Laughing, David strapped her into one of the velvet chairs. "Enough to stock your freezer, I'd imagine. Do your kids like hot dogs?"

"They'd rather eat hot dogs than steak." For which she was deeply grateful. The good Lord knew what he was doing when He invented hot dogs. Without hot dogs and various other peculiar but inexpensive foods adored by teens, parents would be reduced to bankruptcy and wild-eyed despair whenever they stepped into a grocery store.

"Tell me about Deuce and Rhonda. What are they like?"

They passed the flight to San Diego indulging their curiosity about each other's children. Jenny spoke about Rhonda's blossoming toward womanhood, about Deuce's infatuation with computers. Her face lit up as it always did when she talked about her children.

"Computers? Deuce and I are kindred souls. I'm eager to meet him."

Jenny blinked, then hastily inquired about Sara.

"Frankly, I'm worried about her," David admitted with a frown. "She hasn't adjusted as well as I'd hoped. There seems to be a confusion...on both sides." He grinned engagingly. "Perhaps the problem is me. Fathers don't understand such mysteries as green nail polish and holes in the ears."

Jenny nodded and covered his fingers. "Give her time, David. She's been through a lot of changes."

Then the plane, which Jenny assumed belonged to Rob Spenser, was swooping toward the San Diego field. A taxi then whisked them to a Harbor Island restaurant near the airport. "You go ahead," Jenny said. "I want to freshen my lipstick, then I'll join you."

Both men stood as Jenny approached the table, and a surge of pride warmed David's eyes as he drew out her chair. Today she wore her hair in a chignon of twisted gold. The traces of sunburn spread a rosy glow over her cheeks and made her eyes seem impossibly blue. Her perfume stirred his senses as he seated her in a rustle of blue silk. He was certain she drew every eye in the restaurant.

"Rob, I'd like you to meet Jenny Marshall." Lightly, he pressed her shoulder before he returned to his own chair. "I'm sure you've heard of her. Her paintings are hung in galleries all over America and are shown in the collections of modern artists in more museums than I can name."

Jenny's heart stopped. She should have anticipated this, but she hadn't.

Smiling broadly, Rob Spenser said smoothly, "Of course I recognize the name. I wish Ruth, my wife, was here, she'd be thrilled to meet you. Ruth is the art expert in our family."

Oh, no. Eyes wide and stricken, Jenny looked at them. Her mouth was too dry to speak. This was the worst, the very pits. In a flash she realized she'd placed David in a position where now he was lying, too. This had to be the worst moment in her life. Why, oh why, didn't the earth open up and swallow her? What had begun as a dream was plunging toward a nightmare, she thought, as she murmured something she hoped was an adequate response.

They ordered Bloody Marys and Rob Spenser asked polite questions about the art world, which Jenny answered with increasing distress.

Finally Rob spread his hands and smiled at David. "She's as modest as you are, Dave. You have to drag answers out of her."

"I'm sorry," Jenny apologized quickly. "It's just that praise makes me uncomfortable." Oh, Lord. Like everyone else, she thrived on praise. She had reverted to babbling. Always a bad sign. She cast a desperate glance at David, and breathed a sigh of relief when he came to the rescue by signaling the waiter for menus and tactfully changing the subject. He asked for news of Rob's children before he returned to Jenny.

"We talked a little about Sara's problems. How about Deuce and Rhonda—did they adjust well to divorce?" he asked her over bowls of giant shrimp nested in cracked ice.

Jenny smiled, finally on safe ground. "Once they understood we wouldn't be moving and that their lives would continue much as before, they were all right with it. They're sensible kids. I'm sure Sara will be, too."

"I hope so," David said slowly.

"Is she still upset?" Rob asked.

David nodded. "It's been difficult for her. I think she knew things weren't right between Marilyn and me. I think she knew divorce was inevitable." He looked at Jenny. "But perhaps I should have waited longer before moving. Besides having a shy nature, Sara's had to adjust to a new life-style, a new school, new friends. And living with me. We're still adjusting."

Jenny paused with her fork midway to her lips. Confusion furrowed her brow. "Moving? You mean moving out of the house?"

David covered her hand and smiled. "No, I mean moving across country to Denver. I told you last night."

Jenny's fork clattered to her plate. She stared at him for a long, frozen moment, her heart accelerating into overdrive; then she grabbed her napkin and began mopping frantically at the tiny spots on her dress.

Denver.

Oh, my God. David lived in Denver. The anecdotes he'd related about driving across country with Sara had referred to the drive to *Denver*.

When she realized both men were looking at her with polite expressions of surprise, Jenny waved a hand and summoned a weak smile. "A sudden spasm in my wrist. It happens to artists all the time. Occupational weakness." She flopped her hand at the wrist. "See? Sometimes it just ... goes." Babble, sheer babble, while she stalled for time to assimilate the astounding fact that David lived in Denver. "Ah, where in Denver do you live?" she asked when she could breathe seminormally. Surely it would be in Cherry Creek, or the new Polo Grounds, Denver's two most exclusive areas.

"In Columbine. Near Chatfield dam. Off Wadsworth and ..."

"Ken Caryl Road," Jenny whispered. "I know where it is."

She stared into space, watching her life flash before her eyes. David Foster didn't live more than two miles from her house. They probably shopped at the same supermarket, took their clothes to the same cleaner's. Their kids attended the same school. Maybe they had driven past each other or shopped different aisles in the grocery. Sooner or later, as David settled into the community, they would have to run into each other. It was inevitable.

Suddenly she felt as if the air had been knocked from her lungs. "Sara. You said your daughter's name is Sara."

"Yes. Jenny, are you all right?" David leaned forward and examined her with concern. The color had faded from her face and her hands were trembling.

"No." Standing up abruptly, Jenny gathered her purse and her napkin. Carefully she folded her napkin and tucked it into her purse. "I don't feel well," she explained. "Too much sun, perhaps. Forgive me, David, but I think I'll just . . . there's a sofa in the ladies' room."

"Shall I call a doctor?" Standing, he touched her shoulders and peered into her face.

"No, I'll be all right. I just . . ." She glanced at Rob Spenser, then looked into David's anxious eyes. "A touch of sun fever, I think. That's all." Did sun fever exist, or had she made it up? Once the lies started, she thought in disgust, they sprang easily to the lips. She was getting revoltingly good at it. "Don't worry. I'll be all right in a few minutes." David's cool hand rested briefly against her feverish cheek; then she turned and fled.

When she was safely alone in the ladies' lounge, Jenny's shoulders dropped and she covered her eyes with shaking fingers.

Sara Foster was her daughter's new best friend.

She hadn't known Sara's last name until now, or, if she had, it hadn't registered. But the pieces fit. She remembered Rhonda telling her Sara was from California, that Sara's parents were divorced, that Sara needed a friend because she was confused and having difficulty adjusting.

Jenny sagged against the sofa arm. She hadn't realized she could hurt this much without bleeding.

THE MEN WATCHED HER GO, then Rob Spenser smiled at David. "She's lovely." After watching David a moment he added, "she's important to you, isn't she?"

"That is the lady I'm going to marry, my friend. If she'll have me."

Rob considered his steak with pleasure before cutting into it. "As your lawyer as well as your friend, I'd advise you to consider a premarital agreement. In your tax bracket, it's the safest way to go. Need I remind you how deeply Marilyn dug in your pocket?"

"No premarital agreement." However wise such contracts might be, David felt they began marriage with a negative element. How could he or Jenny believe in a lasting commitment if they began a marriage with discussions regarding the fairest way to dissolve it?

"I think you should give this some serious consideration, Dave. You've got a fortune at stake," Rob said.

"It would be an insult to Jenny."

"Nonsense. It's a simple business arrangement. Your holdings are protected and so are hers."

"Forget it, Rob."

"Look, I know how peculiar you are about money. Are you worried about disclosing the extent of your fortune? Is that your primary objection here?"

David's brow lifted in mild surprise. "I'm peculiar about money?"

Rob laughed. "Come on, friend. This isn't some stranger you're talking to. We've known each other for—what?—nine or ten years? You're weird as hell about money. Secretive. It's almost as if you'd rather be poor; an attitude, by the way, that I don't understand for one minute."

"We've been over this before. There's no point in making myself a target for every hotdog salesman, is there?"

"No, but what's the point in having money if you don't enjoy it?" Rob leaned back in his chair and studied his friend. "Mortiz told me you didn't take the suite I reserved for you. And I'll bet you took a taxi from the airport instead of the limo. Dave, give yourself a break. You've earned a few luxuries."

"I've had the luxuries, and I don't like what went with them. Having money has turned into a monumental headache and a lot of trouble." An understatement if he'd ever heard one. He pushed his fingers through his hair. "I've got tax problems I don't want to think about. I worry about Sara's thinking money is the only thing that's important. Managing money is a full-time job. And every salesman in town is beating on my door with the deal of the century. Money has affected my daughter in ways I don't like, has altered my own perspective, and you know what happened to Marilyn when the money came."

"Marilyn didn't change," Rob observed shrewdly. "She was always status-conscious, always a snob."

"Money changes people," David insisted stubbornly. "The minute people learn you have money, they start planning how they can get it."

"Damned right," Rob said cheerfully, "including me. I hope to relieve you of about half a million on this Cancún deal." In a more serious tone, he added, "That goes with the territory. In the end, you make the final decision. You can tell me and the hotdogs to take a hike."

"Maybe I'm not saying this well, Rob, but sometimes it seems as if I'm getting lost in the shuffle of one deal after another. I'm starting to feel like the invisible man; no one sees me—they see my bank account. It's not who I am, but what I can do for them."

"I should have that problem." Rob grinned.

"You wouldn't like it. Tonight you can go home and share a beer with the guy next door. Maybe you exchange tools, or invite him over for a barbecue. You can enjoy his company without waiting for the pitch. That's the life I want. Simple. Up front."

"To each his own." Rob sighed. "Not to complicate things, friend, but what are your impressions of the Palenque?" After discussing the pros and cons of syndication and how the deal would unfold, Rob examined his friend curiously. "Maybe this is reopening a touchy subject, but does Jenny know you're a multimillionaire? Or are you soft-pedaling as usual?"

"I'm sure she knows I have money."

"But does she know you're wealthy?"

David frowned. "I haven't given her a financial statement, if that's what you mean."

They drank their coffee in silence, then Rob sighed. "Well, I guess the lady's in for a nice surprise."

"Believe me, money doesn't matter to Jenny. She has money of her own." He glanced toward the ladies' lounge, then looked at his watch, anticipating the evening ahead.

Rob grinned, correctly interpreting David's quick look at his watch. "You've got it bad, pal."

"You don't know the half of it," David said, smiling. He was thoroughly smitten, as moonstruck as a teenager. And it felt good. Wonderful. For the first time in a year, he'd set aside the suspicions and the search for ulterior motives and all the rest. For the first time, he knew the healing process had truly begun. Life didn't have to be filled with mistrust. As long as Jenny Marshall existed, he could believe the world was a good place to be.

"I'M SORRY, DAVID. My head is killing me," Jenny explained. And her conscience hurt, as well.

For the most part she'd passed the return flight in silence, pleading a headache. She'd stared out the plane window and felt utterly wretched. And when she looked into David's loving, trusting eyes, she wanted to weep.

"Tonight, let's go—" David began when they had returned to the Palenque.

"No." All she could think of was escape. "Forgive me, but I really don't feel up to it. Tomorrow we'll..." Would she have a tomorrow? She looked at him helplessly. "Oh, David. I'm so sorry."

Spinning on her heel, Jenny rushed toward the elevators, leaving David staring after her with a puzzled expression.

Chapter Seven

"I stole a napkin. Can you believe it?" Jenny wrung her hands. "I was so nervous I actually stole the restaurant's napkin. Do you think the international police will come after me? David and Rob must think I'm crazy."

Pam poured two coffees from the room service tray—they had ordered dinner in the room—and handed one to Jenny. "Mail it back if it'll make you feel better. Jenny, are you all right? You look like hell."

Jenny had her hair wrapped in a hotel towel, thick cream lathered her face, and she was wearing her oldest robe, the comfortable, frayed robe she saved for occasions when the world collapsed around her. It had been a stroke of luck that she'd thought to pack it. Always plan for disaster, that was her motto. Hope for the best, but figure disaster is waiting to get you.

Jenny stared into the mirror. Pam was right; she looked like hell. Wide, miserable eyes peered out from a field of white cream.

"No, I'm not all right. I'm a nervous wreck." Usually the cream-and-robe routine made her feel better, but tonight it wasn't working. "Tell me how to get out of this mess."

"Oh, sure. And how about a plan to solve the mystery of black holes while I'm at it?"

"We've discussed the problem and examined alternatives. Of which there are damned few. Now it's time to make a decision."

"There's only one sensible thing to do, Jen. Kill yourself."

"That's the plan I'm leaning toward." Jenny flung herself into a chair and cradled her coffee cup between her hands. "But what would the kids do? After a year or two they'd notice I was gone, and it might upset them."

"No, they'd notice you were gone the minute they ran out of potato chips and soft drinks. Kids don't notice parents until the refrigerator is empty."

Jenny contemplated the ceiling and heaved a sigh. "I'll go home and put my head in the oven. It's decided, then."

"You have an electric oven, Jen."

"So? It will just take a little longer, that's all."

"Dry heat frizzes your hair. You'll look like a punker at your funeral."

"True. Well, I guess the oven's out." After tasting her coffee, Jenny looked at her friend and her shoulders slumped. "Seriously, Pam, what am I going to do?"

"I don't know."

"He's going to find out. He practically lives next door, for heaven's sake. And his daughter is my daughter's new best friend. There is absolutely no hope that I'm not going to be found out. And he's going to despise me."

"You know, something's not right here." Pam poured more coffee. "If David is rich, how come he lives in our area? How come he isn't living in Cherry Creek?"

"I don't think he's rich. Comfortably well off is probably more like it. Maybe ol' Marilyn clipped him good in the divorce. Maybe it's like he said, the media exaggerated IBM's buy-out. Maybe he lost everything at a horse race." Jenny spread her hands. "What does this have to do with anything? Who cares about his money?"

"Am I hearing right? Jenny Marshall scorns money? The same Jenny Marshall who dreams about winning the lottery? Who kisses checks before depositing them? I am impressed. This is definitely a case of true love."

"It might have been."

"I'm just trying to cheer you up, you know that, don't you?"

"Yes, and thank you."

"It's not working, is it?"

They sipped their coffee in silence. Finally Jenny looked up, her eyes filled with pain. "I have to confess, don't I?"

"You can delay. Let him discover the truth when he returns to Denver."

She thought about David saying, "Lying is the refuge of cowards." Whatever else Jenny Marshall was, she'd never been a coward. She'd always tried to do the right thing. Part of this tracked back to her mother-over-your-shoulder theory, but, mostly, doing the right thing was simply a lifelong habit that made it easier to sleep nights. However, more often than not, doing the right thing hurt like the very devil.

"No," she said slowly, hating her decision even as she conceded there had never really been an alternative decision to make. "I have to tell him. As soon as possible. I thought I could see this through to the end, but I can't. Every day it gets worse." She'd always said there was no disgrace in making a mistake. The disgrace lay in continuing to make that same mistake. It was time to stiffen her spine and face the music. Even if the very thought made her stomach feel as if it were churning with spun glass.

Pam shrugged. "It's your funeral, kiddo." But her eyes were sympathetic. "Look, would it help if I talked to him, too?"

"Serve as my character witness?" Jenny shook her head. "Thanks, but I don't want to drag you into this any more than I have already."

"I'm sorry, Jen."

"Me, too. I'm the sorriest person you ever saw."

Before Pam rolled over and buried her head in the pillow, she looked at Jenny, who was standing in the darkness leaning against the doorway to the balcony. "There's one possibility we didn't discuss—maybe he'll understand."

"Go to sleep," Jenny said softly, speaking around the lump in her throat. "It's late."

She swallowed the last of the cold coffee in her cup, then stepped out onto the balcony overlooking the pool area, dark now, and gazed at the sea beyond. Moonlit waves foamed up the beach.

Jenny listened to the soothing whisper of the surf, but her thoughts were a million miles away. The Cinderella story ended too soon. No version she'd read explained what happened when the handsome prince found Cindy in her apron scrubbing out the hearth.

Had he blinked and said, "Kiddo, you sure had me fooled! I thought you were a glamour girl, not a peasant." Had he raised an eyebrow and wondered how this no-account servant girl was going to fit in with his aristocratic friends? Somehow he must have worked out his surprise at the deception as he and Miss Cinderella had ridden off into the sunset.

But the handsome prince hadn't had a sore spot about deceits. His first wife hadn't been a liar.

A deep sigh escaped Jenny's lips. Judging from the moon's position on the horizon, it was past midnight. She looked down at the raveled hem of her robe and permitted herself a wry smile. Boy, was it past midnight. Few traces remained of the glamorous, exciting creature she'd tried to become since meeting David again.

Acting on impulse, because she had to do something other than stand passively by while coaches turned to pumpkins and gowns turned into old robes, Jenny went back into the room and felt through the darkness until she located the burcau. She slipped out of her robe and into a pair of shorts and a T-shirt. In the bathroom, she wiped away the last traces of cold cream and tied her hair in a bandanna.

Then she slipped from the room and passed quickly through the deserted lobby, across the darkened pool area, and finally onto the beach. The sand was soft and yielding, pleasantly cool beneath her bare toes.

She walked to the edge of the water and watched the luminous surf bubble up around her ankles.

She had to tell him. But how?

The water receded and her heels sank in the wet sand. She would look him in the eyes and say, "David, I lied. I didn't mean to, but..."

No good. When people lied they meant to. Lies didn't happen by accident or through carelessness. Lies happened on purpose.

So, she would say, "David, I lied. But there was a reason."

Of course there was a reason. People didn't lie without reason. He knew that. Marilyn probably had dozens of reasons to explain why she lied.

Jenny thrust her hands into her back pockets and stared down at the shells tumbling in the backwash. She watched until the streaming water turned back on itself and rushed up around her legs. Eventually, she turned and walked along the water's edge, kicking aimlessly at the surf, until she reached a stone jetty at the end of the hotel's stretch of beach.

After seating herself on the jetty and dropping her feet in the water, Jenny tilted her head to gaze up at a star-spangled sky. Tiny dots of distant fire flashed through the velvety night. They were millions of miles away, where she wished she was.

"David, I lied. I didn't want to disappoint you, so..."

So, she'd ended by giving him the greatest disappointment of all. Damn, damn, damn!

"David, this has nothing to do with you, not really. It has to do with my inadequacies and lack of confidence."

This uncomfortable admission was nearest the truth, but excused nothing. She doubted anyone as confident as David would understand.

Dropping her head, Jenny stared absently at the dark sand curving along the shore. After a while she realized she was looking at a sand castle. Not just a vaguely formed mound of sand, but a magical cre-

if you liked <u>this</u> story
...try our Preview Service

Get 4 FREE full-length Harlequin American Romance® books

Plus

this eye-catching, storeall cosmetic bag

Plus a surprise free gift

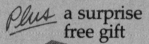

Plus lots more!

Our Preview Service is just that...it entitles you to "sneak previews" of the newest four Harlequin American Romance novels every month—months before they are in stores—at 10%-OFF retail on any books you keep (just $2.25 each)—with Free Home Delivery in the bargain.

Moreover, you can quit any time. You don't even have to accept a single selection, and the gifts are yours to keep no matter what—our thanks to you for loving romance as much as we. A super sweet deal if ever there was one!

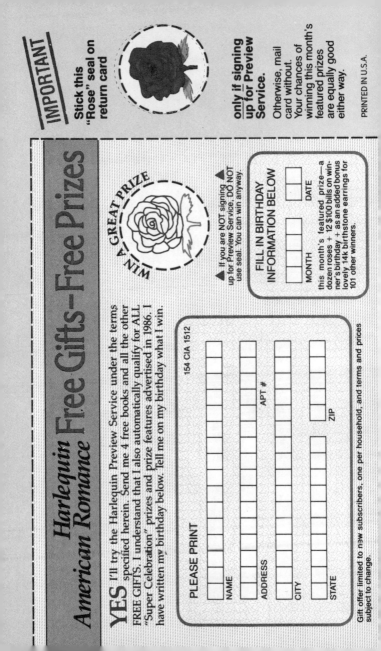
Harlequin American Romance Free Gifts–Free Prizes

YES I'll try the Harlequin Preview Service under the terms specified herein. Send me 4 free books and all the other FREE GIFTS. I understand that I also automatically qualify for ALL "Super Celebration" prizes and prize features advertised in 1986. I have written my birthday below. Tell me on my birthday what I win.

WIN A GREAT PRIZE

▲ If you are NOT signing up for Preview Service, DO NOT use seal. You can win anyway.

154 CIA 1512

PLEASE PRINT

NAME

ADDRESS   APT #

CITY   ZIP

STATE   ZIP

FILL IN BIRTHDAY INFORMATION BELOW

MONTH   DATE

this month's featured prize—a dozen roses + 12 $100 bills on winner's birthday + as an added bonus lovely 14k birthstone earrings for 101 other winners.

Gift offer limited to new subscribers, one per household, and terms and prices subject to change.

IMPORTANT REMINDER:
Use "Rose" seal ONLY IF you are signing up for Preview Service. Otherwise, mail card without seal—and check your favorite store <u>next</u> <u>month</u> for new prizes, new prize features and new opportunities to win.

If card is missing write:
**Harlequin
"Super Celebration"
Sweepstakes**
901 Fuhrmann Blvd.
P.O. Box 1325
Buffalo, NY 14269

Harlequin
"Super Celebration" Sweepstakes

901 Fuhrmann Blvd.
P.O. Box 1867
Buffalo, NY 14240-1867

PLACE
1ST CLASS
STAMP
HERE

ation someone had expended considerable time and talent to build.

The sand castle covered an area perhaps three feet square, complete with moat and a tiny drawbridge fashioned from a flat bit of driftwood. Above the corners of the outer wall rose conical turrets topped by small flags. Swizzle sticks, Jenny realized, identifying the flags she'd seen in poolside drinks. The inner structure of the sand castle reminded her of the Disney castle—splendid, capped roofs, towers, promenades and walled areas. It was an astonishing creation. Sadly, she saw that it would soon succumb to the surf rushing in on the tide.

"You couldn't sleep, either?"

Jenny jumped at the sound of his voice. For a moment she stared up at David as if he were an apparition she had conjured from her thoughts. Guilt, and something akin to panic prevented her from speaking as he sat down beside her and removed his shoes. His bare toes brushed hers beneath the water.

"Are you feeling better?"

"Yes," she whispered. Another lie. She looked at the trust in his eyes and felt the warm strength of his arm slipping around her waist. How could she possibly tell him? Surely she didn't have to do it now. What difference would it make if she waited until morning? She could give herself another hour, couldn't she?

No. This was the moment and she knew it. The longer she delayed, the worse the situation became. She had only to think of Rob Spenser to recall the disaster of further delay.

"I'm glad I found you," David said. "I'm going to be tied up with business most of tomorrow, but I'd like to have breakfast with you. And dinner. And tomorrow night.''

A light kiss brushed her temple and Jenny closed her eyes. She drew a deep, uneven breath. "David, there's something I have to tell you."

"I hope I know what it is," he said gruffly, tilting her face up to his. His wonderfully dark eyes traveled over her lips, made love to her. "I need to hear the words, Jenny, love. Tell me you love me, too."

"Oh, David." Jenny closed her eyes, feeling her lashes tight against her cheeks. "I do love you," she whispered. "I've always loved you."

His kiss was warm and sweet, a confirmation of joy and expectation. "You don't know how I've wanted to hear you say that." He tucked a stray lock of hair into her bandanna and murmured against her lips. "I can't imagine a future without you, Jenny. You're the best thing that's happened to me."

"David, wait. Before you say anything else, there's something you have to know."

His eyes twinkled in the moonlight and his voice teased. "This sounds serious."

"It is, I...I have a confession to make." The words emerged slowly, each an enormous effort.

"Ah, you have a secret?"

He was responding as if Jenny had nothing more serious to confess than that she cut her toenails in bed or chewed ice or forgot to screw on the toothpaste cap. She wished it was as simple as that.

She passed a hand over her forehead and watched the tide nibble the sand castle's outer wall. The builder's dreams were about to be washed away.

"Before I tell you, I want you to know that I do love you. Please remember that." Holding him tightly, she pressed her face against his shoulder. "I love you, David. With all my heart."

He smiled against the top of her head. "It isn't likely I'll forget the happiest moment of my life." Gently, he moved until he could look into her moon-lit face. "Jenny love, it's all right. Whatever your se-cret is, it isn't going to change anything. Don't you know that? We love each other. That's the only thing that's important."

"I hope you're right," she said, her voice cracking on a whisper.

"Jenny—what are you trying to say?"

The gentle patience in his voice broke her heart. As did the innocence in his gaze. He hadn't yet grasped they were talking about something more substantial than an annoying habit. And why would he? He trusted her.

Jenny exhaled slowly, hoping to quiet her racing pulse. This was it. The end of the story. "Do you re-member Cinderella? The fairy tale?" she asked, looking at the sand castle instead of meeting his eyes. And inside, she cursed herself. Even now she hadn't abandoned hope. Instead of coming right out with it, she was hoping she could offer an explanation he might accept.

"Your confession has something to do with Cin-derella?"

She heard the surprise and amusement in his voice and bit her lip before continuing. "I think every woman secretly yearns to be Cinderella," Jenny said quietly, "just once." The lump had returned to her throat and she spoke around it with difficulty. "At some time or another, all of us long to step outside our ordinary lives and become someone else—just for a while. Someone fascinating and exciting, someone more interesting than the person we see ourselves as being in everyday life.''

David's arm tightened around her waist, guiding her into the curve of his body. "Go on."

Jenny raised her eyes to the night sky, unable to bear watching the tide erode the sand castle's outer wall. She wished with all her heart that she didn't have to speak the next words. Please, she prayed silently, let me have misjudged the situation. Let him understand and forgive.

Her breast rose in a long reluctant breath. "David— since meeting you again, I've played at being Cinderella. I've pretended to be things I'm not. I wanted you to think I was successful and glamorous; I wanted to be special in your eyes."

Although Jenny wasn't looking at him, she sensed his bewilderment, felt the smile slowly fade from his lips. "I don't think I understand," David said slowly.

But he was beginning to. Jenny could sense his dawning comprehension in the way he unconsciously drew away from her. She closed her eyes against a threat of tears.

"I thought I wouldn't interest you if I was just myself. So I—" Jenny swallowed and dropped her head "—so I lied to you."

She felt his stare like a hard, accusing force. When he didn't speak, she continued in a barely audible whisper. "I'm not famous, David. No gallery or museum ever heard of Jenny Marshall. I've never painted anything close to a masterpiece. I paint card covers for New Image Greeting Cards. It isn't real art, but it pays the bills. And I need the money."

"The showings and receptions, the interviews...?" He sounded stunned.

"All lies. I've never had a showing, never been interviewed." Jenny closed her eyes, hurting inside at the shock she heard in his voice. It was the sound of betrayal. Whatever happiness she'd enjoyed in the past three days wasn't worth the pain she read in his stare when she dared a swift glance. His arm dropped from her waist and she winced at the chill rush where his warmth had been. Despite the warm night, she suddenly felt cold. Tears pricked her eyelids as she turned quickly aside, blinking rapidly as one of the castle's sand turrets slowly collapsed and trickled into the receding water.

"Lies," David repeated in a strangled whisper. "How much of it was...all that about Frascotti, was that true?"

"No," Jenny said. "I didn't win the prize. I didn't even compete." His toes pulled away from hers beneath the water. She felt a cool space open between them. And she wanted to sob and pull her hair and beg for forgiveness. "I wanted you to be proud of me. I wanted you to think I was as successful as I used to tell you I would be. I just wanted...I wanted you to see Cinderella instead of plain Jenny Marshall."

"You lied," he said dully. "I thought you were different. I thought I could learn to trust again with you."

"Please, David. Can't you understand? Even a little?"

"Understand? How can anyone understand a liar? Do you want to hear something funny? I thought you were open and honest. That's what I most admired about you."

Oh, God, this was worse than she had imagined. The expression in his eyes tore at her heart. She touched his arm and winced when he pulled away.

"Please believe me, David. I'm not a liar. This is the first time I've ever done anything like this." The assertion sounded ridiculous even to Jenny. She'd just confessed to a series of lies, and now she wanted him to believe she wasn't a liar. She tucked shaking hands into her lap and pressed her lips together.

"Oh? Then what is your definition of a liar?"

The sarcasm originated in pain, Jenny knew this, but it wounded her just the same. An inner tower collapsed on the sand castle and dribbled away with the tide. Jenny didn't think she could bear to watch the castle's destruction, but she couldn't look away. Dreams were dying in the flow of tiny sand grains, something wonderful was falling apart.

"What else did you lie about?" David's tone had turned harsh and accusing; his expression was stony. "Was the divorce a lie, too? Was any of it the truth?"

Jenny covered her eyes. "I'm divorced."

"And last night—was last night a lie?"

"Oh, David, no. Last night was beautiful."

"Was it? Or did you fake it?" He was standing over her now, his voice and his pain raining down around her shoulders. "Good God." Sudden realization sank his voice to a whisper. "I told Rob Spenser you were a famous artist. And you let me do it." He stared at her bowed head. "You made a liar and a fool out of me."

"I'm sorry, David. Sorrier than you'll ever know."

"Wrong, Jenny. I know all about being sorry. I've heard it before. I've heard enough 'I'm sorry's' to last a lifetime! And don't bother telling me you'll never lie again. I've heard that one, too!"

Anger stiffened his shoulders as he glared down at her. He started to say something else, then bit off the words and strode abruptly to the end of the jetty. He halted at the stretch of sand leading to the hotel steps.

"Why?" he asked, not looking at her. "For God's sake, Jenny—why? I trusted you. I believed in you. Were you just looking for a free ride? For some sucker to come along and pick up the mortgage? Is that it? Tell the fool anything until he's emotionally sucked in, then maybe he won't care that none of it is true?"

Hurled stones couldn't have hurt more. Jenny watched as the waves carried away the last vestiges of the sand castle. She wanted to scream at the tide.

"I wanted to live in your world for a few days. That's all. I wanted to be the kind of person David Foster would admire." She laced her trembling fingers together and pressed hard. "I...I'm sorry, David."

"Sorry!" After a long silence, she heard him say, "So am I." Then he was gone.

Jenny was never able to remember how long she'd remained on the jetty, blindly watching the waves hiss in and out. When the numbness eased and she could move again, she saw that nothing remained of the sand castle but a smooth depression. Something splendid and magical had vanished forever.

That's when the tears began.

SHE PRETENDED TO BE ASLEEP while Pam got out of bed and dressed for the day. She wasn't ready to talk about what had happened. When Pam had quietly closed the door behind her, Jenny rolled on her back and stared at the ceiling.

She'd made such a mess of it. There was no hope that David would understand. Or that he would believe she wasn't a habitual liar. Why should he? No matter how she tried to excuse herself, she had lied. When push came to shove, there was no acceptable excuse.

The Cinderella stuff was just so much baloney. After thinking about it for most of the night, she could admit that now. She hadn't lied because she'd wanted to be Cinderella; she had lied because she didn't want to be Jenny. There was a world of difference between the two.

Seeing David again had made her take a hard look at herself, and she hadn't liked what she'd seen. She'd seen someone who had failed to reach her potential, who lacked the confidence to reach for her dreams. Someone who made excuses rather than take risks. Who drifted through the years leaning on the word "someday."

The realization shocked her. She'd always considered herself a person who met life head on. She didn't flinch from reality. She knew herself.

That was the original lie. She didn't know herself at all. For years she had believed marriage and babies had prevented her from pursuing her art. Now she knew that wasn't true. She could have found time if that's what she'd really wanted to do. Walter Marshall had had his faults, but lack of support hadn't been one of them. He would have helped her make the time. He would have found the money for a cleaning lady and a baby-sitter if Jenny had told him how important her dreams were.

But she hadn't. She had been afraid of those dreams—afraid that once she admitted to having such dreams, she would have to try to reach for them. Had she done so, she would have put herself squarely on the line.

Jenny made a sound of disgust and covered her face with the pillow. "Jenny Marshall, you've been a damned stupid fool!"

Her stomach rumbled, reminding her that even fools had to eat. She couldn't lay here feeling miserable all day. The clock beside the bed told her it was nine-thirty. Surely David had eaten by now, and had departed to take care of his business. Swinging her legs over the side of the bed, Jenny sat for a moment, gathering courage to face the day. Then she leaned over the vanity to examine the circles under her eyes.

"You look terrible," she said. She drew a long breath. "But you're okay. You got that, Jenny Marshall? You've been an idiot, you've thrown away the best man you'll ever meet. But life goes on. So pull yourself together and show a little pride." It was the only thing to do.

And if she told herself often enough that she could live through this catastrophe, maybe she'd begin to believe it.

"No one ever died of a broken heart," she promised her mirror image. But she felt as if she might do just that. All the brave words didn't chase away the pain.

After Jenny had dressed, she pushed her hand under her pillow and withdrew the tiny Mayan worry people and turned them on her palm. "You guys are frauds," she said softly. "My worries didn't disappear."

If putting worry people under your pillow erased a person's problems, then there would have been more Mayans around today, Jenny decided wearily, and fewer deserted stone cities. She dropped the tiny dolls into their box and secured the lid. So much for worry people.

THE SUN WAS BRIGHT and hot on the terrace. A soft breeze blew off the ocean, rustling the palm fronds overhead, and scattering napkins off the laps of those enjoying a late breakfast. Jenny pushed her dark glasses up on her nose and marveled that life at the Palenque went on as if the world hadn't ended last night on the beach.

If she needed proof that her world had crashed around her toes, she received it when she spotted David across the terrace having coffee with Hernan Mortiz.

With a start, Jenny realized she must have walked past them to reach this table. And David had made no effort to speak or to stop her. So that's how it would be. He was facing her but pretending not to see her, engrossed in whatever Mortiz was saying.

Quick tears blurred his image, but she could still see him. She would always be able to see him in her mind. Sunlight striking silver at his temples. Dark curls tumbled across a tanned forehead. His wonderful mouth, firm with resolve or soft with tenderness.

Unable to bear the ache of watching him ignore her, Jenny turned aside and reached blindly for her coffee.

She finished one cup, then three, and still he hadn't looked at her. Suddenly she missed Deuce and Rhonda and Toulouse and Thedamnedcat. She missed her upstairs studio, and the smell of turpentine and linseed oil. She missed all the familiar things that made up her un-Cinderella life.

If there was one theory overall, one to live by, it was: when it's time to cut your losses, do so with dignity, then hightail it for home.

That moment had arrived. Jenny looked at David's granite expression and knew her vacation had ended. Though morning sunshine dappled her table, the clock was striking midnight.

Chapter Eight

Jenny's house had been built before land developers subdivided the Columbine area. Expensive new homes later had popped up behind her home and to the west, but across the road the area had remained relatively untouched and was still dotted by several of the original old houses.

Her own house had once been a barn, part of a farm that had eventually been sold off into lots. The previous owner had renovated the barn into a comfortable three-bedroom home with a vague look of New England about it.

Nudging the car door shut, Jenny balanced sacks of groceries in her arms. Tender new leaves were budding along the branches of the elm. A spray of yellow forsythia caught the spring sun against the weathered side of the house. The strawberries and the lilacs promised to be abundant this year.

Jenny smiled fondly. If she had all the money in the world, she would still want to live here. Of course, if she had all the money in the world, she'd fix the drainpipes, repair the screen door and treat the house to a new coat of paint. Someday.

She pulled the screen door open with the tips of her fingers and stepped into a large country kitchen. Immediately she braced, seconds before Toulouse hurled his eighty pounds against her chest. His warm, wet tongue lapped her chin and she made a face. The next dog she rescued from the pound was going to be a miniature poodle instead of a gigantic mix of husky and shepherd. So she always said. Before she went soft in the head for a furball of mammoth proportions and questionable parentage.

"Down, boy. I've only been gone an hour." After placing the grocery sacks on the countertop, she reached down and stroked Toulouse's shaggy head. He followed her through the family room to the foot of the staircase. "Deuce?" she called. "There are more groceries in the car. Want to give your mom a hand?"

"In a minute, Mom."

"Now, genius. The computer will still be there in five minutes. Meanwhile, the ice cream is melting."

"Aw, Mom."

Jenny grinned as Deuce appeared at the top of the stairs. Eventually Deuce would resemble Robert Redford, but at thirteen, he still had the look of a child because of his freckles and smooth cheeks. Rhonda had inherited Walter's dark hair and gaze, but Deuce had Jenny's honey-colored hair and cornflower eyes. Jenny understood Rhonda; Deuce was and always had been something of a mystery. But then, how could any woman comprehend a creature who collected ants and worms and knew how to strap on football pads?

"How come Rhonda doesn't have to do anything?" he groused as he passed her on the stairs.

"Rhonda? Come help your brother."

Rhonda's dark head appeared at her bedroom door. "Aw, Mom."

"Vacation's over, guys. It's back to the old routine."

Jenny had been home for a week; the kids had returned from California three days ago. If it hadn't been for the dull ache around her heart, Jenny might have convinced herself that she had dreamed Cancún. And David Foster.

"How'd school go today?" she asked, following them into the kitchen.

"Not so hot," Deuce said, before the screen door slammed behind him.

Rhonda giggled and winked. "Deuce likes Tanya Hubbard, but Tanya likes Bill Grange."

"Tanya?" There was no mother born who would willingly trust her son to a hussy named Tanya. Jenny tried to picture someone named Tanya. She would be built like Dolly Parton and have a killer look in her sexy bedroom eyes.

"Yeah. You've met her. Ugh."

Deuce deposited an armload of groceries on the countertop, then slouched back through the screen door. He wore a teenager's perpetual expression of abject despair. Jenny knew how he was feeling and made a mental note to say something nice about Tanya even if it killed her.

Rhonda stacked canned goods in the corner cabinet. "Mom? Can I have a slumber party?"

"Not until you're thirty. Remember the last slumber party?" Jenny balanced a carton of ice cream in her hand and frowned at the freezer. If she thawed the meat for tonight, the ice cream would fit. But she would need a blow torch to thaw the meat.

"Just a small party. Only my very best friends. We'll be quiet, honest."

Her daughter's words gradually penetrated as Jenny contemplated the problem with the ice cream. "Would this include your new friend?" Jenny asked casually, "Sara, I think her name is?"

"If her dad will let her come. He's awfully strict. Maybe you could call him for us?" Rhonda asked hopefully.

Standing very still, Jenny stared into the freezer. The minute she heard David's voice she suspected she'd fall apart. She imagined little pieces of Jenny all over the kitchen floor. Assuming, of course, that he'd speak to her in the first place. "You try, and if he doesn't agree, well . . . we'll see."

"Does this mean I can have the party?"

Jenny had a feeling she was going to regret this. "Yes."

"Great! Thanks, Mom!" After a quick hug, Rhonda ran upstairs to find the phone, no small chore considering the state of her room. "Friday night, okay?" she called down the stairs.

"Okay."

Friday night. In two days she might see David again. Would he bring Sara to the door, or just drop her off? What would he say? Maybe he wouldn't let Sara come. In that case, Jenny decided that she would call. It wasn't fair to punish the girls for her mistake.

"Mom?" Deuce stared at her. "Ice cream is dripping on your shoes."

"Toulouse will take care of it," Jenny answered absently. Her thoughts had jumped ahead to Friday night.

She'd clean the house from top to bottom. If she could stretch the budget, she'd treat herself to a new hairdo on Friday morning.

Thinking about money reminded her that she'd forgotten to mail the latest batch of picture boards to New York. Damn. Groaning, she flipped some hamburgers on the Jenn-Aire, then ran upstairs to her studio and poked hastily through the clutter overflowing her desk.

"Aha." The thick padded envelope was where she'd left it, taped and stamped. "You don't get paid, dummy, unless they get the merchandise." Tucking the envelope under her arm, she closed her eyes and inhaled deeply, enjoying the tangy scent of turpentine, paint and sunshine.

This was her favorite room. A casual observer would have seen an explosion of clutter, but it was her clutter and Jenny liked it. Wide skylights flooded the studio with afternoon light, playing over her easels, her worktable, her desk and the rambling bookshelves. The far wall was covered with her paintings. Not her real art, but her commercial paintings, the watercolors and acrylics she dashed off for New Image Greeting Cards. There were samples of Easter cards, Thanksgiving cards, Christmas cards and her bread-and-butter staple, the all-purpose cards.

"Mom?" Rhonda shouted from down the hall. "The hamburgers are burning."

"You've got hands, honey. Turn them over." She hadn't seriously thought about her art in a long, long time. She was tempted to open the cabinet doors beneath the bookcases and rummage through the canvases stored there. The canvases were early Jenny Marshalls—still lifes, landscapes and a few wildly exotic impressionistic pieces. But the hamburgers were burning.

"Saved again," she said without humor. After filling her lungs with the clean, sharp scents, she softly closed the door to her studio and hefted the envelope in her hand. It wasn't what she really wanted to paint, but the card covers paid the bills.

Bills were like clothes hangers. They bred and multiplied by some unexplained mysterious process. No matter how hard Jenny tried, she could never catch them at it, but the evidence was irrefutable. There were always new little bills she couldn't account for otherwise. Her theory about bills was simple: Don't worry about them. Either she had the money to pay, or she slid the bills to the next month. Worrying didn't reduce the amount by a single nickel. And there were always more interesting events to worry about—like the coming Ice Age. She paid a little to everybody and did the best she could.

Following dinner and a TV movie that made Jenny wonder why she had bothered watching, she chased the kids upstairs to do their homework, then gave the kitchen a hit and a lick before climbing the stairs to Deuce's room.

"Want to talk a minute?" She poked her head inside a room that was neater than Rhonda's or her own. Jenny didn't nag the kids about their rooms; everyone needed a private space to keep as he liked. Deuce kept his space like a military barracks, with everything in its prescribed spot. Jenny had no idea where this trait sprang from. It had to be a renegade gene.

"I'm kinda tired, Mom, you know?" Deuce switched off his computer and watched the green light wink out.

Jenny crossed her arms and leaned against the doorjamb. ''Hmm.'' The proximity of football equipment and toy soldiers tugged at her heart. She wouldn't have been Deuce's age again for all the money in Columbine First National.

Deuce lifted a pencil and watched it fall. ''Mom . . . do you know anything about girls?''

''A little.'' Her eyebrows arched. ''I used to be one.''

''How do you make a girl like you?''

Jenny repressed a smile. Deuce looked everywhere but toward her. A pink flush climbed from his pajama collar. In three years he would be driving a car. Two years after that, she'd wave him off to college. Where had the time gone? Only yesterday she'd been carrying him on her hip and asking if he'd washed behind his ears.

''Just be yourself, Deuce. That's the best plan.''

''What if being myself isn't good enough?''

Oh, Lord. Out of the mouths of babes. Jenny closed her eyes a moment, then sat on the edge of his bed. ''Being yourself is always good enough, honey. Believe me, I know. If a girl doesn't like you, that's her problem, not yours. If she can't accept you as you are, then she's not much of a bargain, is she?''

Silently, Jenny added: *Do as I say, my son, not as I do. If I'd had the sense to take this advice myself, I wouldn't be feeling so miserable right now*.

His cornflower eyes met hers. ''Are you sure?''

''Absolutely. I'm sure.'' A school picture had been stuck in the corner of his mirror. Jenny examined the shy eyes of a dark-haired girl lacking the barest hint of a chest. ''Is that Tanya?''

''Rhonda told you,'' Deuce accused.

"She just mentioned you had a friend named Tanya." Tanya looked as much like Dolly Parton as a seed looked like an apple. Jenny stared at the school picture and gave her blessing to the match.

"She doesn't like me." Absently, he pulled a comb from his pajama pocket and tugged it through his hair.

Jenny stood up, fearing she'd laugh if she remained another minute. She wondered if all teenage boys took a comb to bed. "Just be yourself, Deuce. Give her a chance to know you."

"Yeah," he said dismally.

After closing his door, Jenny continued along the hallway to Rhonda's room. She ground her teeth and swore she would not think about herself and David in light of her conversation with Deuce.

Rhonda sat cross-legged on the bed, talking into the telephone. A collection of dolls was arranged neatly along the shelves over her bed. Everything else was in awesome disarray.

Rhonda replaced the receiver and smiled happily. "Everyone can come," she announced.

"Everyone?" Jenny swept a pile of laundry off the end of the bed and sat down.

"Can we have real Coke instead of diet drinks? And can we have some of those snacks like you make for adults?"

"Cheese balls?"

"Yeah. And dip for the chips, and maybe bacon wrapped around chestnuts?"

Jenny tried to remember the price of chestnuts. It seemed to her that the last time she'd priced them, she'd concluded a sack of emeralds would be cheaper. "I suppose so." She smoothed Rhonda's dark hair from her cheek, knowing she broke the first commandment of motherhood: Thou shalt not touch thy daughter's hair under penalty of a loud "Aw Mom."

"Aw, Mom," Jenny said along with Rhonda. They both laughed.

"Mom, am I ever going to get boobs?" Rhonda heaved a despairing sigh and gazed mournfully at the front of her nightshirt. "Try it, you'll like it" was emblazoned across the front.

"Of course you will. Don't be in such a hurry."

"I'm almost thirteen," Rhonda wailed. "Everybody I know is getting boobs but me!"

"It will happen. I didn't get boobs until I was nearly fourteen."

"Fourteen! By the time I'm fourteen Brad Engels will be senile. I need boobs by Saturday."

Jenny pulled up the coverlet. "What happens Saturday?"

"Mom, don't you remember? Soccer sign-up. The boys sign up right next to us!"

Good heavens, she'd forgotten all about it. She needed to call Ed Lauper in the morning and make arrangements to pick up her forms before Saturday. Every year she told herself she wasn't going to coach a team and every year she did. Why should this year be any different?

"Sleep well, honey."

Jenny turned out the lights, put Thedamnedcat outside, locked the doors, then climbed upstairs to her room, Toulouse padding along at her heels.

After pinning up her hair, she ran hot water into the tub, and slathered her face with an egg facial, then relaxed in the steaming water, listening to the silent house.

She hated this time of day, when the kids were asleep and the house was dark and quiet. This was the time of day when even the staunchest mind fell prey to lonely thoughts. When hers was the only light burning, and the king-size bed loomed large and empty, Jenny sometimes thought she was the only person in Columbine going to bed with a book. Everyone else was snuggled up to warm, loving partners.

Where was David tonight?

Jenny sank lower in the tub until her chin rested atop the bubbles. She had sworn she absolutely, positively would not torture herself by thinking about David Foster. What was done was done. She couldn't change a thing by agonizing over what might have been.

Was he thinking about her?

"Stop that!"

She sank her chin lower and scowled at the bubbles. Her mind had turned traitorous.

"Think about something else."

She would think about Walter. The kids had told her Walter had remarried. Good old middle-aged Walter had married a college dropout named Susie who was twenty-two years old. A Gorgeous Young Thing. They lived in a school bus they had converted into a house. Susie made jewelry out of beads and feathers, and Walter made leather purses. The kids swore Walter was happy.

"Good for Walter. Right, Toulouse?" Toulouse opened one eye, heaved a sigh and went back to sleep. "Listen, pal, it's no small thing when a woman's ex-husband gets married, and not only that, marries a much younger woman who, according to the first wife's own children, is not only young and beautiful but can bake a lemon meringue pie!''

It was the lemon meringue pie that had depressed Jenny when she heard about Walter's new marriage. In her whole life she had never baked a decent one. Instead of fluffing up as it was supposed to, Jenny's meringue just lay there in the bowl. There were never any little peaks like in the pictures in the cookbook. Her meringue was as flat as Rhonda's chest.

That's what life was all about, she decided, brooding. Lemon meringue pies. Some people had the knack and some didn't, and there you were. Success or failure, simple as that.

"What hope is there for a woman who can't bake a stupid lemon meringue pie?'' Jenny muttered. She thought about Walter living in a school bus making purses and eating lemon meringue pie. It sounded pretty awful in her opinion. On the other hand, at least he had Susie. Jenny released a sigh that began at her toes. "Yes, Toulouse, this is all very depressing.''

As long as she was already depressed, she gave up and let herself think about David Foster. Isla Mujeres rose in her memory, bringing with it the ache of one perfect night. One enchanted evening. Closing her eyes, she remembered the wine-scented warmth of David's breath against her cheek, remembered the strength of his arms wrapped around her.

A single tear cut a track through her egg facial.

THE HUM OF THE PLANE'S engines had lulled most of the passengers to sleep. David turned a moody gaze to the window and stared at a grid of lights far below. They were somewhere over Texas; the plane would land in Denver in about two hours.

He finished the last of his drink and handed the plastic cup up to the stewardess. Tomorrow he had a full schedule, and he wouldn't get home until after midnight tonight. The wise thing to do was take a pillow from the overhead bin and catch a nap while he could.

But every time he relaxed and cleared his mind of business details, Jenny's face appeared behind his lids. He saw her laughing on the bus to Chichén Itzá, saw her eyes soft and shining and smiling up at him from her pillow.

The hell with it, there was no way he was going to sleep. He jabbed the stewardess call button with a short, impatient gesture and asked her for another Scotch-and-water.

He couldn't get Jenny out of his mind. Even knowing she'd deceived him from the first moment, he couldn't forget her.

David stared at the darkness outside the plane's window, turning his drink between his fingers. Even faced with the truth, he found it difficult to accept that Jenny had lied. She simply didn't have a liar's face. There was nothing secretive in her eyes; her face was wholesome and open, lovely. There were even freckles on her nose.

Since when did freckles equate with honesty? Logic was deserting him. He scrubbed a hand over his face, then took a deep swallow of his Scotch-and-water.

Some time ago he had read an article stating that people attracted certain types of other people. He hadn't thought much about the article at the time, but now he remembered and wondered if there was something in him that attracted people who lied. It seemed to stretch coincidence that the two women in his life were both averse to the truth. He wouldn't have guessed Marilyn and Jenny to be the same type of woman, yet it appeared they were.

At least Jenny was creative. Marilyn had never come up with an excuse as far out of left field as drawing on a fairy tale. He shook his head. Blaming a series of lies on Cinderella was a new one. He hadn't heard that explanation before.

Between Texas and Oklahoma, he sipped his drink and tried to find a shred of validity in Jenny's explanation. It annoyed him to realize he was trying to understand a damned fairy tale, and to apply it to a situation in his life. It also irritated him to admit he was looking for some way to excuse what Jenny had done.

But there was none. No matter how he turned her reasoning over in his mind, he continually returned to the basic fact that she had lied. She had invented a background out of whole cloth. All lies.

A weight of memory settled over his shoulders like a sack of stones. He knew what it was like to live with a liar, knew the pain and the frustration. He couldn't do it again.

But, dammit, he loved her.

Walking away from Jenny that night on the beach had been one of the hardest things he'd ever done. Even though he'd been shocked and angry, part of him had wanted to take her into his arms and soothe the utter wretchedness from her face. Experience had stopped him.

He'd known what she would say. She would have promised never to lie again. And the promise of a liar was worth less than an ounce of wind.

Bending, he lifted his briefcase to the table in front of him and removed the syndication papers for the Palenque Hotel. Jenny was part of his past, not his future. There was no point in going over it again. He wasn't going to find a way to forgive. A liar was always a liar. He wanted no part of it.

Then why did he drive past her house on his way home from the airport? He didn't know why, but it annoyed the hell out of him. Curiosity, he decided as he checked her address in the phone book, nothing more. He'd have a look at her house and that would be the end of it.

After cutting the engine of a three-year-old Chrysler, he studied the house across the road from where he had quietly parked.

He liked Jenny's house. This surprised him, as he'd been prepared not to. It had a homey look; a white cat was sitting in the shadows on the front porch. The forsythia and lilac bushes needed to be pruned and he suspected daylight would reveal the house could use a coat of paint. But it was a warm house, an inviting house, one it would be nice to come home to.

The fantasies he'd indulged in in Mexico returned full force. He'd pictured himself and Jenny living in a house like this, laughing with the kids at the dinner table, smiling at each other while the kids sprawled in front of the TV. He'd enjoyed the image of a family, his and Jenny's, together.

After hearing Jenny talk about her children, David knew he would like them. He'd imagined talking football with Deuce, working with him on Deuce's computer; he'd pictured Rhonda and Sara preparing for their first dates. This was the life he had dreamed of, a simple life centered on the people he cared about. A rambling house, a noisy family. And Jenny.

Slowly his gaze swept the upper story before settling on a glow of light behind a curtain. A shadow paused before the curtain, and he gripped the steering wheel. When the shadow passed, David turned his head and stared down the length of the dark street.

What in the hell was he doing? Parked in front of her house like a lovesick teenager. At that moment the car radio played "On the Street Where you Live."

A short burst of humorless laughter broke from his lips, then he snapped off the radio and eased the car from the shoulder of the road. Okay, he'd satisfied his curiosity and that was that. Now he could put her out of his mind.

He drove across Wadsworth and wound through a darkened subdivision filled with custom-built homes. They were impressive, but on closer inspection he decided they lacked the charm and sturdy livability of Jenny's house. Even his own house, a two-story marvel of wood and glass, seemed raw and spare by comparison. It would be years before the trees reached maturity, and before his lilacs needed pruning. At least it was more comfortable than the house in California had been. That house had been surrounded by thick stucco walls and Keep Out signs.

After parking the car in the garage, he carried his suitcases into the hallway, glad to see a light in the family room and the flicker of the TV set. There was nothing worse than coming home to a dark house.

"Sara?"

"It's me, Mr. Foster. Sara's asleep."

"Oh. Hello, Mrs. White. Did everything go all right?" The neighbors had recommended Mrs. White as the best baby-sitter in the Columbine area. She had the additional advantage of being able to live in when necessary. He patted her plump arm as he passed to the kitchen and poured the last of a pot of coffee into a cup. The kitchen was spotless, as he'd known it would be. Mrs. White took pride in her job. "No catastrophes? All quiet on the home front?"

Mrs. White removed a note from her sweater pocket and pushed reading glasses up her nose. "Everything went fine, Mr. Foster." She read from her list. "Your stockbroker called and your accountant wants you to call first thing in the morning. Ed Lauper, head of the Columbine Sports Association, called to remind you soccer registration is Saturday morning. Sara has to go in early tomorrow for a science field trip. And I gave her permission to go to a slumber party Friday night. Was that all right?"

"A slumber party?"

"At Rhonda Marshall's. I've baby-sat for Mrs. Marshall and know the family. I didn't think you'd mind."

It seemed Fate had cast a net to ensnare even his daughter. A week ago David would have been delighted by the news. Now an expression of weariness settled over his face and he drained his coffee in a gulp.

"I'm not sure the Marshalls are the kind of influence I want Sara exposed to."

Mrs. White's eyebrows rose in surprise. "Begging pardon, sir, but I can't think why you'd say that. Rhonda Marshall is a fine young lady; you couldn't pick a better friend for Sara. Mrs. Marshall is divorced, but there hasn't been a breath of scandal attached to her name. She's been active in the community and is well thought of."

Marilyn had been active in the community and well thought of, too, at least for a time. The last he'd heard, Marilyn's propensity to lie, even when the truth was better, had caught up to her and doors were closing. Sooner or later the same would happen to Jenny Marshall. Eventually the truth came out.

"I'm sorry," Mrs. White said when David didn't respond. "I didn't realize you'd object." An anxious line appeared between her brows.

"It's all right. I suppose one slumber party can't hurt." But it was clear he needed to guide Sara toward more suitable friends.

"Well . . . if it's all right with you, I'll stay the night here and go home after fixing Sara's breakfast."

After Mrs. White had retired, David watched TV for a few minutes, then snapped it off and carried his luggage to his room. He'd forgotten how impersonal his room was; it reminded him of a hotel.

A lack of time and interest had delayed him from hanging any pictures or giving the room any small personal touches. He wasn't good at that kind of thing anyway. Yet tonight he would have liked to come home to a room that was warm and welcoming. He dropped his suitcase on a bedspread that didn't match anything else in the room and cast a glance toward the clean surface of the bureau dresser. What was needed were the bottles and brushes and clutter of everyday living.

It surprised him to realize suddenly that he was missing a woman's belongings. Women made a house a home. The idea was so blatantly chauvinistic that he laughed out loud. He could just imagine what Jenny would have said about that.

Jenny.

He sat on the side of the bed and pushed his hands through his hair. Had it been Jenny's shadow behind the curtain?

Standing abruptly, he unpacked his suitcase and scattered his brushes and toiletries across the bureau surface. Tomorrow he would find time to hang some pictures, or to hire an interior decorator.

Chapter Nine

"My God," Jenny breathed. "Do normal women wear this stuff?" She stared at racks of filmy lingerie that impressed her as appropriate for strippers and ladies of the night.

The saleswoman smiled. "Honey, where have you been? Sexy is in. Tummy control is out; garter belts are back."

"I didn't know they'd been gone." Jenny swallowed and touched a slip as wispy and insubstantial as a cobweb. "Look, I'm a mother. Do mothers of teenagers wear see-through lavender?"

The saleswoman placed her hands on her hips and tilted her head. "Divorced, right?" Jenny nodded. "There's a new man on the scene and all you've got are white cotton bras you bought when the kids were babies, right?"

"That's amazing. You're a mind reader."

"That, my dear, is typical." The saleswoman pushed Jenny toward a fitting room. "We're going to take care of you, honey. And you won't believe how good you're going to feel. Like a new woman."

Forty-five minutes and two hundred dollars later, Jenny conceded the saleslady had been right on target. She was wearing hot-pink dance pants with a matching teddy and bra. And she felt wonderful. Ready to open the door tonight to David Foster, secure in the knowledge that she was as perfect as she could be from the skin out. Her theory regarding morale building was simple: Buy new underwear. Nothing did more for a woman's state of mind than knowing she was wearing something slinky and silky, something that had not seen the inside of a washing machine two million times before.

"Now," the saleslady said, "you go see Hilda in sleepwear and let her fix you up."

Jenny frowned uneasily at the charge slip. "I don't know...."

The saleslady regarded her with a knowing look. "Granny gowns, right? Faded and starting to unravel? Maybe pajamas?" Her lip curled.

"Point me toward Hilda." Jenny sighed. David might be lost to her, but she could dream. And she would dream better in something filmy, sexy and morale-building.

An hour later, Jenny staggered from the store, weighed down with parcels. She prayed the house didn't burn down in the middle of the night. If it did, she was going to be standing in the road half naked. But clad in see-through black and gorgeous.

And probably half dead from the extra work she was going to have to do to pay for all this splendor.

She looked at the spill of packages on the car seat beside her and made a face. Her purchases fell in the category of locking the barn door after the horse had run off. There was no man in her life and she had absolutely no need for sexy lingerie and slinky nightgowns. But knowing she had them made her feel better. Heaven knew she needed a boost right now.

At the hairdresser's, she tried to relax and think of what remained to be done for Rhonda's slumber party. She still had to clean the house. Ugh. And she had to pick up the snacks, which would cost a fortune, at the grocery. She thought of the money she was spending on this party and groaned. Who would have imagined that a slumber party for a group of preteens would require new lingerie and a hairdo? But then, who would have imagined that she would ever see David Foster again?

"Is everything all right, Mrs. Marshall?"

"Fine." She followed the hairdresser back to the chair and stared into the mirror.

"All right now. What are we looking for?"

"Something chic and appealing. Something that cries out for forgiveness." Jenny studied herself hopefully. "A hairdo that says 'I'm sorry.'" Whoever said loving meant never having to say "I'm sorry" was nuts. The phrase made a great opening line, but it was about as true as saying spiders are a girl's best friend.

"Sort of like Farrah?"

Jenny bit her lip. "I don't know."

"You look sorta like Farrah. I think that would be good on you."

Naturally Jenny had a theory to account for hairdressers. Hairdressers saw everyone in terms of someone else. Customers looked like Farrah or Elizabeth or Joan or the Plain-Jane character actress whose name nobody could remember. The resemblance might consist merely of a curve in the ear. But it was enough. You paid your money and you walked out looking like Farrah or Elizabeth or Joan or Plain Jane.

Jenny had never known a woman who left the hairdresser looking as she had hoped to look. It was always a disappointment no one admitted to. The hairdresser was praised lavishly, lies were exchanged and the woman went home to stare despairingly in the mirror and contemplate suicide.

When the hairdresser stepped backward and beamed, Jenny swallowed hard and summoned a brave smile. "I love it," she said in a wobbly voice.

Oh, God. She looked like Sheena of the Jungle. Spiky curls exploded from her head in all directions. So much lacquer coated her hair that she could have strolled through a hurricane without disturbing a single strand. This hairdo didn't say "I'm sorry," it shouted a Tarzan call.

"Simply love it," she repeated. If the gods smiled on her, she wouldn't encounter anyone she knew between here and home. Thank heaven she'd remembered to bring her dark glasses. She paid, then ran to the car wondering if she could make it through tonight without drowning herself.

"Mom! What happened to your hair!" Rhonda's eyes widened as Jenny ducked through the kitchen door.

"Never mind." Jenny pushed Toulouse's paws off her shoulders and hung her sweater in the closet.

Slowly, Rhonda walked around her. "I think I like it. It's sorta punk, you know? If you dyed it green on one side and pink on the other, you'd look just like that girl on Duece's poster."

Jenny cast a grim look toward the oven, remembering it was electric and not gas. She reached for the phone and dialed, hoping Pam was home. "Pam? This is an emergency. Get over here immediately and bring your curlers and a bottle of Scotch."

When Pam walked through the screen door, she stared at Jenny and burst into laughter.

"We have six hours to repair this," Jenny said briskly. "You mix us a Scotch-and-water; I'll wash the lacquer out, then we will both pray for inspiration."

JENNY RAN HER HANDS over her skirt and nervously glanced around the family room. The lights were low, music from the FM waltzed through the room. Even Marilyn Cody, previously perfect person, could not have created a more comfortable setting.

After Pam left, Jenny had worked like a dog to remove any lived-in look, striving for the *House Beautiful* gloss of perfection that told the viewer no teenager had ever passed this way.

Unfortunately, hers was not a *House Beautiful* home. Toulouse had teethed on the chair legs, the sofa sagged slightly to fit the contours of Duece's favorite TV-viewing position and the slipcover on Rhonda's chair had been made in her home economics class. Jenny was proud of Rhonda's accomplishment, but she doubted that *House Beautiful* would have cheered. The chair looked a bit like a wrinkled, yellow toad. It was a friendly toad, but it was a toad.

Never mind. Leaning toward the hall mirror, Jenny inspected herself with a critical eye. Pam had tamed the Sheena hair to soft waves that were discreetly silent and said nothing, thank God. A whisper of gray eye shadow arched over her eyelids, rosy-pink lipstick covered her mouth. After tearing her closet apart searching for something fantastic, she'd settled for a gray skirt and a rose-colored silk blouse, beneath which a sharp-eyed observer could see hints of the lace edging her new rose-colored teddy.

What on earth would she say to him?

"Hello, David. If you don't forgive me I'll hurl myself into the briar patch." No good. Maybe she should throw herself at his feet, wrap her arms around his legs and cry, "I'm sorry, I'm sorry. Please give me another chance." This plan appealed to her, but it was a bit dramatic.

Maybe he wouldn't come; maybe he'd have someone else drive Sara over. In which case the new hairdo, the slumber party and the frenzied housecleaning would have been for nothing. But she would feel vastly relieved. Feminine wiles were not her strong suit. She'd never liked game playing.

On the other hand, she guessed the new lingerie and hairdo constituted game playing. Russian roulette, maybe. She had one shot at this, one last chance to see David and hope that being together again—if he brought Sara—would move him to forgive her. That was the game plan, such as it was.

The doorbell rang and Rhonda ran past Jenny to throw open the door. "Come in, Kelly Ann. Did you bring the purple nail polish?"

Pam followed her daughter into Jenny's family room. "Okay, I'm first, as planned. Does David know you're inviting the parents in for drinks as they drop off the girls?"

"I didn't talk to him." Jenny rubbed her hands nervously. "Maybe this wasn't such a good idea, Pam."

"What are you talking about? This was my idea and it'll work. You'll see David again. That's what you want, isn't it?"

"What do I say to a man who hates me?"

"Is this a trivia question?"

"There must be a masochistic streak in me. I mean, look at the evidence. I married Walter, I actually volunteered to run for PTA President, I'm coaching soccer again this year, and I'm torturing myself tonight. I need a shrink."

"What you need is a drink." Pam approached the pass-through from the kitchen and mixed a Scotch-and-water from the tray Jenny had prepared. "To success!"

Jenny raised her glass. "I'm not sure what would constitute success, if you want the truth. If he could forgive, Pam, he would have phoned."

"Maybe he just needs a little nudge."

"Maybe," Jenny said doubtfully.

She spilled part of her drink when the doorbell rang again. Hating her anxiety, she peeked through the curtains while Rhonda and Kelly Ann raced for the door and pulled Marcie Taylor inside. Gene and Anne Taylor followed, and Jenny mixed drinks. In a few minutes the kitchen had filled with giggling girls and the family room buzzed with the conversation of their parents. Soon, Jenny thought, fixing drinks and passing nibble food, soon the bell would ring and it would be David. And she would drop to the floor in cardiac arrest and the ambulance would come and haul her away and David would leave without their having exchanged a word. That's what she got for playing games. When you interfered with Fate, Fate zinged you hard to teach you a lesson.

DAVID STOOD on the porch behind Sara and pressed the doorbell. "Is this the right night?" he asked Sara. Half a dozen cars lined the driveway, and it sounded like an adult party inside. He shifted Sara's overnight case to his other hand and glanced at his watch. He had a dinner date with his accountant tonight, and he was already late.

"Hi, David, it's nice to see you again."

"Hello, Pam."

Sara released a squeal of delight and rushed inside, leaving David on the porch with her overnight case.

"Come inside," Pam said, smiling and holding open the door. "We parents are having a drink to celebrate the fact that this slumber party is at Jenny's house and not ours."

"Thanks, but I'm late for an appointment. Shall I give Sara's case to you?"

Pam blinked innocently. "You'd better bring it inside. I don't know where the girls are putting their things."

A hint of a smile touched the corners of his mouth. "Pam," he said quietly, "please don't play matchmaker."

"I wouldn't think of it, friend." Pam opened the door wider, stepping aside to let him pass. "But . . ."

"No buts, okay?"

"Everyone makes mistakes, David. And Jenny made a big one . . . but she loves you."

"She has a funny way of showing it. Look, Pam, I appreciate what you're trying to do, but let's just leave it alone, okay?"

They were standing in Jenny's foyer. Over Pam's shoulder David could see a large, comfortable room with an inviting, lived-in look. A low bookcase was crammed with books, games and puzzles. The furniture had been chosen for comfort rather than compatibility. The colors were warm and harmonious, and good artwork adorned the walls. It was a room that invited one to sit down, kick off his shoes and relax. This was what David imagined when he heard the word "home." He hadn't lived in a house like this since he was a child.

"David, can't you give it another chance?" Pam asked in a low tone. "Jenny meant no harm."

He tried to keep his voice light. "Everyone is a product of their experience. My experience is that once trust is broken, it's impossible to reclaim. I like things up front and open. No surprises." He met her eyes. "And no lies."

Pam said something more but her voice was lost in a nearby burst of laughter. David looked around for a place to put Sara's overnight case. As soon as he'd set it beside the door, Pam took his arm and tugged him forward, introducing him to the Taylors and then the Bradfords. Like it or not, it seemed he would be staying for a few moments.

Then he saw Jenny. She was standing beside a couple who looked vaguely familiar, a half smile on her lips. She'd done something new with her hair and it fell in soft wheat-colored waves around her cheeks. Her rose-colored blouse cast a pink glow over her face, and her eyes were as blue as the Colorado sky. She was beautiful and animated, soft and yielding. David stared at her and thought her the most desirable woman he'd ever seen.

A wave of resentment stiffened his body. It could have been so good between them. Jenny would have brought warmth into his life. She could have thawed that small, frozen kernel inside him. With Jenny, the world would have been a playground, filled with lightness and laughter.

If she had been what he'd thought she was. If she hadn't lied to him.

JENNY SENSED his presence the moment David stepped into her house. Though she didn't see him immediately, she felt him. The air around her seemed to quiver with expectation. Her pulse quickened. She placed a hand on her heart and expected the FM to swell with "Some Enchanted Evening." For one wild instant, hope raced through her. Maybe, just maybe...

But when she turned and raised her eyes, meeting his stare above the heads of her other guests, she almost flinched. He hated her. She saw it in his narrowed eyes, in the hard lines framing his mouth. Everyone else was dressed casually, but David was wearing a gray silk three-piece suit. And beneath the silk his shoulders were tense.

The smile faltered on her lips and a dull ache radiated from her chest. Inviting the parents inside had been a terrible idea, abysmal. Why couldn't she just accept that David was lost to her? Why did she have to torment herself with hope? All she'd accomplished was to make David uncomfortable and herself miserable.

Pam appeared at her side. "Offer him a drink," she urged between her teeth.

Jenny closed her eyes, listening to the sounds of party chatter, to the giggles and squeals emanating from the kitchen, where the girls had gathered. It was time for a pep talk, a rah-rah session to stiffen her spine and help her see this through.

All right, she told herself. *This is no time to fall apart. This is your house, dammit, and you don't hide from people in your own house. Remember: You are wearing hot-pink undies. And a woman in hot-pink undies can do anything. You may not be a famous artist, but you've built a good life. Didn't you just make a double payment to Visa? You're holding it together and raising two nice kids. You have a lot to be proud of. Now lift your head high, march over there and give him a drink.*

"I have climbed the side of a Mayan pyramid," she mused aloud. "In my day I've changed hundreds of dirty diapers."

"Damned straight." Pam grinned. "And don't forget, you have lived through two garage sales."

"I have triumphed over waxy yellow build-up."

"You have whipped the PTA into shape."

"Once I made brownies for Rhonda's band class out of melted chocolate chips and bran flakes. I killed a garden snake last summer without screaming."

"You can do anything."

"You're damned right," Jenny said firmly. "I can certainly offer a guest in my own home a drink."

"It's a dirty job but someone has to do it." Pam laughed.

Midway across the room, David's drink in her hand, Jenny paused. David was seated on the sofa beside Deuce, head to head in animated conversation. Deuce was wearing a fascinated expression that told her they were discussing computers. She watched them, having already imagined a similar scene, and an ache closed around her heart.

"Deuce," she said as she reached the sofa, "would you do me a favor and empty Pam's ashtray, please?"

"Aw, Mom." He shook David's hand. "Thanks a lot, Mr. Foster. I'll try the program you told me about. Maybe we can talk again sometime."

"I'd like that, Deuce."

When Deuce left, Jenny drew a breath. "Hello, David." The slight tremble in her fingers made the ice tinkle in his drink glass.

The pleasure faded from David's eyes and he looked up at her, his face expressionless. "Hello, Jenny."

The coolness in his tone wounded her. "I brought you a drink."

"Thank you, but I can't stay." He stood, and she felt suddenly diminished by his height. "I have an appointment."

"Oh."

An appointment or a date? She didn't know what to do with the drink in her hand or what to say to him. Words failed her.

"What time shall I pick up Sara in the morning?"

"All the girls plan to sign up for soccer. I thought I'd drive them to the field, and the parents can pick them up there."

He nodded and glanced at his watch, then toward the door. *Say something,* Jenny told herself. *This may be your last chance. Ask his forgiveness.*

Instead, pride firmed her backbone. The look in David's eyes made her feel like a criminal. And she wasn't. She hadn't set out to hurt him or to destroy whatever chance they might have had. She had made a mistake, that was all. A bad mistake, granted, but it wasn't the crime of the century.

She watched him edge toward the door. And she remembered telling Deuce that a person who wouldn't accept someone as he was was no bargain. Her head inched higher, and a flush spread across her cheeks. What kind of man was so pigheaded that he couldn't forgive an innocent error? Maybe David Foster was no bargain.

She didn't believe it for a minute, but the thought helped her through the moment. "Goodbye, David."

He looked at her for a long minute and something flickered in the depths of his eyes. Regret? Longing? Resentment? The look passed before Jenny could identify it.

"Goodbye, Jenny."

As he walked to the door, she suddenly remembered she had forgotten to vacuum the sofa. David's gray-silk fanny was liberally coated with white cat hair. Jenny covered her eyes and sighed. Damn. Well, it served him right. She bent to pat Thedamnedcat, who sat on the hearth licking a paw and surveying the party with regal disinterest, before she excused herself to investigate the crashes and bangs coming from the kitchen.

The girls were making popcorn and fudge, and destroying Jenny's kitchen. As far as they were concerned, the slumber party was just getting started.

Jenny heard the spin of gravel as David's car pulled from her driveway. She cast a dismal glance toward the window. As far as she was concerned, the evening had ended.

Chapter Ten

Ed Lauper had become the president of the Columbine Sports Association for one reason. He was the only person who had volunteered for the position. He'd been unanimously elected by a room full of relieved parents. Ed was now serving his third term, and, all in all, Jenny thought he'd done a good job. But no one had ever accused Ed of being organized.

She parked her station wagon at the edge of the soccer field and the girls spilled out. Jenny could see at a glance that this year's registration was going to be as disorganized as last year's. Long tables were arranged at the end of the field, and signs had been taped to their surfaces that identified age groups. But it had been done by no discernable method. The eight-year-olds would sign up next to high-schoolers, and so on. There were two teams in each age group, but instead of the tables being placed side by side, one had to go in search of the additional team.

Well, at least this was a nice day. No signs of the rain there had been last year. A hot spring sun shone from a cloudless sky. Jenny was glad she'd worn shorts and a T-shirt. She collected her clipboard and sign-up sheets and walked across the field toward the table that would be hers. And she smiled as Rhonda and Sara and Kelly Ann and the other girls puffed out their flat chests as they passed the lines forming in front of the boys' sign-up tables.

Jenny greeted Celia Jenkins, who would be her assistant coach this season, and spread her papers on the table in front of her. Somewhere, in the midst of kids and milling parents, she could hear Ed Lauper shouting that sign-up would begin in fifteen minutes.

"There must be two hundred people here," Celia said, opening Diet Cokes for herself and Jenny.

"Ed's doing a good job," Jenny commented, and they both laughed.

"No, he isn't!" Rhonda cried.

Rhonda and Sara rushed to the front of Jenny's table. Both were flushed and angry, expressions of deepest betrayal darkening their faces.

"What's wrong, honey?" Jenny looked at them, puzzled.

"Mr. Lauper says relatives can't be on the same team!"

"What?"

"He says it's a new rule!"

Celia opened the booklet listing the rules for registration. "It's here, Jen. See?"

Jenny read the ruling, then stared at Rhonda. Rhonda was her best player. Without Rhonda, she didn't see how she'd have a chance of a winning season. "Why would Ed do such a dumb thing?"

Celia shrugged. "You know how it is. Coaches play their own kids the most, and the other parents scream favoritism. Ed got tired of parents calling him in the middle of the night to complain. So he changed the ruling."

"It isn't fair!" Rhonda said hotly. "I can't play on my own mom's team!" She and Sara stared at Jenny.

Jenny read the ruling again and sighed. She should have gone to the coaches' meeting. But she'd been in Cancún. "Well," she said slowly, "I guess you'll have to sign up on the other team."

"You don't understand, Mom. Sara and I want to be on the same team," Rhonda said. Sara nodded solemnly, her large, dark eyes fixed on Jenny.

"You can both be on the other coach's team."

"No, we can't, Mrs. Marshall," Sara said. "I can't play on that team because my dad's coaching it."

Jenny blinked. "David is coaching a soccer team?" Leaning forward, she stared down the row of tables and her heart lurched in her breast. She saw his dark head bent over the forms, the silver at his temples catching the sun. A tight golf shirt defined his shoulders, tanned, muscled legs emerged from a pair of navy shorts. He looked like an advertisement from a sports magazine. She was incredulous. "You father is coaching a girls' soccer team?"

"He thought I could be on his team," Sara explained, "but I can't." She caught Rhonda's hand and turned pleading eyes on Jenny.

"Mom, can't you do something?"

In a flash Jenny grasped what was about to happen. Rhonda would end up on David's team, and Sara would be on hers. "I'll try," she promised firmly.

But Ed Lauper wouldn't budge. "Jen, baby," he said, shifting a wad of gum to his other cheek and patting her shoulder. "You know Rhonda is the best player on your team, and I know it. Everyone here knows it. Nellie Byers is the best player on Gene Byers' team, and you and I know it. But all those other parents—'' he waved a hand toward the people crowding the field ''—they don't believe it. They're convinced their own kid is the best, and they want their kid out there kicking his or her way to glory. Boy, do I hear about it.''

''But, Ed—''

''Believe me, Jen, baby. This is the best solution to the problem.''

''Maybe for you, Ed, but this is going to cost me a winning season.''

Deep down, Jenny acknowledged he was right. She'd had calls from irate parents, too. She made one last halfhearted try for an exception, then gave up.

''I'm sorry, girls,'' she said when she'd returned to her table. ''We're stuck with the new rule.''

Romeo and Juliet had not parted with more pathos than in the parting between Rhonda and Sara. Jenny rolled her eyes at Celia as the girls hugged and pledged eternal loyalty, even though they were to be on different teams.

''Will we ever have to play against each other?'' Rhonda asked tearfully.

Jenny checked her game roster. ''Only one scrimmage toward the end of the season.''

''I'll let you win,'' Rhonda promised Sara.

''No, I'll let you win,'' Sara insisted.

Ed Lauper's voice boomed through the bullhorn. ''Sign-up begins now!''

''Well,'' Jenny said, raising a smile for Sara as Rhonda ran toward David's table, ''looks like you get me.'' The thought of coaching David's daughter raised conflicting emotions. On one hand, she welcomed getting to know Sara. On the other hand, Sara would be a constant reminder of what might have been.

This had little to do with Sara herself, Jenny thought, studying the girl. Shiny dark hair framed Sara's delicate face; her body was long and coltish. Unlike Rhonda, who responded warmly to any stranger, Sara suffered from shyness and a lack of confidence evident by her bitten nails. Jenny's heart went out to this appealing waif with the troubled eyes.

"I don't mind, Mrs. Marshall, it's just that..." She leaned forward to look down the row of tables toward David. "My dad agreed to be a coach so he and I could spend more time together."

Jenny thought about Rhonda and sighed. "I understand perfectly," she said. "I'm sorry it didn't work out." She filled in Sara's name and address on the first form.

"That's okay," Sara said, looking at Jenny with David's dark eyes.

Jenny printed David's name on the form, then paused at the next line. "What's your dad's occupation?"

When Sara didn't answer, Jenny looked up, surprised at the high color in Sara's cheeks. Sara didn't meet her eyes.

"Honey, what's your dad's occupation? He's an investment broker, isn't he?"

Sara shook her head. Her slender fingers picked at her sleeves. "Maybe...I don't think so."

Jenny frowned. "I'm sure I heard him mention something about being an investment broker."

"He's mentioned real estate and oil, too. I...I know this sounds weird, Mrs. Marshall, but I'm not sure what my dad does." An agony of embarrassment darkened her eyes. "He used to own a computer company but he sold it. I think he's retired now." She looked at Jenny anxiously. "If my dad is unemployed does that mean I can't play soccer?"

"Of course not. You can still play." Impulsively, Jenny reached across the table and gave Sara's hand a reassuring squeeze. Something wasn't right. "Honey, your father is a successful man. He manages investments, I'm sure of it."

"The phone rings all the time, but...he doesn't have an office like he used to." Sara bit the inside of her cheek and the next words tumbled out in a rush. "After Dad sold the company, things went bad for us, Mrs. Marshall. Mom left and we moved out of our house. I'm going to public school, and Dad sold the Rolls-Royce and bought an old Chrysler. We have to watch our money very carefully now."

The girls and their parents who were waiting behind Sara faded from Jenny's vision. Though she was aware of a twelve-year-old's candor, Sara's perspective astonished her. Sara seemed to believe the Fosters suffered money problems. "Sara, honey, there's a misunderstanding here." And Jenny could guess what it was. Lack of communication. She would have bet all she owned that David didn't realize a problem existed, that he hadn't fully explained his business or situation to Sara, believing her too young to understand. "I think you should talk to your dad about this."

"Oh, no, Mrs. Marshall." The girl's eyes widened and she cast a quick glance toward David's table. "My dad never talks about money or work. Not anymore. He says the whole world is too focused on money, that other things are more important."

"You think he says that because he doesn't have a job and he's broke?" Jenny asked gently, ignoring the impatient looks from the others in line.

"We aren't broke," Sara insisted with fierce loyalty and pride. "We're just . . . It's different now."

"Sara . . ."

Embarrassment flamed the girl's cheeks, and she moved from foot to foot. Jenny stared toward David, seeing the sun flash from his Rolex. Her immediate urge was to take Sara by the hand and lead her to David, and ask him to straighten this out right now.

"Jen," Celia said, "do you want me to start another line?"

"Thanks." Jenny bit her lip in hesitation, still watching David. Was it possible Sara was right? Of course not. The thought was too ludicrous to entertain.

"Mrs. Marshall? Can I go now?"

"What? Oh, yes, Sara. I'll collect the fee from your dad."

"No, I have it right here." Sara dug in her pocket and produced a wad of bills. "I saved it from my allowance."

Because she thought the fifteen dollars would strain her father's financial resources, Jenny thought, looking at the small pile of crumpled bills. The sun beat down on her head as she watched Sara run off to find Rhonda and Kelly Ann.

"Mrs. Marshall? It's me, Lydie Adams. I want to be on your team again."

"I'm glad, Lydie." Jenny smiled blankly and pulled another form in front of her.

She filled in the registration forms automatically, her mind not fully on the task. Occasionally, she glanced down the row of tables, and once her eyes met David's. Their glances held for a moment, then David turned and smiled at the next girl in his line. Jenny tilted her head and frowned.

When the field had cleared and Ed Lauper was directing a clean-up crew to fold the collapsible tables and pick up the pop cans, Jenny stretched and looked at Celia. "Well, that's it. Looks like we'll have a good team this year."

"We'll miss Rhonda." Celia stood, then collected her purse and papers and fell into step beside Jenny as they walked toward their cars.

Jenny scanned the tables, noticing David had gone. She wished she'd noticed when he had left. Sara's blurted confession stayed in her mind, and she wished she'd seen what kind of car David drove. She had supposed he now drove the Porsche he'd dreamed of in college, but maybe, if Sara was right, maybe he did indeed drive an old Chrysler. She had imagined she knew David, but Sara's words preyed on her thoughts. Maybe she didn't know him at all.

"The first practice is Tuesday," she said, waving goodbye to Celia and sliding behind the wheel of her station wagon. She called out to Rhonda, who was talking to a knot of girls, all of whom were busily pretending not to notice a similar knot of boys who were pretending not to notice them.

Rhonda slid down in the car seat until her head rested on the back of the seat. "I would kill for some boobs." She groaned. "I'm never, ever going to get boobs."

Jenny laughed. "Yes, you will." After backing out of the parking lot, she slid a look toward her daughter. "Think you'll like being on Mr. Foster's team?"

"Yeah, he's neat."

A pinprick of betrayal stirred in Jenny's chest. "What happened to all that indignation and outrage? How about good ol' Mom's team?"

Rhonda shrugged and grinned. "Like you say, Mom. 'If you can't beat 'em, join 'em.'" She cast a dreamy look at the ceiling of the car. "Mr. Foster is sooooo handsome. Don't you think so? He says he used to know you in college."

"He said that? Did he say anything else about me?"

"Nope. I like the way Mr. Foster smells. He smells like Christmas, kind of. You know?"

Jenny knew. "What does Christmas smell like?"

"Oh, spicy and happy. Sort of lemony like the yellow candles. But outdoorsy like the tree. He smells good." Rhonda rolled her head on the car seat. "Can I skip my clarinet lesson today?"

"No. Children should have some musical background. Someday you'll be at a party, and someone is going to say 'Gee, I wish there was someone here who plays the clarinet.' And you will modestly admit that you play a little. Then you will perform masterfully, dazzling everyone, and everyone will say, 'I never heard Gershwin played like that before.' You will be a star, the hit of the party."

"Aw, Mom. First, I'm not a kid anymore. I'm practically grown up. And second, nobody is ever going to ask me to play the clarinet at a party."

"They might. Besides, if you don't play the clarinet, you can't be in the school band. And if you aren't in the band, then I won't get to bake brownies for the band fund raisers. And I've learned to love making brownies at midnight because you forgot to tell me you had to have them." Jenny returned Rhonda's grin, enjoying the moment and her daughter. "Okay, scoot. I'll pick you up later," she said, parking in front of the school.

After Rhonda dashed toward the gymnasium, Jenny sat for a while as her thoughts returned to David and his daughter. The whole thing was puzzling. Finally she nodded to herself and drove to the library.

When Jenny had explained what she wanted to Mrs. Adams, the librarian, Jenny took up a position by the copy machine and copied the material Mrs. Adams brought her without reading it. She would save that task until she could do so in private. An hour and a half later, she had copies of everything in print that mentioned David Foster.

"MOM?" DEUCE SAID when Jenny popped into his room to say good night. He took his comb from his pajama pocket and ran it through wheat-colored hair. "You were right. I think Tanya Hubbard likes me. Even though I'm not on the football team or the baseball team."

"I knew she would," Jenny said, smiling.

"She likes computers. She has her own modem. Did you know girls could like computers?"

"No, I didn't know that." Jenny shot the computer a suspicious look. Machinery defeated her. You couldn't depend on it. The minute you thought you knew your vacuum, it turned vicious and started coughing out clouds of dust. She'd never been on compatible terms with anything mechanical. "Tanya must be a special girl."

"She is," Deuce agreed seriously. "Mom?" he said as Jenny snapped out the light. "How do you know when you're in love?"

When you hurt inside, she thought. But she didn't say it. "You'll know, honey," she answered softly. The process started so young. Love truly did make the world go around.

Toulouse followed Jenny into her bedroom and watched her choose her old ratty robe instead of one of the new filmy confections. Tonight she wanted comfort rather than glamour.

When the house had quieted, Jenny sat on her bed and slanted the reading light over the papers spread across her quilt. Then she drew a long breath and started reading.

At the finish, she lay back on the bed and stared at the ceiling, her eyes glazed with shock. David Foster was definitely not poor. He was filthy rich. Not just rich, but extraordinarily wealthy. If David Foster wanted a genuine Mayan pyramid in his backyard, he could afford to transport it, stone by priceless stone, and would never miss the money.

Jenny gazed at nothing and tried to imagine money like that. What would it be like to walk into a store and buy something without once glancing at the price tag? How would it feel to get a pencil from the desk drawer without trying to ignore the stack of bills surrounding it? Were there really people in this world who received their VISA bills without clutching their hearts and staggering around the family room? She couldn't imagine it.

But that was David's life. He was a modern-day Midas. He didn't worry about a ten-dollar tag on a piece of canvas. If he worried at all, he worried in the millions.

The concept boggled her mind.

She sat up and read through the copies again, thinking she must have misinterpreted what she'd read. But that was impossible; it was all there in black and white. He'd made one fortune on Foster/Beta computers and another fortune or two when IBM bought out the company. After the IBM purchase, David had faded from the news except for two small items. One reported his divorce, and the other mentioned David as the owner of an oil company that had made a mammoth oil strike drilling in the North Sea.

He had lied to her.

Anger filled Jenny's eyes as she remembered him telling her he was an investment broker, and telling her that the media had inflated the price of the IBM buyout. He'd told her he didn't have any more money than anyone else she knew.

"Wait a minute," she said slowly, and let her anger sink to an acceptable level.

He hadn't exactly said he was an investment broker. He'd said he was something like an investment broker. And, of course, he was. But he was investing his own money, not money for clients. So he hadn't really lied. Not by a strict interpretation of the word.

And maybe the media had exaggerated the IBM purchase price by a few thousand dollars, for all she knew. The figure mentioned in her copies was in round millions. So maybe that wasn't a lie, either. Not in the strictest sense.

And he hadn't told her he wasn't rich; she'd simply made the assumption that he was comfortably well off, instead.

But something was very wrong here.

She remembered David buying Sara the shell necklace instead of the expensive gold earrings. He'd had a room like Jenny's at the Palenque instead of one of the suites. His home was across Wadsworth Boulevard instead of in Cherry Hills or the Polo Grounds. He didn't have a Mayan pyramid in his backyard, or a swimming pool or a tennis court. His own daughter thought he was unemployed and practically destitute.

Jenny's brow knit in a baffled frown. If David was wealthy—and the papers strewn around her removed all doubt—then why wasn't he enjoying his money?

She folded her legs up under her and absently scratched behind Toulouse's ear. Then she closed her eyes and concentrated.

She remembered David's baritone voice as he told her about his life with Marilyn after the money came. Remembered passing the villages on the road to Chichén Itzá, and how David spoke wistfully of a simpler life and a return to values that meant something.

"Good Lord," she breathed softly.

David hadn't come to terms with being wealthy. That had to be it. Having money hadn't brought him pleasure; it had brought him problems.

"So..."

So he pretended he wasn't wealthy. Somewhere in David's mind, he equated money with phony values and a way of life he wasn't comfortable with. Money meant false impressions and pretentious houses. Money was snobbery and expensive labels.

"Oh, David."

Long after Jenny had turned out the lights, she lay in bed sleepless, watching a bar of moonlight creep across the carpet. We're all liars, Jenny thought. One way or another.

We tell polite lies, like the lie she had told the hairdresser. And we tell it's-good-for-you lies, like the one she'd told Rhonda about the clarinet lesson. And we tell protective lies, like the pride-based lies she had told David.

There were white lies and black lies, egregious lies and innocent lies. Polite lies, helpful lies, the lies you told friends because you didn't want to hurt their feelings.

And there was the silent lie. David hadn't lied outright, but he'd let Jenny believe a false assumption and had done nothing to correct her impression.

Then there was the worst lie of all. Self-deception.

"He's lying, too," she whispered, feeling the anger begin again.

When she'd told David she was a famous artist, she had known it was a lie. But she sensed in her heart that David didn't grasp that he was lying by minimizing his fortune. He was guilty of the silent lie. And by trying to live as if money wasn't important, he was deceiving himself. And Sara.

Furious and hurt, Jenny pressed her face into the pillow and wished life weren't so complicated.

ACTUALLY, DAVID ENJOYED grocery shopping. But he hated doing it alone. He always felt like the only man within miles. This feeling was reinforced by the glances he sometimes received as he pushed his cart along the aisles. A few of the women gave him sidelong stares, a combination of mild surprise and some resentment, as if he had invaded a territory exclusively their own. He didn't mind that type as much as he minded the motherly type, those who assumed that because he was shopping alone he was in desperate need of assistance.

A motherly type was watching him now as he dropped potatoes into a sack. Her lips were turned down in disapproval. Finally, she shook her head and observed, "You're doing that wrong."

"Beg pardon?"

"You're supposed to look at them."

"Why?" He could never think of a polite way to discourage them.

"To see if they're bruised or spoiled." The woman took the sack from his hands and dumped it out over the potato bin. "See?" she said triumphantly. "You had three that are already starting to go." He watched helplessly as she began selecting potatoes for him and placing them in the sack.

"Please, I can do that."

"It's no trouble."

He released a sigh of exasperation and looked toward the dairy section. Jenny Marshall was watching him. Smiling. It was inevitable that, living this near, they would run into each other on occasion. He'd been prepared to nod coolly and go on about his business. He wasn't prepared to be caught in the embarrassing position of having some strange woman steamroll him while Jenny looked on. Her smile told him she knew exactly the frustration and vulnerability he was feeling. He could see that she was enjoying it.

"I can do this," he said firmly, his voice sharper than he'd intended as he took the potato sack from the motherly type.

She stared at him. "Well, I never! That's what you get for trying to help someone." Her nose lifted in the air as she sailed toward the lettuce. "Ingratitude."

Grimly, he stuffed potatoes into the sack without looking at them.

"Next time, cough. Coughing will discourage them," Jenny said sweetly as she pushed her cart past him.

He stared after her as she rounded the corner. She was wearing jeans and a paint-splattered shirt. Her hair was tied in ribbons in mini-pigtails behind her ears. She looked no older than twenty. A smug twenty.

In the meat department he thought, *What the hell?* and doubled over in a coughing fit as a helpful-looking woman moved toward him. She stared at him, then veered toward the fresh fish. "I'll be damned," David marveled.

"It worked," he said to Jenny as he approached her in aisle three.

"I thought it might," she said.

They passed each other and turned their carts at the end of the aisle.

He stopped his cart beside hers in front of the pasta section. It wasn't that he wanted to talk to her, he told himself, he needed pasta. Pasta wasn't on his list, but he was certain he didn't have any at home.

"I think it's time you talked to Sara," Jenny said without looking at him. She selected a package of spaghetti and weighed it in her hand.

David arched an eyebrow. "Sara knows about woman stuff."

"Woman stuff?"

"You know."

"Oh. That's not what I meant." Jenny looked at him then, a long, level look. "I think you should talk to her about money. She's very confused, David."

Immediately he bristled. Money was one subject he didn't care to discuss. Especially not with Jenny Marshall, and especially not in a grocery store. His eyes cooled and his voice was distant. "Excuse me." He dropped two packages of pasta shells into his cart and turned to the other side of the aisle.

"David, Sara paid her soccer fee out of her allowance."

"Good. She's beginning to learn the value of a dollar." It pleased him to hear it.

"That isn't the point. Sara thinks—"

"That's exactly the point," he said sharply.

An unreasonable anger swept over him. He was trying to forget this woman who invaded his dreams when he was asleep and his life when he was awake. After every soccer practice, Sara sang Jenny's praises. It was Mrs. Marshall this and Mrs. Marshall that. And every time he heard her name, he remembered how her eyes looked in candlelight, remembered the touch of her lips on his body. He was beginning to think there was no escape from the dull ache he felt whenever he thought about her. He couldn't even shop for groceries, for heaven's sake, without falling over Jenny Marshall. She was everywhere.

"David, please. I really think—"

"You think," he repeated coldly, interrupting her. "I don't recall asking your advice. But perhaps you specialize in family counseling when you aren't painting masterpieces or giving interviews."

The color drained from her face as she stared up at him. The spaghetti dropped from her fingers and fell into her cart. "That was a cheap shot," she whispered.

"It's your fairy tale, princess."

The sarcasm appalled him. Whatever anger he'd felt evaporated as he watched the color flare back into her cheeks. She gripped the cart handle and pushed past him toward the checkout counter, her back very straight and stiff.

Dammit. Lashing out at her didn't solve a thing. It made him feel ashamed for acting childishly. He knew what he was doing, of course. The cutting remarks were a protective device. It would be so easy to say, "Let's give it another chance." Then where would he be? Did he really want to go through all the frustration and upset again? The eternal sifting of every word to find the grain of truth? No.

But he wanted her. God help him, but he wanted her. He wanted the sunshine in her eyes and the warmth of her laughter. He wanted her silky hair on the pillow next to his, wanted her there when he woke in the morning. It was idiotic and it was driving him crazy.

"Hi, Mrs. Marshall." The checkout girl leaned across the counter and winked at Jenny. "Did you see that guy in aisle five? Wow. He can put his celery in my fridge anytime he wants to."

Jenny instinctively looked toward aisle five. For a moment her gaze held David's and the hurt in his eyes was as great as the hurt in hers.

"That's the best-looking guy I've seen in years," the girl gushed.

"If you like that type," Jenny answered faintly.

"Are you kidding? Tall, dark and handsome, and steaks in his basket? Who doesn't like that type?"

Knowing David was still watching, Jenny paid her bill without muttering about extortion, as she usually did; then she fled.

Chapter Eleven

It was time, past time.

Jenny stepped into her studio and rubbed her palms across her plaid shirttail.

This was it. The big day.

The kids were in school, a tuna casserole was made ahead and ready for dinner. Her latest batch of card covers were in the mail to New York. There was no soccer practice today. She had the phone on the answering machine. She'd fed Toulouse and Thedamnedcat, and had made a pot of fresh coffee for herself, which she had carried upstairs and plugged in over her worktable.

The morning light streaming through the skylights overhead was perfect. She had new tubes of paint and she'd already stretched and primed a fresh canvas. She was as ready as she would ever be.

She was flat out of excuses.

But this was a significant moment, one worth savoring. One didn't launch a moon shot in a day, and, in Jenny's mind, what she was about to attempt was comparable. After filling her coffee mug, Jenny perched on her work stool and studied the blank canvas waiting on her easel!.

White, she decided upon reflection, was the color of challenge. The color of dreams. Some art experts claimed white was not a color at all, but Jenny didn't accept that. Brides believed in white, so did Frosty the Snowman, and so did she. No one would convince Jenny that white didn't exist.

It was the color of fear.

If she doubted, she had only to notice the tremor in her fingers as she sipped her coffee and stared at the empty canvas. Nerves were creeping up on her as she thought about what she wanted to do, and with the nervous tremor came the old, familiar anxiety that had stopped her so many times before.

After all, who was she to think she could paint a masterpiece? What made her think she was that good? Or possessed that kind of talent and ability?

Jenny's confidence, such as it was, wavered, then plummeted to her toes. She covered her eyes.

This was a mistake. She wasn't ready for this; she'd forgotten everything she'd ever known about technique, balance and all the rest. Too much water had passed under the proverbial bridge. A sign painter had more talent than she did.

Face it, she told herself glumly. *Jenny Marshall is no artist; Jenny Marshall is a dauber, a person who dashes off card covers by the dozen.*

"And a person who can talk herself right out of anything," she said aloud, her lips turning down in disgust.

Squeezing her eyes shut, Jenny blotted out the bright room and the blank expanse of canvas. "You can do it," she muttered. "You can at least try. So you don't paint a masterpiece, so what? At least you'll be working on real art, and that's something in itself.

Food for the soul, girl. Something you've needed for a long time."

Drawing a deep breath, Jenny reached inside herself to pull forth a measure of resolve and determination. But finding the confidence to proceed was no easy thing.

According to the Jenny Marshall theory, confidence was as elusive as a spring wind. About as substantial as a lover's whisper. Confidence rested on the frailest of frameworks. A mere thought could blow it away like a leaf in a hurricane.

Her theory insisted there was no such thing as true confidence. Jenny had concluded this long ago. A person could only pretend to be confident, and after a while the pretense was almost as good as the real thing. If you were lucky, you started to believe it. And when you did, the courage to try followed behind.

Okay. She'd begin by reminding herself that she had sworn to accept no more excuses, no more self-deception. From now on, she'd concentrate on the reasons why she could instead of why she could not.

What were those reasons? Panic blotted her mind.

"Calm down, dummy." She drew another deep breath and slowly the panic receded. After all, what was the worst that could happen? She could fail. Okay, she had failed before. And the world hadn't screeched to a halt. Besides, no one would have to know she'd failed unless she decided to tell someone. And if she failed, where would that leave her? Right where she was now, and that wasn't so bad. Her greeting cards were some of the best in the industry; she was making a living.

But it wasn't what she really wanted to do. The thought brought her full circle.

"Frascotti believed in me. He thought I could take the Italian prize." *Yeah, but that was years ago.* "Doesn't matter. Talent doesn't disappear." *Who says?* "I do, dammit."

The inner voice sneered. *Put your money where your mouth is, kiddo,* the voice challenged. *Put the paint to the canvas and let's see what you can do.*

"I can do it," she said firmly, pretending the confidence that would, please God, lead to the real thing.

Setting aside her coffee mug, she pushed from the stool and gazed at the canvas, seeing in her imagination the finished product. It would be a large painting. The canvas was three feet by four feet.

She continued to gaze at the canvas and she laid out tubes of paint and squeezed a wheel of color onto her palette. The sharp, clean scent of oil paints rose to her nostrils. There was no perfume to compare with the tang of oils and turpentine. This was how artist's heaven smelled.

Finally she was ready to approach the canvas. She had studied her anatomy books, had framed the scene in her thoughts, had prepared a dozen sketches. Now it was time to transfer her vision to the canvas.

Jenny stood before the blank expanse of white, brush in hand, her palette at her side.

She stood without moving as the canvas blurred and shimmered before her eyes. One moment her vision was there—the next moment it was gone. Not faded, but absolutely gone.

Jenny bit her lip and shifted her weight, feeling a nervous pulse flutter in her throat. A light coating of moisture dampened her palms.

Frowning, she stared hard at the canvas and willed her vision to reappear. The window would be here; the old teakettle there. Lace curtains. Hands on the table, weathered hands that had known hard work. She had sketched the scene a hundred times, had produced a dozen charcoal copies.

It wouldn't come.

A trickle of perspiration zigzagged down Jenny's side. Whatever creativity she possessed seemed to have evaporated. She had no idea where, or how, to start.

"The background," she muttered frantically, "lay in the background."

But her hand wouldn't move; the dream was crumbling. She closed her eyes and swayed dizzily, feeling the threat of defeat behind her lids.

She couldn't do it.

She had only been fooling herself. Once again she had built a dream spun from gossamer yearnings instead of based on anything substantial.

She lowered her palette and covered her eyes with a shaking hand. Like the sand castle in Cancún, her dreams were wonderful and splendid, but, oh, so fragile. So achingly vulnerable to the tides of reality.

The scene from that night rose vividly in her memory. Again she watched the sand castle's tower spilling silvery grains of sand into the water that foamed up around its fragile fortification. And she experienced the same stunning regret, now as she had then, that the castle would fall to reality, taking with it the dreams and illusions of its builder.

A tiny thrill shot down Jenny's spine. Goose bumps rose on her skin.

Her eyes blinked open and she stared at the canvas, not seeing the empty sweep but seeing, instead, a sand castle standing deserted and forgotten against the night tide. A dream abandoned.

Excitement sparkled in her eyes. *Yes. Oh, yes.* She could see it.

Setting aside her palette and canvas, she snatched up a stick of charcoal and quickly sketched a rolling line along the left side of her sketch pad. The tumbling rush of the tide. Unstoppable, inexorable. Then, working feverishly, her hand flew, creating the walls and towers of the castle. The fantasy, the dream.

She stepped back and squinted before she rubbed out a tower with the heel of her hand. Not right; do it again. Make it beckon; make it promise. The charcoal raced over the paper.

"MOM? I'M HOME."

The screen door slammed, and Jenny heard the distant sound of the refrigerator opening and closing. Startled, she lifted surprised eyes to the clock over her worktable. Where had the hours gone? It seemed she had just stepped into her studio. It couldn't be five o'clock.

But it was. A tension she hadn't been aware of drained from her shoulders. After stretching, she reluctantly stepped away from the easel and began scrubbing the paint from her untouched palette. Before she was ready for paint, she would sketch the scene dozens of times, until her fingertips knew the lines by rote, until the paint would flow by instinct rather than design, until the magic pulsed in her heart and flowed from there to the canvas. But she'd made a start.

And it was good. It was damned good.

Before closing the door to her studio, she studied the rough sketch on the paper. She hadn't caught what she wanted, not yet—but it was coming. She could feel the scene in her fingertips, could see it in her mind.

"Hot dog!" A wide smile curved her lips, a smile of sheer happiness.

"Hot dogs for supper?" Rhonda called up the stairs.

"Nope, tuna casserole and champagne. I've been saving a bottle for a special occasion."

"What's the occasion?" Deuce asked as Jenny danced into the kitchen.

"We're going to toast Cinderella and sand castles and new beginnings."

The kids looked at each other, then shrugged and made little circles near their heads with their index fingers.

Jenny laughed. "No, I'm not crazy. Just happy."

For the first time since returning from Cancún, she'd spent an entire day without thinking about David Foster. But she didn't realize this until later, when she was preparing for bed. Right now, her eyes were starry with excitement.

She'd done something for herself today. She'd given herself hope. And, by heaven, it felt good.

ON THE OTHER SIDE of Wadsworth, David had covered the dining room table with blueprints and renderings of the office complex he planned to build. The ground-breaking ceremonies would be held next month.

"Hi, honey," he said, looking up when Sara came in the door carrying her schoolbooks. "How was school?"

"Fine. I got an A on my science paper."

"Great." He followed her into the kitchen, smiling as she made a sandwich and poured a glass of milk. This was his favorite time of day. He made a point of being home when Sara returned from school so they could talk. He was sharing his daughter's life as he hadn't when they had lived in California.

In California, Sara had attended a posh girls' school. She hadn't worn jeans, as she was wearing now; she'd worn outfits assembled from boutiques along Rodeo Drive. The school's limo had picked her up in the morning and delivered her home in the late afternoon. She'd received grades for such things as deportment and social graces. In David's mind, these were about as valuable as plastic apples.

"Do you like your new school?"

"It's different. But, yeah, Dad, I like it a lot."

"How about you and me going out for dinner tonight?" he asked, leaning his elbows on the kitchen counter. "We'll go somewhere fabulous, and you can wear one of those terrific outfits I never see anymore."

Sara put her sandwich aside and examined green fingernails that made David smile. "We don't have to go anywhere fabulous, Dad. A hamburger or a pizza would be okay." She gave him a quick look. "We have to watch our money."

David smiled with pleasure. Thank God. Slowly, Sara was beginning to understand money. Nothing could have pleased him more. He felt a surge of pride that she understood it wasn't where one dined but with whom that was important. They could enjoy each other's company over a pizza as easily as over chateaubriand.

"I think we can afford a night out," he said, grinning. "But if you'd prefer a pizza, that's fine with me."

Her relief was so obvious that he was momentarily puzzled. Suddenly he recalled Jenny's advice. Was it possible there was something here that he wasn't seeing? Perhaps he should have allowed Jenny to at least state the topic of concern.

"Sara, is there anything you'd like to talk about? Is anything troubling you?"

Her eyes flared and she glanced toward the door. "No."

"Honey, if something's on your mind, let's talk about it." The flush on her cheeks and her refusal to look at him hinted that something was bothering her. "Do you miss your mother?" he asked gently.

"Not so much anymore. Besides, I'll be seeing her this summer."

So that wasn't the problem. And she'd already told him she liked her new school. The phone rang constantly, so she was making friends. But he sensed something was amiss.

"Sara..."

"We're going to be late for my piano lesson, Dad. I need to change clothes, then we'd better go."

"Okay," he agreed absently, "I'll meet you in the car."

He supposed she'd tell him when she was ready. That is, if something really was bothering her and he hadn't just imagined it. It wasn't easy being both mother and father to a girl on the brink of young womanhood. His daughter fascinated him, but he didn't pretend to understand such things as green fingernails and a yearning for pierced ears. Soccer was something he understood, and he was glad Sara was also interested. But he wouldn't have agreed to coach if he'd known Sara wouldn't be on his team.

"Dad, can I ask you something?" Sara asked in the car.

"Sure, honey." So he hadn't imagined that something was troubling her.

She hesitated, pretending great interest in her thumbnail. "Is it true that boys only like girls with big boobs?"

The car swerved toward the center line before David brought it squarely back into the lane. He stared at his daughter, seeing the scarlet in her cheeks. "Ah, well, I guess some boys do." This wasn't what she wanted to hear. An annoying heat rose in his own cheeks. "But some don't." He'd managed to answer without answering, dammit.

She studied her thumbnail with minute interest. "When am I going to get boobs? Karen Kowalski already has boobs; she wears a bra. And I'm three months older than she is, and I don't have anything." Her face was a crimson beacon.

Oh, Lord. What did men know about boobs beyond an appreciation that women had them? What he recalled of adolescence was that one day the girls were flat, and one day, miraculously, they had sprouted curves. He had no idea how it happened or when.

"Well, uh, soon. You'll get boobs soon."

"How soon?"

All he could think about was Jenny. He wished to heaven she was here. She would know about such things and why they were important and how to answer Sara. At this moment he needed Jenny and wanted her; he couldn't for the life of him remember why they weren't together. He needed her and Sara needed her.

"Very soon," he said helplessly, thinking of Jenny until he saw the disappointment in his daughter's quick glance. Letting her down devastated him.

"So," Sara said finally, too brightly, "how did your day go?"

"About the same as usual." He felt guilty and angry at the relief he experienced when the topic veered away from boobs.

"Did you go out today?"

"No, I'm studying plans for an office building."

Her large, dark eyes studied him without expression. "Are you going to get an office, Dad?"

"I have an office," he said, looking at her with surprise.

"You never go there."

He smiled. "I think it runs better without me. I handle most business by phone." He turned the car into the parking lot in front of the school gymnasium.

"Then why are you looking at office plans?"

He wasn't sure how much she would understand. "I'm going to build it."

"Oh." Her eyes brightened. "You must be a carpenter."

He laughed. "Hardly. Remember the bookcase I built? Not exactly a hallmark of craftsmanship." To his amazement, her eyes filled with quick tears. "Sara? What's wrong?"

Anger flashed behind the tears. "I wish you wouldn't treat me like a child! You want me to talk to you, but you don't talk to me!" She struggled with the car door. "I wish you wouldn't lie to me!"

"Lie to you?" David's mouth dropped open.

"All that stuff about the office. And...I just...I... Oh, never mind!"

He stared after her in astonishment as she ran across the lot toward the gymnasium door. He didn't have the foggiest notion what she was upset about or talking about. Lie to her? He'd never lied to her.

David wrapped his arms around the steering wheel and stared out the windshield. Women were amazing creatures, moody, contrary and as prickly as cactus. Delightful, mysterious and ever-changing. That's what made them so irresistible, he supposed. But it certainly made them difficult to live with.

A long sigh escaped his lips. This was probably a phase, something Sara would outgrow. Still, it wouldn't do any harm to leave the office blueprints where she would see them. For some unfathomable reason, she seemed to doubt he was going to build it. Or maybe Sara's outburst had something to do with breasts and the way he'd bungled answering her questions.

He shook his head, hurt by Sara's accusation. It had to trace back to Marilyn. He wasn't the only one Marilyn had lied to. Maybe, in Sara's mind, anything she didn't understand equated with a lie. Was that it?

HE WAS STILL WONDERING how best to handle this as he drove her to soccer practice the following day. Casually, he asked, "Did you happen to notice the blueprints for my office complex? If you like, I'll explain them to you."

She looked at him with a sullen expression, defensive. "Dad, do you have a job?"

The words emerged in a rush, as if they were hard to say. David smiled. "Not a regular job, no. Not like I had in California with Foster/Beta. Mostly I work out of our house now."

"That's what I thought." Her voice was low and choked. Then she lifted her head and squeezed his hand. "You're doing fine, Dad; we'll get along okay. And I like the work you're doing at our house. I love the bookcase you built!"

"Well, thank you, honey." But she was gone, her eyes teary again, her voice on the edge of sobs.

For a moment he just sat behind the wheel of the car, too bewildered to move.

If this was a phase, it was more baffling than those that had preceded it. He watched Sara run onto the soccer field and hurl herself into Jenny Marshall's arms. He had an idea Sara was crying. Frowning, he watched Jenny smooth back Sara's hair and kneel beside her. Even from this distance, he could see Jenny talking and Sara's bowed head. A rush of relief relaxed his shoulders when Sara finally looked up at Jenny and smiled.

Slowly, he got out of the car and walked toward the adjacent field where Rhonda and the rest of his team were waiting. But his mind wasn't on soccer. Before he organized the girls into practice squads, he looked back toward his daughter, but it was Jenny who caught his attention.

She was standing, hands on hips, staring at him. He spread his hands in a helpless shrug, wishing he could talk to her and discover what had happened. Then, as he watched, Jenny mouthed the words, *"You insensitive idiot."* A dark flush spread over his face and his shoulders stiffened. Whatever was going on, it was between him and his daughter. It didn't concern Jenny. He turned abruptly from Jenny's glare and blew his whistle.

"Rhonda, you'll be captain of Squad A; Mary, you'll be captain of Squad B."

When he glanced over his shoulder, Jenny was still sending him poisonous looks. They glared at each other. It wasn't until Rhonda tugged his sleeve that he looked away, frustrated that it was he who dropped the stare first. It crossed his mind that this was an adolescent reaction. Jenny brought out the worst in him, no doubt about it. The thought didn't make him feel any better.

Periodically throughout the practice, he found his gaze straying to the other field. He had to admit that under Jenny's tutelage Sara was developing into a skilled player. This annoyed him even as he admitted he was being unfair.

His stare followed Jenny as she kicked a ball into the net, showing the girls a new maneuver. Her legs were long and shapely, golden with the tan she'd begun in Cancún. When she laughed, as she did frequently, her breasts strained against the pink sweatshirt she wore. He felt a tightening in his thighs and knots ran up the line of his jaw.

"Dammit."

Rhonda giggled and looked at the other girls, and he cursed beneath his breath.

"Sorry," he muttered. "Let's play ball."

Before they scattered onto the field, he heard one of the players say, "Boy, is Mr. Foster in a bad mood today!"

Frustration lay on his face like a thundercloud. If he lived to be a hundred, he would never understand women. They were as alien as a species from another planet.

He shot one last look toward Jenny Marshall before he cleared his mind and concentrated on his team's practice session. And he wondered if she had ever painted her fingernails green or made her father crazy with unexplained crying spells. Or missed a perfect goal shot because a pimply-faced boy chose that moment to smile around his braces.

"Pay attention, ladies," he shouted, as much for his own benefit as theirs.

Chapter Twelve

The weeks flew by. The promise of spring blossomed into early summer; petunias replaced the tulips, crocus and daisies peeking out of Jenny's garden. In a week, school would end for the summer. Soon after, Deuce would depart for computer camp and Rhonda to Girl Scout camp. After they returned, they'd spend a week at home, then fly off to California for a month with Walter and Susie.

For the first time since her divorce, the prospect of an empty house didn't dismay Jenny.

"Are you sure?" Pam asked, pouring more coffee from Jenny's pot. "Usually you don't know what to do with yourself when the kids are gone. You get weird and start cleaning house and talking about funeral plans."

"Not this year," Jenny said.

"So, what's different?" Pam studied her across the sunlight streaming through the kitchen window. "You look fantastic, by the way. Like a woman with a delicious secret." Her green eyes narrowed. "Does this have anything to do with a certain gorgeous man I occasionally run into at the grocery store?"

Some of the radiance faded from Jenny's expression. "I only wish it did." She sighed and pushed at the jelly doughnut in front of her.

She couldn't believe her own foolishness in having imagined she would never see David Foster again. Nothing could have been further from the truth.

She saw him twice a week at the practice field, ran into him at the grocery store, at the cleaner's, at Pizza Hut. Every Friday night they both attended Ed Lauper's meeting for the soccer coaches. She drove Rhonda to David's house; he drove Sara to hers. They had stood three feet apart during parent-teacher night at the junior high. Everywhere she turned—there was David Foster. Sometimes she thought the only way she could see more of him was if they lived in the same house.

But if they inhabited the same house, they wouldn't need to make such a point of ignoring each other. They wouldn't pass with coldly polite nods and impersonal murmurs.

"Want to talk about it?" Pam asked.

"There's nothing to talk about. Nothing has changed."

In a broad sense that was true. And yet . . .

Something was building, Jenny could feel it. Whenever she encountered David, it seemed as if the very air became charged with tension. Her body tightened, her breathing turned shallow, hot pink flooded her cheeks. All the while she was pretending to be unaware of him, she could hardly think of anything else. It was as if tiny antennae had sprouted on her body and were bent toward David Foster, blanking out all else around her. And she would have bet her last dime that David experienced the same phenomenon.

Take the past week for instance. They had faced each other across Ed Lauper's living room. Jenny had gritted her teeth and sworn she wouldn't look at him. But she had, drawn irresistibly to the silver streaks in his dark hair, to the stretch of cotton swelling over muscle, to a voice and mouth that sent shivers down her spine. And she'd caught him looking at her. Caught his eyes on her lips, moving over her breasts and thighs. Later, Celia had laughed and teased, "Talk about sizzle! Watching you two is like watching the buildup for an X-rated movie. Wow." Jenny blushed. She would have promised to clean every oven in Columbine before admitting to the explosive attraction between herself and David. But it was there. Oh, yes, it was there.

But the overall picture hadn't changed. David steadfastly remained aloof. When it was absolutely necessary for him to speak to her, he did so with an ultrapoliteness that said it all. He hadn't forgiven her for lying to him. Jenny had abandoned hope that he ever would.

What made it so awful was that she still loved him; Jenny couldn't deceive herself about that. The loving didn't change. Whenever she saw him, her heart banged against her rib cage and a bittersweet longing jumped into her eyes.

But she had to admit that gradually a slight alteration was taking place. In addition to love, she also experienced flashes of intense anger. Once she'd comprehended David's self-deception, seeds of resentment had taken root. She didn't excuse her lies to him—that wasn't possible—but she was finding it harder to excuse David for his deceptions. Who was David Foster to withhold forgiveness? He who daily practiced the silent lie? Whose own daughter was confused and worried?

Whenever she thought about Sara, Jenny felt an uneasiness deep inside. During the past weeks of coaching Sara, Jenny had developed a genuine fondness for David's daughter. Sara was bright and eager to please, and she had a shy humor that Jenny loved. But at times, Sara's gaze would drift to the adjoining field where David's team practiced and anxiety would wrinkle her small brow.

A deep sigh made Jenny's shoulders drop. A hundred times she had considered showing Sara the clippings she had copied from the library. And a hundred times she had reached the reluctant conclusion that it was not her place to do so. It would be interference of the worst kind. The one time she had tried to discuss Sara with David, he had made it crystal clear that his relationship with his daughter was none of Jenny's business. And Sara had turned scarlet with humiliation when Jenny had attempted to talk to her about David. The situation tugged at Jenny's heart. Sara was utterly convinced her father was unemployed and on the verge of bankruptcy.

"She needs new tennis shoes," Jenny said. Frowning, she licked powdered sugar from her fingertip and eyed the jelly doughnut. Should she, or should she not eat the jelly doughnut? Or should she just rub it on her hips and apply it directly? That's where it would eventually end up. She had a theory to account for the fact that three ounces of jelly doughnut instantly transformed to five pounds of fat, once it passed the lips. Sugar was devious and magical; once it came into contact with the stomach, it exploded, gaining weight and density. The man who discovered an antidote would be an overnight gazillionaire.

"Who needs new tennis shoes?" Pam asked. "Jen, you might as well eat the doughnut. You know you're going to."

"I have to torture myself first. It's in the jelly-doughnut rules. First torture, then remorse." Jenny poked the doughnut and licked the sugar off her finger. "Sara needs new shoes. I'll bet my bathroom scales she thinks David can't afford to buy new tennies."

"You're kidding! He could buy the factory."

"I know," Jenny agreed unhappily.

When she thought about Sara, she wanted to take David by the shoulders and shake him until his bones rattled. It was one thing for him to drive a three-year-old car and live in a middle-priced subdivision and pretend he wasn't filthy rich. It was another thing entirely to deceive his daughter.

Pam stared. "You don't think he's misled her on purpose, do you?"

"No. That's what's so sad, Pam. And so damned frustrating. I don't think he has any idea what's going on in Sara's head." Jenny leaned over the table. "He probably thinks she's too young to understand business. Every time she mentions saving money, he's pleased. He thinks she's learning the value of a dollar. I'm sure he doesn't realize she's trying to keep them afloat by not spending a single dime that isn't necessary." Jenny covered her eyes. "This thing breaks my heart. And makes me mad as hell."

"Hey, what happened to the happy Jenny Marshall?" Pam coaxed. "When I came in here, you were on cloud nine. Let's go back to that."

"What?"

Pam spread her hands. "Something had you floating about two feet off the ground. So, give. What's going on with you? Did you win the lottery? Bake a decent lemon meringue pie? Inherit a windfall? Invent a new line of greeting cards? What?"

Jenny smiled, and an uncharacteristic shyness entered her eyes. "Well," she said slowly, almost reluctantly, "I've been working on something."

"Does it have anything to do with a new slipcover for the toad chair, I hope?"

Jenny laughed. "Nope. It has to do with..." She drew a breath and clenched her fists in her lap. She hadn't realized she would be this nervous.

"You're making me crazy. Tell me what's got you so weird or, so help me, Jenny Marshall, I'll force that jelly doughnut down your throat bite by bite!"

"Pam... I have a *real* painting."

There. It was out. Lightning didn't flash and the floor didn't wobble under her feet.

"A *real* painting? The card covers are real painting, aren't they?"

Jenny shook her head. "No. The covers are a living. But they aren't *real* art."

A flattering curiosity sprang into Pam's eyes. "You mean art as in famous-artist-type art?"

"Well... yes."

Pam smiled. "Good for you, Jen. When do I get to see it?"

"Now, if you want to."

"I want to."

Silently, Jenny led the way upstairs to her studio. Outside the door, she paused and bit her lip. Was she ready to show *Sand Castle*?

"Jenny?"

She'd done everything she could. *Sand Castle* was the best she could do. If this wasn't real art, then she was incapable of ever realizing her dreams. She opened the door and walked to her easel.

"Stand there," she said to Pam, "by the door."

"Jenny? Are you all right?"

No, she wasn't. Inside, she was shaking. Her fingers trembled as she lifted the dustcover from the painting. Then she closed her eyes, unable to look at Pam.

She heard Pam gasp, and a long silence followed. When Jenny could bear it no longer, she opened her eyes. Pam had sunk to the floor. She was sitting in the doorway staring at Jenny's painting.

"Oh, my God," Pam whispered, transferring her gaze to Jenny.

And then they were hugging each other and Jenny was laughing and crying and Pam kept looking at the painting and saying, "Oh, my God," over and over as if she couldn't believe what she was seeing. It was one of the finest moments in Jenny's life.

As NEITHER JENNY'S TEAM nor David's had had a winning season, neither made the playoffs. The scrimmage between the two teams was the second-to-last game before the girls scattered for the summer. In ordinary circumstances, the final score of the scrimmage wouldn't have mattered, as scrimmage scores didn't count toward the win/loss record. Normally, Jenny would have been relaxed and wouldn't have cared about the final outcome. She would have told the girls to have a good time and play for fun.

But David was coaching the other team and that made all the difference. She wanted her team to beat his into the dust. The way she had it figured, Rhonda would score most of the goals for David's team, so Rhonda wouldn't mind terribly when David's team lost. It was awkward coaching against Rhonda, but she couldn't let that influence her.

"Okay, girls," Jenny said, gathering her team around her. On the other side of the field, David was doing the same. "Just because we didn't have a winning season, doesn't mean we aren't good. Right?"

"Right," they chorused.

"So we aren't going to let up just because this is a scrimmage. We're good enough to win this game and end the season on a high note."

"We still have one more game that counts on our score, Mrs. Marshall."

"I know. But this game counts, too. Not for our win/loss record, but for our confidence."

The girls looked across the field, identifying friends on the opposing team. In a regular game, the opponents were strangers from a rival school.

"Okay, here's how we're going to do it." Jenny consulted her clipboard. "We'll play Sara, Kelly Ann, Jeanie, Kimberly—"

"That's our first squad," one of the girls interrupted.

Jenny nodded. In scrimmage games, she ordinarily played the girls who were less skilled, giving them a chance to develop and gain experience. She cast a glance toward the parents and friends sitting on the sidelines. Ed Lauper would probably receive a few complaints after the game today. But she needed her first squad to beat David's team.

The girls looked at one another then back up at her. "We're going to win, right?"

"Right," they said.

"Okay, Sara. Let's go out for the coin toss."

She and Sara walked toward the referee in the center of the field, both watching David and Rhonda approaching from the other side.

"I feel kinda funny playing against Rhonda and my dad," Sara admitted.

"You can't think of it that way. Think of it as just another game. One we're going to win."

Jenny spoke the last words loud enough that David could overhear. He looked at her, and Jenny narrowed her eyes. Okay, he was handsome. And her nerves had zipped to the surface of her skin as he stopped beside her. She was going to beat his socks off. What did she care that he smelled like Christmas? Or was bronzed from the sun? It was nothing to her that he looked sexy as hell in his shorts and plaid shirt.

She turned and fastened her gaze to the coin that caught the sunlight as it pinwheeled out of the referee's hand.

In fact, she thought, lots of men had sexy lopsided smiles. And lots of men had broad shoulders and muscled thighs. And most of them weren't so damned pigheaded they couldn't forgive a mistake. Most of the men she knew wouldn't be so stubbornly committed to a stupid idea that they couldn't see themselves or their own daughters.

The referee bent to the grass and examined the coin before picking it up. "Blue team kicks, red receives."

Jenny's team would receive. Good.

Rhonda and Sara thrust out their hands for the traditional handshake; both were solemn and clearly uncomfortable.

Then it was Jenny's turn. It was customary for the coaches to shake hands after the coin toss.

She clasped David's hand reluctantly, feeling a jolt of electricity shoot up her arm at his touch. Hoping nothing of her reaction showed in her eyes, she squeezed his hand firmly.

He squeezed her hand, too, pressing until she felt like wincing. Then, as if he'd read her mind, he grinned. It was that damned lopsided smile she found so sexy, but today there was no humor in it.

"We're going to beat you," he promised in a low voice.

"Not a chance," Jenny snapped.

They stared at each other above their clasped hands and suddenly Jenny wondered if this was the confrontation they'd been building toward. The tension she'd noticed in previous encounters crackled between them, almost tangible.

The referee lifted his whistle and raised an eyebrow. "You guys gonna hold hands all day or are we gonna play ball?"

Feeling the heat rush into her cheeks, Jenny jerked her hand away, then spun on her heel and strode toward the sidelines. To her great annoyance, her heart was thundering and her knees felt wobbly. His touch had left her light-headed.

She wiped her hand across her shorts in irritation and knelt within the circle of her team. "Okay, guys," she said as they leaned into the circle to join hands. "Go out there and give me your best. What are we going to do?"

"We're going to win!"

"What? I can't hear you." ·

"Win, win, win!" they shouted.

"Let's do it!" Smiling grimly, she watched her first squad run onto the field and take their positions. She adjusted the whistle around her neck, tucked her clipboard under her arm and stared across the field.

David was watching her, his expression as determined and unyielding as hers. Their eyes locked and held; then the referee's whistle blew and the game was on.

At first, both teams were loose and somewhat careless, talking on the field, exchanging shouts and laughter with friends on the opposing team. But it soon became apparent to players and spectators that this was no casual game. Both coaches stalked the sidelines, shouting angrily at their players, waving furiously, urging the players to settle down and play winning ball.

By the end of the first quarter, the score remained zero to zero, but the laughter had died from the field. The girls faced one another as fiercely as they had faced players from rival schools.

"Come on, Sara," Jenny shouted. "Block her!"

It didn't occur to Jenny that the person she wanted Sara to block was her own daughter, Rhonda. At this point, Rhonda was simply a player on the other team, a very good player that needed to be blocked.

From across the field, she heard David's shout. "Pass it, Rhonda!"

"Run, Marcie! Intercept!"

By halftime, Jenny was hoarse from shouting.

The girls flung themselves on the grass while Celia passed out Gatorade and oranges. They were red-faced and panting, their wet hair was plastered to their scalps.

"Hey, Jenny," Celia said while the girls gulped Gatorade and peeled oranges. "What's this all about?"

"Winning."

"This is only a scrimmage, remember? Not a championship game. Scrimmages are supposed to be relaxed and fun."

Jenny turned away from Celia's frown and shoved at the damp tendrils of hair that were sticking to her temples. "I'm having fun," she said between her teeth.

On the other side of the field, David was helping his assistant coach pass out drinks and oranges. His shirt stuck to his spine, and the silver at his temples glistened damply. The day was hot, Jenny thought grimly, and it was going to get hotter.

When the whistle blew, signaling the end of the half period, the girls resumed their positions on the field. This time the play wasn't careless or loose. Both sides were playing to win.

Rhonda worked the ball downfield, weaving in and out before she passed to a tall girl named Mary, and Mary shot. Jenny didn't release her breath until her goalie came up with the ball and kicked it back down the field. "Good," she screamed, pacing along the sidelines. "Stay with her, Sara; don't give her an inch."

Sara shadowed Rhonda every step, feet flashing as she tried to penetrate Rhonda's defense and steal the ball. The ball soared out of bounds, and Jenny's team brought it back in. They lost the ball, retrieved it, lost it.

Then Rhonda scored and David's team went wild.

On Jenny's side of the field there was silence. She bit her lip as everyone wearing blue screamed and jumped up and down and hugged one another.

She cupped her hands around her mouth and shouted. "It's not over yet! Not it's our turn, Reds. Let's play ball!"

Sweat dripped from the players, their faces were scarlet as they worked the ball back and forth, in and out. Not a single spectator remained seated. All were crowding the markers, stepping back only when Jenny ran down the sidelines, tracking the ball.

"Take the shot, Sara! Now!" Jenny screamed.

Sara's kick shot the ball past the Blue goalie and into the net. Jenny's side of the field erupted into frenzy. The second- and third-string players spilled onto the field and hugged their teammates. When the referee restored order and the game resumed, the score was tied.

It was still tied as the fourth quarter began, and the minutes started counting down.

Rhonda had the ball again, moving it downfield in a series of skillful maneuvers, but Sara was making her pay for every inch.

"Hands!" Jenny yelled at the referee, pointing furiously. Her voice was almost gone. "Are you blind?"

The tall girl named Mary had the ball now, her face intent as she shouted Rhonda's name before she kicked, passing the ball across the field. Immediately both Rhonda and Sara dashed forward, running at full speed and concentrating on the ball. They collided at full force, and sprawled in the grass. Both girls lay where they had fallen, gasping for breath.

"Foul!" David shouted. "Red fouled Blue!"

Ignoring him, the referee pulled the girls to their feet. Immediately they faced off and Rhonda accused Sara of tripping her. Sara hotly denied it, claiming loudly that Rhonda had tripped her.

"You're damned right it was a foul," Jenny yelled toward David's side of the field. "Any fool could see that your player tripped mine!"

"The hell she did!"

Face dark, David marched onto the field with long, angry strides. Jenny threw down her clipboard and plunged across the markers toward center field. She didn't halt until the tips of her Nikes pressed against the toes of his Adidases.

When they were nose to nose, Jenny planted her hands on her hips and shouted up at him. "What are you trying to pull? Any idiot who knows the rules of this game knows your player fouled mine!"

He leaned forward until the heat of his body enveloped hers. The cords rose on his neck, his jaw tightened and his breath flowed over her lips. "Oh, yeah? Well, what sort of idiot sees only what she wants to see instead of what really happened?"

"Don't talk to me about idiots when you're so blind you can't see what's right under your nose!"

Jenny's face was flushed and hot, her trembling body felt on fire. A hard intensity burned in her eyes, her breath was rapid and shallow. Tension wound her muscles tight.

She was no longer aware of the spectators watching silently from both sides of the field. She didn't know the players stared at them openmouthed. She only saw David. Dark, damp hair curled from his collar, his shirt stuck to his body, emphasizing bulging muscle.

He looked at her mouth. "My player was going for the ball and your player came up behind her!" His voice had sunk to a deep baritone, husky from shouting.

Jenny's voice cracked and emerged in a throaty croak. "My player has as much right to a free ball as yours does!" She glared into the tawny heat in his eyes, her nails cutting into her palms. The heady scent of clean, honest perspiration made her feel giddy and weak-kneed.

His stare dropped to the rapid rise and fall of her breast, and his eyes darkened to black before returning to her lips. "What kind of fool do you think I am? Do you think I'd take your word for anything?"

The tension between them exploded. Jenny reacted mindlessly, responding to an involuntary protective instinct. She swung at him, her one thought to slap the face just inches from her own. To touch him.

David caught her wrist as her hand came up. His quick movement pulled her hard against his body. For one eternal moment Jenny pressed against him and her eyes locked to his. She felt his immediate response, and a wild shock of heat erupted through her senses. She stared into his eyes and saw the sudden blaze of passion. His stare penetrated her own; his hair was damp at the temples, as it would have been after lovemaking. His shoulders tensed, and his rapid breath scalded her lips.

The most intensely physical moment of Jenny's life was happening in front of a hundred people.

A similar thought must have occurred to David, because he suddenly blinked and looked toward the sidelines. Then he stepped backward at the same moment Jenny snatched her hand out of his grip. They turned toward the girls.

Sara and Rhonda were wide-eyed and staring.

The referee stormed forward, jerking his thumb in the air. "Okay, you two, you're out." His scowl was filled with disgust. "This is the most unsportsmanlike conduct I've seen in years!"

"Out?" Jenny repeated in disbelief.

"What do you mean out?" David demanded.

"I mean out, buddy. A double coaches' foul. You two are out of the game."

"You're benching us on the sidelines?" Jenny asked, her ruined voice a croak of indignation.

"Out, lady. O-U-T, out. Turn it over to your assistant coaches and go home. Both of you."

They protested vehemently.

The referee leaned forward from the waist, his face tight, his eyes in slits. "One more word from either one of you and this game ends right here. You got that? Both teams take a coaches' loss."

Jenny cast an apologetic look at Rhonda, who was staring anxiously back and forth between her and David. Both girls were. They were holding hands, their own differences settled.

Jenny's shoulders slumped. Embarrassment set her face on fire. She didn't remember ever being this ashamed of herself. Feeling like slime, like the world's worst example of a coach or a mother, she turned without a word and walked swiftly toward the sidelines. She could feel a hundred pairs of disapproving eyes examining her; it felt as if the field had suddenly expanded to cover miles, and she would never reach the bench.

"Oh, Jenny," Celia said as Jenny silently handed over the clipboard and her whistle. "What in heaven's name happened to you?"

"I'm sorry," Jenny whispered. She bent for her purse.

"Look," Celia said, frowning, "I'll finish up here; then I'll get Rhonda and I'll take the team for ice cream or something. Give you some time to settle down. Okay?"

"Thanks."

"I'll bring Rhonda home about five. That'll give you a couple of hours."

"Thanks, Celia, I owe you one."

As she walked toward her car, Jenny heard the referee's whistle blow, and the game continued, but it didn't matter anymore. She didn't look back and she didn't look at David, who was walking beside her. When they reached the parking lot, he veered toward the car parked on the other side of hers.

After finding her keys, she discovered her hand was shaking so violently that she couldn't get the damned key into the lock.

"Jenny?"

She drew a long breath, then glanced over her shoulder and looked at him from expressionless eyes.

"We have to talk. That was appalling."

She nodded. David looked as weary and upset as she was. "Now?"

"Okay, but not here. We've made enough of a spectacle."

Jenny wholeheartedly agreed. "Follow me to my house, it's closest."

"Is Deuce home? I don't want to do this in front of the kids."

Do what? Did he think she was going to attack him again? She'd never hit anyone in her life. What had happened on the soccer field was a humiliation, a once-in-a-lifetime occurrence. It horrified her to think about it.

"Deuce is spending the afternoon at Tanya's house working out a new computer program."

"The one he asked me about?"

David didn't seem to expect a reply and Jenny didn't answer. When she'd wrestled open the car door, she glanced toward the cheers rising from the field. One of the teams had scored. "My house. Five minutes."

David was looking toward the field, too. "You got it."

Chapter Thirteen

She was magnificent when she was angry. The thought was so trite that David's mouth curved in a humorless smile. Trite it might be, but it was also true. In his mind's eye he continued to see her flushed and furious, her chest heaving, her eyes flashing blue fire. Remembering how her nipples had risen against her shirt aroused him again. And this rekindled his anger. He didn't want to be aroused by Jenny Marshall. What he wanted was to get her out of his system, out of his thoughts and out of his fantasies.

He would be the happiest man in Columbine when school ended next week and Sara left for California. No more driving her to Jenny's house, no more calls from the Marshall household. The first thing Monday morning, he would do what he should have done weeks ago. He'd hire a permanent housekeeper to handle the grocery shopping and the dry cleaning. It wouldn't entirely eliminate the possibility of encountering Jenny and reminding him of stubborn wounds that refused to heal—he would still run into her when Sara returned for school next year—but a housekeeper would minimize accidental encounters.

But that wasn't enough. Unless they cleared the air between them, every chance meeting would continue to be traumatic. They'd proven that today.

He parked his Chrysler behind Jenny's station wagon, then slid out and followed her around to the kitchen door.

"Brace," she said dully, stepping inside.

He caught the screen door, then was knocked back into it as one of the biggest dogs he had ever seen jumped on him. A warm, wet tongue lapped his cheek.

"Down, Toulouse," Jenny said.

"Does he bite?" Cautiously, David removed the giant paws from his shoulders.

"I wish he did," she said, glancing at him, "but he doesn't." She opened a cabinet and placed two glasses on the table, then swung open the refrigerator door and removed a pitcher of iced tea. "Sit down."

David sat at the kitchen table and Toulouse promptly nestled his shaggy head in David's lap. He stroked the dog as he glanced around Jenny's kitchen. It had the same comfortable lived-in look he'd noticed in her family room. The thought crossed his mind that Marilyn would have gone crazy here. What he considered a neurotic urge for perfection would have prompted Marilyn to remove the schoolbooks from the countertops and the drawings and notes from the bulletin board. Marilyn wouldn't have been able to resist picking dead leaves from the plants on the windowsill all the time they were trying to talk. It had driven him crazy.

Jenny seated herself across from him and cupped her hands around the glass of iced tea. "Okay," she said in a throaty whisper. "You wanted to talk."

"First, I owe you an apology. I'm sorry about what happened on the field."

Some of the resentment faded from her gaze. She pushed at her hair. "So am I. Look, I... I'm sorry I tried to slap you."

David remembered the sudden heat of her body pressed against his and his own swift reaction. The moment had been powerfully erotic. He'd stared into her challenging eyes and had wanted to pull her down to the grass and make violent love to her then and there. He looked at the damp tendrils of hair drying around her forehead and at the pink flush still on her cheeks.

"It's all right. I provoked you."

"Yes, you did. But that's no excuse." She dropped her eyes and caught her lower lip between her teeth. "I don't know what came over me. I've never done anything like that before." When he didn't respond, she looked up at him, her eyes cool and challenging. "You don't believe me, do you?"

"Should I?" The words were out of his mouth before he could halt them. "How do I know we aren't playing Cinderella again? Cinderella, part two: Our heroine puts on the gloves and goes three rounds."

It was the wrong thing to say and he knew it. But the bitterness—his anger and disappointment—was just a pulse beat away. If only she hadn't lied, things would have been so different. But she had. And he'd believed her, dammit, every word. She'd played him for a fool, and he'd gone along with it. He'd fallen in love with her and not once had it entered his mind that Jenny Marshall was a liar.

"You just can't leave it alone, can you?"

"Would you in my place?"

She stared at him and the heat in her cheeks deepened. "If I were in your place, I hope I'd try to understand. I hope I'd be big enough to forgive."

"Oh, I understand all right. You forget that I've played this scene before. Now, let's see if I have it straight." He hated the sarcasm and bitterness in his voice but was powerless to stop it. Something in him wanted to hurt her as she had hurt him. He wasn't proud of this urge, but he couldn't prevent it, either. "You're usually as honest and truthful as the day is long, right?"

Scarlet flamed up her throat, and she pressed her lips together.

"All you wanted to do was be Cinderella for a while. Do I have it right, so far? Of course, I don't remember Cinderella being a liar, but that's beside the point isn't it? Or am I remembering the story wrong?"

"I don't think I like you very much right now," Jenny said quietly.

"Did you ever, Jenny? Did you like me when you let me lie to Rob Spenser? Did you like me when you were playing me for a fool and listening to all those idiotic things I was saying about being proud of you? Did you like me then, Jenny? When I was swallowing all the lies?"

"Dammit, David, I'm not Marilyn. I made a stupid mistake, but that doesn't mean I'm a habitual liar! You're transferring your hurt and anger at Marilyn to me. Can't you see that?"

"You're dead wrong. I've considered that possibility, but it doesn't wash. Sure, I was angry and hurt to discover I'd married a liar. But that was years ago.

You have to care about someone to be hurt by that person, and I haven't cared about Marilyn for years. At the end, her lying was a frustration and a damned complicating inconvenience, but it didn't hurt anymore. It was different with you. With you, it hurt!''

"And the reason doesn't matter?"

"What reason? There's no acceptable reason for lying!"

They were both leaning forward, faces angry, sore voices raised. Jenny met his stare, and his intensity and pain sliced across her heart.

"Oh, David," she whispered, her anger draining away in a rush. "What are we doing?" A plea entered her eyes. "The last thing I ever wanted was to hurt you. I know you don't believe that, but it's true." Tears stung her eyelids. "I love you."

"Don't, Jenny. Don't say it." Pushing from the table, he brushed Toulouse aside and stood up.

"I've always loved you." Slowly Jenny pulled herself to her feet, facing him. "Why do you think I left Frascotti's? Do you really want the truth, David?" He stared at her. "I left when I received your wedding invitation. It hurt so much that I couldn't paint, couldn't think. I couldn't function. I kept picturing you with Marilyn." She closed her eyes. "And, God, it hurt."

What she said stopped him from reaching for the door. "You left Frascotti's because...? But if you cared that much, why did you go to Rome in the first place? Why didn't you tell me?"

She looked at him. "Why didn't you ask me not to go? Or why didn't you come with me?"

"I thought you wanted to study in Rome."

"I did, but I wanted to be with you, too."

He covered his eyes with his hand, then looked at her over the top of his fingers. "When you left, I thought it was over."

"When you let me go, I thought it was because you didn't care anymore. And then, when I received the wedding invitation, I..."

"Oh, Jenny. How foolish we were. How filled with pride and foolishness."

Later she could never remember who moved first, but suddenly she was in his arms, her head on his shoulder, his strength wrapped around her.

The faint scent of Christmas filled her nostrils, a fragrance she now identified with David. His fingers were pressed to the small of her back, and she felt the heat of his hand as if her clothing had melted beneath his touch.

His lips murmured against her hair and his arms tightened. "God, Jenny. I've missed you so much."

"Every night. Every long, endless night."

"I think about you a hundred times a day. I can't get you out of my mind."

"Nothing helps. Even when I'm painting, I think about you."

He kissed her then, a kiss that began as a gentle caress, then exploded into fiery passion. The moment she felt his tongue part her lips, a rush of weakness overcame her. Afraid that her legs would no longer support her, Jenny pressed against him and wrapped her arms around his neck. She could feel his hard thighs against her own yielding flesh, could feel his rigid need. When his urgent mouth released her, she stared up into his eyes, shaken, her breath emerging in ragged gasps.

"David..."

"Is there somewhere...?"

"Upstairs."

Taking his hand, she led him upstairs, past Rhonda and Deuce's rooms, past her studio and into her bedroom. There was no need for words, just a desperate need for each other. Not taking her eyes from his face, Jenny threw off her shirt and slid her shorts over her hips. She dropped the rest of her clothing, then looked at him, loving his long, hard body, loving the silver in his hair, the firm curve of his mouth.

"Come here, Jenny, love," he said, his voice hoarse with desire.

She ran into his arms, crying out at the warm shock of his naked skin against hers. Her fingers flew over his shoulders, his face, the thick hair tumbling over his forehead. "David, oh, David."

"I've wanted you every night."

"I thought we'd never be together again."

He swung her into his arms and crossed to the bed, his mouth hungry on hers. And then his weight was over her, his hands caressing her naked body until she trembled and twisted beneath him and whispered his name in mindless repetition.

And finally he entered her, the first deep thrust bringing a cry of joy from her lips. Her hands tightened on the swell of his shoulders; she pressed her face into the wildly beating hollow at his throat. She met each punishing, blissful thrust with a passion that overwhelmed her. Nothing existed but this moment. The world dropped away, and she was conscious of nothing but the waves of rapturous pleasure following one after the other in rapid succession.

There was nothing gentle in their lovemaking. It was wild and urgent, an expression of explosive need. Without her awareness, Jenny's nails raised pink tracks down his back. His fingertips left tiny bruises on her hips and shoulders. Her head thrashed across the pillow, and her body arched to meet his thrusts.

And when an almost unbearable tension built toward eruption, when she trembled and her teeth bared, when she felt his body gather and tense above her—finally, finally the release came, and it seemed to Jenny that the universe expanded over her, contracted and flew outward again.

They lay beside each other, panting for breath, exhausted. When Jenny's breath finally quieted, she turned to smile at him. She'd pictured his head on her pillow a thousand times, seeing him as he was now, his hair damp with exertion, his wonderful mouth relaxed and smiling, his long frame filling her bed.

Gently, she touched his cheek, reassuring herself that her happiness was real, that he was actually there. "I love you, David."

He covered her hand with his own and pressed her fingers to his face. "I've loved you from the moment I first saw you." A smile moved against her palm, and his eyes twinkled. "Would you really have slugged me?"

She closed her eyes and laughed softly. "I can't believe I did such a thing. Can you ever forgive me?"

And there it was. The worst possible choice of words, words that placed the problem squarely between them again. Yes, they'd been foolish those long-ago days, when they were in college and pride counted for all. But that was then, and this was now. And

Jenny saw the struggle in his eyes, watched his happiness fade to a troubled expression.

"If I could, Jenny, love, I would," he said softly, his voice deep with regret. "You must know I've tried."

A chill rippled up from her toes as she slowly removed her hand from his cheek. "Then, you're saying..."

There was an uncharacteristic helplessness in his eyes, but it didn't make her feel better. She couldn't believe this was happening.

"If I could just understand. But I've tried and I can't."

"I told you what happened."

"You told me you didn't mean to lie." He sat up and swung his legs over the edge of the bed, holding his head in his hands. "You said you just wanted to be someone else for a little while." He looked into space, then bent down for his clothing. "What I can't understand is why you had to lie to do it."

It was all unraveling, coming apart again before her eyes. Stunned, Jenny held the sheet to her breasts as David dressed. Why was he doing this? Hadn't he felt the same things she had? How could he tell her he loved her and then walk away?

"It was a dream, can't you understand that? I wanted all those things to be true for a little while. I pretended my life was really what I wished it was."

He shook his head, and she knew he would never grasp what she was saying. She couldn't put the explanation into words he could understand. The tight, cold knot in her stomach grew. In silence she watched him finish buttoning his shirt, and her face grew stony.

Emotions aroused by lovemaking and hope swung in a stormy arc and her voice emerged icy. "I'd think you of all people would understand an innocent deception."

"What is that supposed to mean?"

Anger blossomed in her cheeks. "You're no stranger to deception, David, and I'm not talking about Marilyn. I'm talking about a man as rich as Fort Knox who drives a three-year-old car and goes coy when money is mentioned. Who lives in a middle-income neighborhood and does his own grocery shopping. Your whole life is a deceit, David. You work hard to give people false impressions. You play down your successes and suggest that IBM bought Foster/Beta for a pittance. You pretend to be something you're not. Is that honest?"

The color drained from his face, then flooded back. "It's protection. You can't guess how many people latch onto someone with money. There's no point in making myself an easy target."

"You could always say no, have you thought about that? Or is it easier simply to lie and pretend you're only an investment broker? It's not your money, oh, no, it's your clients' money." She stood beside the bed, still holding the sheet to her breasts, her anger increasing by the minute.

"I am an investment broker!"

"With one client. Yourself. It's not an outright lie, I'll give you that. It's a silent lie. The lie of encouraging a false impression, of not bothering to correct an erroneous assumption. But it's every bit as damaging and as patronizing as any other lie!"

He looked at her as if she'd struck him. "That's how you see it?"

"Of course that's how I see it! You deliberately mislead people. How is that any different from what I did?"

"You don't understand."

"I do understand, that's the sorry part of all this. I do understand. You haven't come to terms with having money. So you deceive people by pretending you're just like everyone else, up to your eyelashes in bills." The anger poured out of her, anger deeper than she'd known she felt. "I have a desk drawer stuffed with bills, David. What would you have thought if you'd known that up front? Would you have thought I was interested in you only for your money?"

"I might have," he admitted slowly, not proud of it. Then his voice turned acid, "It's been known to happen."

"And that justifies hiding the truth? From me, from the world at large, even from your own daughter?"

"Leave Sara out of this."

"No, David. You wanted the truth and you're going to hear it. Sara is worried sick about money. She thinks you're unemployed, did you know that?"

He stared at her. "Unemployed? That's utter nonsense!"

"She paid her soccer fee out of her allowance because she thinks you can't afford it. She needs new shoes in the worst way, but she hasn't asked you for the money, has she? No, because she thinks you don't have it. She thinks you're sitting home worried about how you'll pay the light bill, or that you're out looking for work. Sara thinks you're practicing to be a carpenter. You've done such a good job of deceiving yourself, and everyone around you, that even Sara thinks you're broke!''

"That isn't true. It can't be." But his mind whirled with fragments of conversation. The pieces fell into place if Jenny was right. If.

"It is true." She stared at him. "You talk about values, David. Have you taken a hard look at your own? You're being dishonest with yourself and those who care about you. You're suspicious of everyone around you. You're punishing yourself and Sara by denying the pleasures money would buy. Is that a terrific value system?" She passed a hand over her eyes. "Values are inside a person. They aren't dependent on a person's bank account, or on how he lives or what kind of car he drives. Can't you see that?" Now she met his eyes. "You talk a good game, my friend, but every word is false. You say people are important, but you either push them away or deceive them. You want a simple life, yet you've made it unnecessarily complicated."

The sheet had pulled from the bed and dropped to the floor, exposing her breasts. David looked at her, and, God help him, but he wanted her again. Wanted her, despite the sharp accusations ringing in his head. Despite the fact that she was lashing out at him, saying things he wanted to deny.

It had been a mistake to come here. He should have known better. How many times had he watched Marilyn do exactly what Jenny was doing? How many times had Marilyn shifted the emphasis from her transgressions by attacking him? He made a sound of disgust. Would he ever learn?

"David?"

There was nothing more to say. Instead of answering, he stared at her for a long moment, then opened the door and shut it firmly behind him. Blindly he strode forward, passing what were obviously kid's rooms, then stepping over Toulouse, who was sleeping across a doorjamb, half in and half out of a large sunlit room.

He might have missed it. He might have rushed past the door Toulouse had nudged open, and he might never have glanced inside. He might have missed a moment he would never forget.

But he lifted his head at the right instant, and he glanced into the room as he passed. And he stopped midstride to retrace his last two steps and stand in the doorway of Jenny's studio. He stared at the painting resting on an easel beneath the skylights.

It was magnificent.

Waves tipped by moonlight and faintly luminous tumbled forward from the left side of the painting. He could almost smell the sea, could almost hear the distant whisper of surf. It was that real. And yet, there was also an ethereal quality to the painting, a suggestion that this scene was seen through a dream, something magical and so fragile it could vanish in a blink.

Drawn by the painting, he stepped farther into the room, his mind swept clear of anything but this moment, overwhelmed by the painting before him.

The sand castle whispered of enchantment, of filmy dreams and days lost in the mists of time. The towers beckoned, promised moonlit secrets. Visions lingered within the castle walls, dreams of splendor touched by distant stardust.

The painting stirred his emotions, though he didn't usually respond strongly to art. It troubled him, disturbed something inside, that the tide was about to wash away the sand castle. Silvery grains caught the moonlight, spilling toward the water's grasp. The dreamer's vision would ultimately, inevitably, yield to the tide's reality.

Emotions and half-formed images flashed in his mind, impossible to put into words.

Childhood dreams . . . the touch of warm, wet sand against his palms . . . romantic illusions of chivalry and jousts . . . reality tugging against fantasy . . . the whisper of surf . . . the silence of a deserted beach . . . the remnants of a long day, a forgotten pail, a small pile of shells—and a castle built from sand and dreams . . . abandoned now to the fingers of water reaching toward it.

Overlaying all was a deep and tragic sense of loss. Silently and unobserved, the moonlit sand castle would be swept away. Mourned by no one, for it wasn't real. Just a castle made of sand, a structure as insubstantial as an illusion. It had never been intended to endure, but only to give pleasure to the builder.

And then he understood.

A small sound rasped in his throat as he covered his eyes.

What Jenny had done in Cancún was to build a sand castle out of words. She'd fashioned a splendid structure of dreams and ambitions from long ago. She hadn't done it for him, but for herself. And her castle had never been intended to endure; he saw that now. Her illusion had been as transitory as the castle she had painted. A momentary fantasy, one that would yield to reality when the moment had passed.

"Good God," he whispered, staring at the painting.

What had he done? How could he have been so blind?

At the door, he turned back for another look at the painting. It was unquestionably masterly. Jenny hadn't lied in Cancún; she had predicted her future. This painting would make her reputation and place her on the road to greatness, if that was the direction she wanted to go.

And David Foster? His jaw tightened. He, too, had built a castle from material no more substantial than sand. With a rush of insight he gazed at the painting and understood that everything Jenny had said about him was true. He, too, had set reality aside.

In the hallway, he paused and glanced at Jenny's closed bedroom door. Then he descended the staircase and walked to his three-year-old Chrysler.

The engine coughed and rattled to life. But he didn't hear it. In his mind he heard the oncoming rush of the tide.

WHEN SARA RETURNED from the soccer game, the living room floor was covered with shoes. Track shoes, running shoes, saddle shoes, loafers, high-heeled pumps, sandals, boots, thongs. She stopped in the doorway, her ice-cream cone midway to her mouth, and she stared at the array in astonishment.

"I didn't know your size and what you wanted, so..." David grinned and shrugged. "Who won the game?"

"It ended in a tie," she said, still staring at the shoes. She lifted large, dark eyes. "Dad?"

"Sit down, honey," he said gently, patting the sofa beside him. "There are some things I want to tell you."

Chapter Fourteen

If there had been someone special to share the evening with, tonight would have been the most perfect moment in Jenny Marshall's life. She turned sparkling eyes toward the throng jamming the Melton Gallery. All these people—the cream of Denver's society, the elite of the art world—were here to view her work and honor her. Well, not her alone. Thornton Melton had arranged the showing to feature five local artists. But she was one of them. And *Sand Castle* was prominently displayed and causing a stir.

Smiling, Thornton Melton introduced yet another gushing couple who wanted to meet the artist. They shook Jenny's hand effusively and enthusiastically praised her painting.

Dazed with happiness, Jenny smiled after them.

"You're the success of the showing!" Thornton said, refilling her glass with champagne. "So, when can I expect to feature you alone?"

It was a dream come true. "I'm starting work now on a series."

"Wonderful! I'll want an exclusive, my dear. May I have my attorneys contact yours next week?"

She didn't have an attorney, but she would hire one. As soon as she finished the latest batch of card covers for New Image Greeting Cards and was paid for them. She anticipated having the money by August.

Thornton Melton leaned toward her ear. "I have a buyer for *Sand Castle*. It seems you were quite right to insist on a high price."

A buyer? She lifted stricken eyes. "I priced it at ten thousand because I didn't really want to sell it," she said. Despite her need for the money, *Sand Castle* was part of her. It represented beginnings old and new, and losses of an intensely personal nature.

"My dear, I confess I, too, thought ten thousand outrageous for a debut work. But obviously there is someone, other than myself, who sees the value in owning an early Jenny Marshall."

"Who?" She searched the room, seeking out the person willing to part with ten thousand dollars for her painting.

"Mrs. Stanford Van Allen, of the Illinois Van Allens." Melton's eyes glowed. "You met her earlier, remember?"

"Oh." For a moment, for just a moment, Jenny's heart had leaped with hope. There was another person who, if he saw the painting, might see in it something intensely personal.

"Must I sell it?" she asked in a low voice.

"No," Thornton replied slowly. He straightened his tie and smoothed his cummerbund. "But I'm afraid your reputation might suffer if the painting was withdrawn after such a generous offer."

She nodded. Though he didn't say so, she suspected her reputation would suffer most with Thornton Melton. While it was clear he loved art, the Melton Gallery was expected to turn a profit. Jenny sighed. The path ahead would not be smooth, there were hidden obstacles waiting to trip her up. There were things she didn't know. But she would learn. Unfortunately, the learning process had just cost her *Sand Castle*.

Thornton moved away to murmur compliments in the ears of the other artists, and Pam took his place beside Jenny.

She sipped her champagne and looked at the gowns and tuxedos thronging the gallery. "Nice crowd. Did you see the sable on the woman with the orange hair?" She rolled her eyes. "Sable in July?"

Jenny laughed. "You left yours in storage, right?"

"I should be so lucky." Pam smiled fondly. "Congratulations, Jen. Everyone's talking about *Sand Castle*." She tilted her head and looked at Jenny with an odd expression. "Your life is going to change, isn't it? Tonight is the beginning. All that stuff you said in Cancún—it's going to be like that, isn't it?"

"Maybe. I hope so." Jenny took Pam's hand and pressed it. "But some things don't change, Pam. Like good friends. Is that what you're worried about?"

Pam watched a news photographer kneel in front of Jenny. They both blinked as the flash exploded. "I guess so," she admitted, looking into her glass.

"Well, don't be so stupid. Remember me? I'm the person who still writes to friends I had in high school a hundred years ago. I don't let go easily, Pam. You should know that. For example, who else do you know is still in love with a man she met fifteen years ago? A man who seems to have vanished into thin air." Jenny bit her lip and ducked her head, wishing she hadn't said that. She'd sworn she wouldn't wear her heart on her sleeve.

But he was always there, always on her mind. She hadn't heard from David since the day of the great soccer match, five weeks ago, and she hadn't seen him. He appeared to have dropped from the edge of the earth. But he was always in her thoughts. A certain men's cologne could bring him rushing to mind. Or a lopsided smile. Or a love scene on TV. Or the empty space beside her when she slid into bed each night. Hiding her expression, Jenny drained her champagne glass and tried to think of her aching feet instead of her aching heart. Was it against any rule for the artist to sit down?

"That's right," Pam agreed. She smiled. "I'd forgotten your friendship theory."

"Friendship is like tooth decay. Once it starts, you can't get rid of it. It may go into remission, but you know it will come back. Sometimes it spreads, and sometimes it hurts. But you can count on it being there. The Marshall theory of true friendship." They smiled at each other. Then Jenny blurted, "It's sold. Someone named Van Allen paid real money for *Sand Castle*."

Pam didn't look surprised. "Did you ever doubt? Of course it sold, Jen. It's a fabulous piece of art."

Was it? Or was it a one-time fluke? A piece of her soul that she'd converted to paint.

Don't falter now, Jenny told herself. *Remember the confidence theory? Quit worrying about tomorrow and enjoy tonight. It's been a long time coming.*

She smoothed her hands over her black silk gown—courtesy of VISA—and smiled at a woman who grabbed her hand and pumped it.

"Splendid, my dear, simply splendid! I made a bid, but your work has already sold."

"Thank you," Jenny murmured, starting to get the hang of this. All that was expected of her was a gracious thank-you and a pleasant smile.

And then, all too soon, the showing was over.

There were blank spaces on the walls where featured paintings had hung. The gallery floor was sprinkled with discarded napkins; empty goblets littered the ledges. Two of the artists sulked; the others were like Jenny, tired but wearing dazed smiles of happiness.

She looked at her painting, her *Sand Castle*, luminescent beneath soft spotlights. Tomorrow it would be shipped to an address in Chicago.

"I can't bear to part with it," she whispered. Relinquishing *Sand Castle* was like amputating part of herself. It hurt.

Thornton made a sympathetic sound. "Most artists feel that way about their first successful work." He kissed both her cheeks. "Think about your triumph instead, my dear. Jenny Marshall is the new sensation!"

Her feelings surprised her. She should have felt on top of the world. Someone had paid real money for a Jenny Marshall painting; finally and truly she was a *real* artist. Dreams were becoming reality.

Instead, Jenny experienced an inexplicable rush of depression. And she felt very alone. The kids were in California visiting Walter. Her friends had apparently assumed she'd made other plans and had departed, leaving Jenny behind. There was no one waiting to share the biggest moment in her life or to help her celebrate. In a few minutes she would climb into her station wagon and return to her dark house. Alone. She would open the bottle of champagne waiting in her refrigerator and drink to her future. Alone.

She wondered what late movie was featured tonight on TV. And decided that this was the loneliest thought in the world.

"Thank you, Thornton."

"Good night, Jenny Marshall. You'll be hearing from me. And the world will be hearing from you!"

She managed a smile, then lifted the hem of her black silk gown and stepped into the warm July night.

He was leaning against a car parked at the curb, his arms crossed over the lapels of a black tuxedo.

Some men were born to wear a tuxedo, and David Foster was such a one. Her heart jumped at the sight of him, at the long elegant lines of his body, at the sight of that familiar lopsided smile.

He bowed low, then opened the door of the car, holding it for her. "Your carriage awaits, my princess."

"David! What...?"

Dark eyes sparkling, he placed a finger over her lips, his touch a brief caress. "Not yet, Jenny, love."

It was a Porsche, low-slung and luxurious. It had that new-car smell of leather and perfection.

She turned wide eyes to him as he slid behind the wheel. "You bought a Porsche? David, that's wonderful! You always wanted a—"

"Not a word," he said, smiling into her eyes. "Soon."

She didn't understand, but she didn't need to. She was with David again, and that was all that mattered. And he had come to her. In a Porsche. He held her hand as he drove, and she knew something had changed, something important that he would explain in his own time.

For the moment it was enough to be with him, to feel the warmth of his hand laced with hers, to feel the familiar hunger for him when their legs touched.

She was too dazed to notice where they were going until the Porsche turned off Wadsworth into the Columbine division where David lived. "Your house?" she asked, smiling. Until now she hadn't thought about it, but she'd never seen the interior of David's house. She'd dropped Rhonda out front and picked her up without going inside.

"The palace," he said, returning her smile as he guided the car to a halt in the driveway.

It was his house, but it wasn't exactly as she'd remembered. It took Jenny a moment to identify what was different. An addition had been added upstairs, altering the roofline; a row of new skylights reflected the moonlight. Behind the fence, where the top of a bush had once been, rose the roof of what looked to be a poolhouse.

"You remodeled?" Whoever had done the design had eased the stark lines Jenny recalled. The house looked warmer, more inviting. "And added a swimming pool?"

"I've been busy," he admitted, eyes dancing.

A dozen questions jumped to Jenny's lips, but he would say no more. Shaking his head and smiling, David escorted her to the door. Then he turned and gently pulled her against his body and into his arms.

"I'm very proud of you," he said huskily, gazing at her lips. "Can you ever forgive me for being such a fool?"

"Forgive you?" She stared into his eyes as her breasts and hips melted against him. "I don't know what you're talking about...but yes. Yes, David. I love you."

"I can't imagine why, after the way I've behaved, but you've made me the happiest man in America."

He kissed her then, a long, lingering kiss that spoke of love and the passion that would come later. Then he touched her cheek and pushed open the door.

"Surprise!"

Jenny blinked. David led her into a large, sunken room filled with everyone she had ever known in her life. She was convinced of it. A banner stretched across the vaulted ceiling, its gilt letters reading Congratulations Jenny Marshall! Confetti rained down around her, and a hundred champagne glasses toasted her success.

"I...Oh, David," she said, when she could speak around the lump building in her throat.

"I love you, Jenny," he said, his hands on her shoulders. Then he nodded to the crowd, and at his signal, the guests parted, forming an aisle to clear her line of vision.

And she saw the old man and the horse she had painted for him in college. The large canvas dominated the room, mounted beneath soft spotlights that enhanced the subtlety of the work.

The canvas blurred behind the tears springing to Jenny's eyes. She leaned heavily on David's arm, steadying legs that were suddenly trembling.

"I wanted *Sand Castle*, Jenny," he murmured against her hair. "But Melton sold it to his aunt, a collector."

"Mrs. Van Allen is Melton's aunt?"

"The painting was sold before the showing opened."

She looked at the study of the old man and the horse, tears sparkling in her eyes. "You kept it. All these years."

Then Pam emerged from the crowd and embraced Jenny, holding her tightly. "I'm jealous," she said. "When do I get a Jenny Marshall painting?"

"Soon," Jenny promised, looking at David over Pam's shoulder. She smiled into his dark eyes, tears of happiness hanging on her lashes like diamonds; then Rhonda and Deuce and Sara ran forward to hug her. "I thought you were all in California!" she said, laughing and wiping her eyes. David stood against the wall, smiling and watching her.

"We were, Mom," Deuce said.

"Mr. Foster flew us home for your party." Rhonda's eyes were bright with excitement.

"Dad says there's no point in having money if you can't enjoy it," Sara added happily.

"Your father said that?" Jenny asked. She tried to find David in the crush of friends and neighbors, but he had disappeared. She returned her attention to the three young people who made her joy complete. They looked very pleased with themselves for having kept the secret.

Sara leaned forward to shyly kiss Jenny's cheek. "You were right about everything, Mrs. Marshall," she whispered. "When you have time, if it's okay, Rhonda and I need to talk to you about boobs."

"First thing tomorrow," Jenny promised, holding Sara tight.

Then she was surrounded, as well-wishers converged on her, wanting to discuss *Sand Castle* and the untitled old man and the horse and to drink to her health. A glass of champagne appeared in her hand, and later a plate of canapés. She saw David during the next two hours, but always at a distance. When she understood, she gave him a dazzling smile, which he returned from near the doors leading to the lighted pool. The evening was hers, a triumph not yet to be shared. His smile told her to seize her moment and savor it. His time would come.

She was waiting when his hand lightly touched her elbow. "Do you think I could steal you away for a few minutes?"

Jenny smiled up into his dark eyes, loving him, hurting inside with the intensity of loving so hard. He led her into a wide hallway and up a sweeping curve of stairs, then into a room washed by starlight falling softly through the bank of skylights. The room would be a perfect studio. It was vacant, except for a love seat and a small table.

He led her to the love seat and bowed as he had when he'd opened the car door. Jenny smiled at him, then seated herself, wanting to stroke his beloved face.

David reached into his pocket; then he cleared his throat and knelt on one knee at her feet. "M'lady," he said, gazing at her mouth and then into her moist eyes, "I have searched the realm for the princess to whom this belongs. I have reason to believe it is yours."

He opened his hand, and Jenny caught a breath as her fingers flew to her mouth.

Resting in the center of David's palm was a miniature crystal slipper. It drew the light from above and sparkled magically as if cut from dreams.

"Oh, David," Jenny whispered through a rush of tears. "You understand! You really understand."

"There's a final test," he said, smiling up at her. Then he tilted the slipper and an exquisite diamond ring dropped into his palm. It caught the starlight and flashed brilliant fire. Reaching for her hand, he slipped the ring onto her trembling finger. "As I suspected," he said softly, "a perfect fit."

"David..."

"Will you have me, Jenny? And let me spend the rest of my life making up to you whatever hurt I've caused?"

"David, I...I'm not a perfect housekeeper and..."

"I despise perfection," he said laughing.

"Everything I own is covered with cat hair..."

"I'm crazy about cat hair."

"And I have a desk drawer stuffed with unpaid bills..."

"We'll pay them."

"And I can't bake a lemon meringue pie to save my life!"

"I hate lemon meringue pie."

"Oh, David," she said, staring at him with shining eyes.

"Say yes, Jenny, love. Say yes."

She slid to the floor beside him and threw her arms around his neck, covering his face with a thousand kisses before she leaned back to look at him, her face radiant.

"Yes, yes, yes!" She held out her hand and laughed with sheer happiness. "This is the biggest, most pretentious ring I ever saw in my life." He grinned at her. "And I love it!"

Her lips met his, and he lifted her to the love seat, murmuring her name as his fingers found the zipper of her gown.

Before Jenny sighed blissfully and surrendered to her prince, she gazed at the crystal slipper twinkling in the starlight. It didn't surprise her to glimpse a shadowy winged figure standing beside the slipper. She knew who it was.

"Thank you, Fairy Godmother," Jenny whispered.

Then, because fairy godmothers are noted for their discretion, Jenny's tactfully withdrew to find Sara and Rhonda.

But not before she and Jenny exchanged a wink.

Harlequin American Romance

COMING NEXT MONTH

Harlequin "Super Celebration"
SWEEPSTAKES

NEW PRIZES—NEW PRIZE FEATURES & CHOICES—MONTHLY

1. To enter the sweepstakes, follow the instructions outlined on the Center Insert Card. Alternate means of entry, NO PURCHASE NECESSARY, you may also enter by mailing your name, address and birthday on a plain 3″ x 5″ piece of paper to: In U.S.A.: Harlequin "Super Celebration" Sweepstakes, P.O. Box 1867, Buffalo, N.Y. 14240-1867. In Canada: Harlequin "Super Celebration" Sweepstakes, P.O. Box 2800, 5170 Yonge Street, Postal Station A, Willowdale, Ontario M2N 6J3.

2. Winners will be selected in random drawings from all entries received. All prizes will be awarded. These prizes are in addition to any free gifts which might be offered. Versions of this sweepstakes with different prizes may appear in other presentations by TorStar and their affiliates. The maximum value of the prizes offered is $8,000.00. Winners selected will receive the prize offered from their prize package.

3. The selection of winners will be conducted under the supervision of Marden-Kane, an independent judging organization. By entering the sweepstakes, each entrant accepts and agrees to be bound by these rules and the decision of the judges which shall be final and binding. Odds of winning are dependent upon the total number of entries received. Taxes, if any, are the sole responsibility of the winners. Prizes are not transferable. This sweepstakes is scheduled to appear in Retail Outlets of Harlequin Books during the period of June 1986 to December 1986. All entries must be received by January 31st, 1987. The drawing will take place on or about March 1st, 1987 at the offices of Marden-Kane, Lake Success, New York. For Quebec (Canada) residents, any litigation regarding the running of this sweepstakes and the awarding of prizes must be submitted to La Regie de Lotteries et Course du Quebec.

4. This presentation offers the prizes as illustrated on the Center Insert Card.

5. This offer is open to residents of the U.S., and Canada, 18 years or older, except employees of TorStar, its affiliates, subsidiaries, Marden-Kane and all other agencies and persons connected with conducting this sweepstakes. All Federal, State and local laws apply. Void where prohibited or restricted by law. Winners will be notified by mail and may be required to execute an affidavit of eligibility and release which must be returned within 14 days after notification. Winners consent to the use of their name, photograph and/or likeness for advertising and publicity in conjunction with this and similar promotions without additional compensation. One prize per family or household. Canadian winners will be required to answer a skill testing question.

6. For a list of our most recent prize winners, send a stamped, self-addressed envelope to: WINNERS LIST, c/o Marden-Kane, P.O. Box 525, Sayreville, NJ 08872.

No Lucky Number needed to win!

Take 4 books & a surprise gift FREE

Explore love with Harlequin in the Middle Ages, the Renaissance, in the Regency, the Victorian and other eras.

Relive within these books the endless ages of romance, set against authentic historical backgrounds. Two new historical love stories published each month.

HIST-A-1

Shay Flanagan is Gypsy,
the raven-haired beauty who inflamed passion
in the hearts of two Falconer men.

Carole Mortimer

GYPSY

Lyon Falconer, a law unto himself, claimed Shay—when he didn't have the right. Ricky Falconer, gentle and loving married Shay—when she had no other choice.

Now her husband's death brings Shay back within Lyon's grasp. Once and for all Lyon intends to prove that Shay has always been—will always be—*his* Gypsy!